Brewster Daggit

Other books by L. L. Layman

Tom Livengood

Paxton McAllister

Jesse Buxton

Tyler James

Buck Moline

Lema

Jose Baca

Brewster Daggit

An L. L. Layman Western

L. L. Layman

iUniverse, Inc.
New York Bloomington

Brewster Daggit
An L. L. Layman Western

iUniverse books may be ordered through booksellers or by contacting:

iUniverse
1663 Liberty Drive
Bloomington, IN 47403
www.iuniverse.com
1-800-Authors (1-800-288-4677)

ISBN: 978-1-4401-4110-2 (pbk)
ISBN: 978-1-4401-4111-9 (ebk)

Printed in the United States of America

iUniverse rev. date: 6/4/2009

Acknowledgements

For my seven previous novels already in print I used the same acknowledgements, thanking the thieves and crooks who remained abed affording me hour upon hour of peaceful penning in the front seat of a police cruiser. I then thanked the command personnel of the Peoria Police Department who ignored my literary endeavors.

After more than ten years of writing stories between calls for service and periodically having to rise to the occasion, along came the devil himself. We got a new chief of police who actually expected officers to be productive. His new demands became time consuming quotas.

The once indifferent sergeants and lieutenants became minions from hell. They installed satellite positioning electronics in the squads along with cameras and video recorders. Daily activities were constantly monitored. All officers, but mostly me, were under constant surveillance. We were badgered, harassed, and prodded to become "fiscally" productive. This new chief was serious. He actually expected me to do police work all day long.

No choice did I have but to retire; but not a day before I finished book number eight.

Larry Layman
Peoria, Illinois

For

George "Bud" Fulton

No man could ask for a better friend.

Chapter 1

▼

It was but a short walk from my night camp through the dew soaked prairie to the stream where I intended to fill my coffee pot. Five minutes no more would be the time away from Julius, my old, near worthless horse. He was busy attempting to chew grass with his few remaining teeth. Julius had no desire to be bothered; I had no desire to divert his grazing. Long would be our days trail. Home before dark was my goal. Julius needed his strength.

Carefully I made my way, ever watchful. Sioux were about; I'd seen sign aplenty the day before, and a man alone is easy pickings. Me, Julius, and old Irving, my one shot, rusty, near ancient shotgun would be just that; picked over and scalped. Not that the Sioux and I were at war or even mad at each other for that matter; simply put, a man alone is a man alone. Those thieving rabbit chokers would take what you had, this was gospel. No help from the militia would I get; most had already been conscripted and sent south to fight the Rebs.

"Going to free the slaves," they had said as they marched away. I had never given much thought to their plight or their need to be freed. My life was tough enough as it was. I did not need further complication. I had bought some cows cheap, drove them nearly a hundred miles, sold them for a profit and was now headed home with the proceeds.

As I walked I planned my day. After my repast, Julius and I would finish crossing what was left of this Minnesota prairie and then make our way through the pine. I envisioned less than a three hours ride to the wood; then maybe ten more hours travel in the forest. I would be home; back at Crow Creek, back with Helga and Hans. A man like me did not deserve such a fine wife and son, but I had them and was thankful.

The travel across the prairie was faster but more dangerous. The Lakota lived on the prairie. The forest travel was much slower as deadfall often times blocked the trail, but the danger from Indian attack was much less. It seemed that the Sioux avoided the timber for most of three seasons and for obvious reasons. The number one reason was the mosquito and black flies; number two was the mosquito and black flies, and number three, the same. Anyone with any sense at all avoided the Minnesota wood in the summer. The insects would and often did eat men alive.

Why my old man had chosen to build a life up here was the big question. Why I chose to stay after he died was an absolute mystery. All this land offered was nagging, biting, blood sucking, buzzy things and snow; cold, miserable, knee deep, blowing, face cutting, finger numbing snow.

If it were not for my wife and her family, I would take her and the boy, our stuff, and head south; Illinois or lower. Tennessee was good country; civilized too. Tame country they called it, no Sioux.

I needed to get home. I had gold coin in my pocket and Helga wanted to use it to purchase real glass windows for our home. It was hard to believe that so much coin could come from the sale of one cow and three heifers, but they say there is a fool born every minute. That captain at Fort Ridgely was an idiot; he had paid twice the going rate. All I had to do was push those four cows south through Lakota country four days, make my delivery; and then race home with the money.

Lucky I had been thus far not to have encountered any problems, especially with so many tracks about. Plenty had been the signs; unshod horses and moccasins. Caution was the day.

I could hear the sound of the water as it fell over the rocks. From this same spot I had filled my pot the previous night. I had been wise not to sleep so close to this babbling brook; the noise of which might cover the advance of some unknown danger.

I was far from a woodsman, but over the past twenty plus years I had learned a thing or two. Never leave camp without Irving was another absolute. Only one shot did I have, but at close range I would not miss. Always keep a blade close to hand was another rule. Mine was but a small sheath knife, as old as Irving, but most utile and well sharpened. Little else was there to do on those cold winter nights.

Strange how the mind works; I was mentally installing glass windows as I filled my pot. Cold was the water. Silent was the prairie. Those windows really muffled the drone of the crickets. I could not even mentally hear the birds.

"Yeow!"

I had been hurt. Something had pierced my butt. Something was still in my butt.

"Son of a," my retort was deafened with the noise of yipping and yelling savages.

I rose running, right through the stream, crashing through the willow brake on the other side. I made a sharp right hand turn and headed down stream. All I was showing was the bottom of my boots.

"Run Brewster run," was my brain screaming at my legs. I was picking em up and putting em down.

Chapter 2

▼

As I raced along the wall of willows that bordered the stream, most of the savages ran along the other side. Arrows were shot as they ran but the willows did much to divert their flight.

The arrow stuck in my right buttock was not only hindering my race for life, but also my pride. If I had not been so terrified the scene might have offered some humor. Somehow in mid stride I was able to pluck the stick from my butt, and surprisingly gaining some extra speed for the effort.

If I was bleeding badly I could not see, as all focus was given to the obstacles ahead. Were I to fall, my pursuers would be upon me, I would certainly die.

Yet, look I did, not at my throbbing buttock, but at my pursuers. To my right on the other side of the creek were six or seven very small Indians. They were incredibly small. They might not yet be teenagers. They were none the less keeping the pace and shooting their arrows as they did. The little Indians were shooting little arrows and they were trying to stick them in little old me. I ran all the faster.

Behind me were three older boys, all well into their teens, all brandishing some type of weapon. They too, were keeping the pace; no they were gaining.

All of them, the boys to my right, the savages to my rear, were yelling and screaming at me. What they were saying I had not a clue. For sure it was something to do with my demise.

I ran for my life.

My lungs were laboring now. My legs were feeling heavier. I'd left the younger boys behind, no longer were their arrows sailing past me. I needed to cross back over the stream, get back to camp, find Julius, and make tracks for home.

One shot was all that I had, as I still carried old Irving as I ran. I had my shot, a long barreled club, and my knife. Boys or not, a Sioux was a Sioux. They were all Lakota. A lot of little cuts could kill as easily as a few big ones. These three savages from hell and their little arrow slinging friends had made their intentions clear; but I was not ready to die.

Gasping now, I knew I was in big trouble. Perhaps a mile we had run, maybe more. I started to stagger forward, I started to fall, yet somehow my feet caught up with my body. No choice did I have. I stopped, turned, pointed old Irving and fired.

Loud was the roar from that shotgun. A cannon blast could not have been louder. The load caught the first boy square to the chest and down he went, hard to the ground. He hit totally limp, slithered forward, and moved not a muscle. I knew he never would. Some shot from the barrel had passed by the first boy and hit the one behind him in the face. His hands went to his eyes, his knees to the ground. The third continued his charge. He gave some blood curdling high pitched scream as he raised his hatchet. This boy charging was bigger than the other two, his charge continued without hesitation. Down came the axe as I whipped the shotgun barrel across the side of his head. He was game, but I hit first; and I hit hard. My blow spun him wide to my left. He went down, rolled, and came back up. He still had his axe. He still tried to use it. I hit him again, this time I bashed him again and again until he went down. Then I butt stroked him a good one to the noggin, he didn't get up.

One was for sure dead, one was thoroughly bashed; the third was still on his knees holding his hands to his eyes. He was crying.

I left him in his agony and went looking for Julius. I had no idea when the smaller boys, the arrow shooters, would catch up, but they were coming, I was sure of it. What worried me most were their older brothers and fathers; I needed distance, a lot of it.

Chapter 3

▼

Julius was in no mood to travel, pleasant thus far had been his morning, but I had him saddled and north bound in record time. What good it did I wondered as I knew all to well I could walk faster than Julius could trot. Irrespective I put the boots to him; old Julius gave me his best.

Not a minute too soon either as those miniature little creatures had almost caught up. They were now within arrow shot. I could see them break into a sprint. Seven mad little Indians were charging me.

Irving was a useless piece of iron that weighed me down. I had not yet had time to reload. Powder and shot for two other loadings was in my possible bag tied to the saddle. To stop and reload would leave me surrounded with but one shot if ever I could manage that.

As Julius found his gait my butt began to bounce. The more I bounced the more I bled. No matter if I could out distance them; I left a trail even a white man could follow. They would surely catch up with me when I leaked out.

I needed time to plug my hole.

Hutchinson was a long eight miles away. Since I had gone cross country instead of along the traveled road I could expect no help.

"Zip," a little arrow shot by a miniature Lakota sailed past my head "Zip, zip," came two others.

I put the boots to Julius, though there was little result. Julius was already giving me his best.

Now I'm near six feet in my socks if ever I had any. Julius was 13 hands high in his youth. So low was his sway back now, my feet were near dragging the ground. It must have been amusing to see us run, the horse with his four legs, me with my two. We became a six legged, two headed, beast running for its life.

A mile, two we kept the pace. My pursuers gradually fell behind. They had slowed to a walk; I could see five now. Two had probably gone looking for their big brothers or fathers. If I had thus far been in trouble I would pale in comparison when the big boys came for revenge.

After another mile Julius began to seriously labor for breath. He slowed to a walk. Ahead, perhaps a quarter of a mile, I could see the willow brake that bordered Buffalo Creek. My life seemed to depend on getting to the other side. I gave Julius a kick. He snorted, staggered, fell to his front knees, gasped, and died.

It was as simple as that, and I was left standing astride him. My faithful old Julius, my first and only horse was dead.

"Zip, thwack," an arrow now stuck from Julius's rump.

"Yip, yip," five little kids from hell were closing in again.

"Zip," another arrow sailed past me and stuck in the ground ahead.

I grabbed my possible bag, broke off the arrow in Julius's rump, and started running again. I grabbed the other arrow as I passed, breaking it in half. Two less arrows to shoot at me was all I thought. Another minute of flight had me well out front of them again, but they were still coming. I was breathing in great gasps, I was still bleeding, and Hutchinson was still three or four miles away.

I needed to pace myself; I needed to get home.

My butt ached constantly. Then my right leg began to throb. Eventually I was forced to a walk. My walked turned into a fast limp. My situation was not improving. The only plus was that the slower pace had allowed me time to reload my shotgun. My consolation was the fact that one of those miniature dog eaters from hell would bite the dust.

My deductions, however, left me with four other little arrow shooters to stay back and put more holes in me. Perhaps they just wanted to pin me down until their big mean daddies could get here. Who knew, the only thing for certain was that my butt hurt real bad.

I waded across Buffalo Creek; cold and dark were its waters. The water was not over my head but it was near chin deep. On the north side of Buffalo Creek I stopped, turned, and got myself ready. It was my intention to catch those little devils in the water which would be over their heads. I was going to shoot one of them then drown the others. I was going to rid myself of each and every one of them. Right here in the middle of Minnesota, in the middle of Buffalo Creek I was going to choke the life out of all of them.

I sat down on the bank and just waited.

I waited and waited. They never came. It was hard to believe that they had given up the chase, but apparently they had. It was near dark when I started my limp through the mosquito invested wood toward Hutchinson.

As I smacked and swatted this new blood sucking horde I developed some respect for my earlier pursuers. At least they were smart enough not to have ventured into the Minnesota forest at night.

Chapter 4

▼

Hutchinson was not much of a town, but a welcome sight it was. I was exhausted, limping, blood covered, and mosquito eaten. My walk of only a few miles had taken me most of the night, or so it seemed.

My shirt was now sleeveless, the material I had used to bandage my bleeding arrow hole. Twice I had to apply the padding before somehow my butt quit leaking. My hands were often times blood covered. As I had over a hundred times smacked the biting night bugs on my face and torso I was well blood smeared. I must have been a sight as I stumbled into Svenson's tavern, a place I had visited many a time. The door was never locked. My money had never been accepted.

A lamp was lit but no one was astir. Old man Svenson was slumped over the corner table, sleeping for sure. A bottle stood upright, close to hand. Several empties, dead soldiers, lay where they had fallen. Another man, a stranger, possibly a real soldier by his dress, was curled up on a floor mat. He was snoring in unison with Svenson.

Svenson was my wife's uncle. He was family. He was good people.

There was a coffee pot on the stove. As I made my way towards it, Ulla Svenson, Helga's aunt, came into the back door from their rear apartment.

"Eeeeh, my god!" she screamed.

The elder Svenson jumped to his feet knocking over the table in the process. The falling table caught the sleeping soldier on the head.

"Oh my God is that you Brewster?" she pleaded.

"Brewster, it's Brewster" yelled the old man "It's Daggit."

"Yeow, what the hell!" yelled the man on the floor. He was big, blond and now bleeding, a gash he had over his right eye.

9

"Oh my God!" Ulla was leading me to a chair. "Papa, go fetch the doctor. Mayo is down at Neva's house. Oh my God"

"What happened?" the old man wasn't leaving until he knew there wasn't a bear or worse outside his door.

"Dakota's," I replied. "I was ambushed."

"What happened?" he asked again either not comprehending or denying my reply.

"Who hit me?" yelled the big blond.

He was holding his hand to his head though little good it did to stem the flow of blood.

"What happened?" the old man again inquired, refusing to leave.

"Papa, go get Mayo, do what you are told." Ulla was gaining control. She now had me seated. "Get."

Svenson went out the door just a yelling, "Indians! Alarm! Indians! Brewster Daggit has been scalped!"

At that announcement the big bloody blond soldier stopped in his tracks, turned and stared at me. He had concern. He apparently did not care much for the Dakota. He and I had that in common.

Within the span of not less than five minutes the entire tavern was filed to near bursting. There must have been more than fifty people; men, women, boys and girls. All were clamoring for a view of the scalped man.

"See, I told you, scalped and near dead. My nephew by marriage he is, and dying right as I speak."

Everyone was yelling at once.

"Injuns! Injuns are coming!" prevailed over most other screaming.

"Someone send for the army, they are camped just north of town."

"Where is the doctor?"

"There is another man scalped." Someone had noticed the big blond.

"Make way, make way, it's Doctor Mayo. Make way."

"Injuns Doc, Injuns scalped two men!"

"Over here, this one is dying!" yelled Ulla who was now trying to cradle me to her breast.

Total was the confusion.

Then, through it all, in the door from the rear apartment appeared a vision. I thought I must have died. She was just the most beautiful girl I had ever seen. She was young, maybe sixteen, but full grown in all respects, that was for sure. Strange it was that I had noticed her in all this bedlam, and I was old enough to have been her father.

Not a word did she say. She just stood back and took notice. Her eyes were dark and her expression stern. If she saw me looking at her I could not say. The room was wild.

"Let me through. Make way." It was the Doctor. "Now Ulla, let go, I need to examine this man."

He looked me over.

"This man has not been scalped. Where are you hurt mister? Show me."

The whole room was quiet now. Everyone was listening and watching.

"Quick man, where are you hurt? There is a bleeding man over there"

I bent to his ear.

"What, I can't hear you?"

I bent to his ear again.

"Where, speak up!"

I bent again.

"Your what, did you say your butt. You had an arrow in your arse!"

What had been initial concern became hysterical laughter. Never mind that an arrow is an arrow, but apparently its final lodging caused amusement.

It was old man Svenson who silenced the crowd. "Where did it happen?"

"In his arse," yelled someone from the crowd.

Again the crowd went to laughing.

"South of Buffalo Creek, maybe three or four miles," I said, hoping to divert their jeering.

"How many were there?" asked Svenson.

"Ten I think." Not mentioning their diminutive size. "They came up on me early yesterday morning; arrow shot me from behind, and then gave me a run. Killed my horse in the process."

"Julius?" questioned a voice.

"Yes, he gave his best and I am here to tell about it because of him."

Immediately, what had been hysterical laughter turned somber. It had been okay to be amused by my misfortunate injury, but Julius's demise was a different story. No one kills a man's horse, even a poor horse. I did fail to mention that it was I who ran the horse into the ground; besides there was a broken arrow in his rump. Someone would certainly take note of the arrow and report back.

After all, this was serious business. An Indian attack was concern for everyone on the prairie. Everyone was in jeopardy. Riders would be sent, plans for reparations would be made. This was survival. This was war.

Chapter 5

▼

War brings soldiers and this day with amazing speed. As the big blond soldier and I were being helped out of the tavern door, in route to the doctor's for treatment the morning's sun was rising. At the same time, a cavalcade of southbound mounted troopers appeared. They were riding their horses through the center of town. There were more than fifty of them, led by a red headed man. I saw that he had a single golden bar over his shoulder, a lieutenant I assumed. Upon seeing us on the porch he and the Sergeant behind him wheeled their horses to the rail.

"Continue on," he ordered. "Sergeant Howell, take the lead. Sergeant Maher, remain with me."

The troop continued on, but all eyes were to the porch as they passed. A bloody sight we must have been.

"What have we here?" the Lieutenant inquired. There was indignity in his tone. He was looking at the soldier first, then at me. "That man is one of my ranks."

The doctor, who was taking us somewhere for treatment, took the lead. "Hurt men here sir. This bleeding soldier of yours had the misfortune to be bashed with a table. Daggit here, the other man, was arrow shot yesterday. He said they were Dakotas."

"Who?" he inquired, now looking directly at me.

"Daggit," I replied.

There was something that was not quite right. He had a wounded soldier and a man that had been attacked by savages. His concern for my name was just out of context.

"Maybe three or four miles south of Buffalo Creek," I offered, trying to refocus the Lieutenant.

"How many hostiles?" he inquired.

His look was intent, but somehow the question and his eyes were saying different things.

"Ten."

"Are you sure?"

"I can't read a lick but I have fingers."

"Don't get smart with me mister. We have not had an Indian problem here in Minnesota for years. I'm not so sure you are making this up."

The crowd from inside the tavern had moved to the porch. Everyone could hear the brash speaking red headed officer.

"Are you calling me a liar?"

"Oh no, but more than one man has prevaricated to attract the attention of a beautiful young lady."

"What!" I retorted, still very much puzzled by the indignity of this officer.

I could see that he was looking past me. He was looking into the crowd behind me. I turned; he was looking at that same girl I had seen inside the tavern. She was standing on the porch just outside the door. In the early morning light she looked even more beautiful than she had earlier.

I turned back to the problem at hand, a most indignant officer. I was mad enough to jerk him down off that horse and slap that smirk right off his face, something I knew I could do. Lucky though he was; I had mastered simple mathematics. I had earlier showed him I could count to ten. What I hadn't shown him was my ability to comprehend the number fifty. I really couldn't recite all the numbers exactly, but I had a very good idea what fifty or so soldiers could do to me.

"He has made his report Lieutenant." said the doctor. "You will make yours."

There was authority in the doctor's tone, and recognition of the same with the Lieutenant.

"We are on our way to Mankato. A report will be made at Fort Ridgely, rest assured."

The Lieutenant then turned his attention to his Sergeant.

"Sergeant Maher, see that Corporal Matthews is properly treated then catch up."

I saw the Lieutenant give both men some unnecessary eye contact, perhaps it was a message. He then reined hard right and put the spurs to his mount. There was a clamoring of hooves and he was gone.

A few minutes later I was standing on the rear porch of someone's house.

The doctor looked me over, "You sir are a bloody mess. Before I can examine and treat you, you will need to cleanse yourself."

"What?"

"You are no longer bleeding; you are not going to die. But I surely may if I am exposed to the filth you carry with you. Simply put, take a bath in yonder tub. The water is still hot; I just used it."

"Out here?"

"Out here, and be quick about it. I will be in here treating the soldier."

The doctor went inside the house with Matthews following him. Matthews had his hand covering the gash to his face; he was trying still to stem the flow of blood. He used the uncovered eye and the sergeant used his two good eyes to glare at me as they disappeared through the doorway.

Apparently soldiers did not like men who were recently arrow shot without cause. Perhaps my condition would result in a call to arms which would necessitate their involvement. Who knew? I shrugged them off as I contemplated my next trial; a bath in the middle of Hutchinson on someone's porch in broad daylight.

There was indeed a tub on the porch; it was metal and full of water, hot water. It sat back in an alcove of sorts but offered total vantage on one side. Not that anyone would be looking or concerned, I was still a bit nervous. There was soap and a reasonably dry towel close to hand. On the same porch was a wood stove. On the stove was a pot of hot coffee. There was cup on a hook. I availed my self of both. I made myself at home. Within no time at all I was naked and nestled deep into the tub of hot soapy water. The coffee was strong; I savored it as I drank. If it were not for the stinging hole in my butt I might have enjoyed the moment. As I closed my eyes I saw visions of Helga and home, not twenty more miles did I have to go.

Chapter 6

▼

Metal bath tubs, what would they think of next. A far cry it was from the hogshead Helga and I used back home. I was just amazed, my sore butt and my feet were in the water at the same time. And a back rest, I could actually lean back. Most of my lanky six foot frame was at least partially submerged.

Glad I was too; as there in the porch opening was that girl; over her arm hung some clothing.

"Ah hum," she said. "Excuse my intrusion, but Ulla sent these clothes for you to wear. She said that they were left by a traveler. She said to tell you that they were clean and for you to keep them. I was also to tell you that Papa Svenson is getting his buggy ready. He is taking you the rest of the way home.

I was much startled by first her presence then next by her boldness. I reached for the towel, though I had not a clue what good it would do.

"Thank you," was all I got out.

"Not a worry my dear cousin," she laughed.

"Cousin?" I was stalling as I strategically placed the towel over my still submerged private parts. It was a terribly small towel and did little to help.

"Yes, cousin, your wife Helga's mother, my mother, and Ulla are sisters. That makes us at least cousins in law or something like it. My name is Lydia."

"Brewster."

"I heard."

"So you are Lydia. Helga has mentioned your name many times. You are the girl who writes to her, her pen pal.

"Yes, that is me. Helga and I have never met but so many have been our letters I feel I know the two of you very well. I have just recently arrived from the Empire State for a short visit. It is my intention to meet with Helga before I return home.

"Home?" I asked.

"Back to Hoosick," she replied.

"Who's sick?"

She was laughing, but before she replied there was an interruption.

"I'm ready for you now," It was the doctor standing next to Lydia in the opening of the porch. "I do hope you are clean. Hurry up now, be quick about it, I've a long drive home, especially with the Lakota unrest."

He turned and left. Lydia still stood in the opening.

"Ah hum." It was my turn.

"Oh, I'm sorry. You need your privacy. Tell Helga that I wish to meet with her soon.

Then, she was gone.

It took but two minutes to wash what looked important, pat my butt dry, towel off, dress, and report. Still, a sight I must have been. My new trouser legs were barely calf high. The shirt was obviously from a different man yet as the sleeves covered both of my hands. Grateful I was though as both were clean, blood free, and pleasant to the smell. Most important, however, was the seat of the trousers. It was intact and without an arrow holing.

The bath had done little for my pain and physical condition. I limped from the tub into the adjoining room from which the doctor had appeared. I was in a kitchen. Seated at the table was the head bashed blond. The sergeant stood the wall. The doctor was at that moment admiring his handiwork.

"Now in two weeks have these sutures removed." He said. "Any physician can do it.

I could plainly see that the doctor had much to work with and little had he accomplished sans the bleeding which seemed to have stopped. I could tell right off this man would have a whopper of a scar.

As I looked at him, he glared at me.

"You have a problem?" the man said most challengingly.

"That will be enough Matthews. We will have no fisticuffs in here."

"I will be watching for you Daggit," said Matthews.

I did not respond, but nor did I break eye contact. If this man or both men for that matter wanted a piece of me I was ready. I was good and ready. Both men were bigger but I doubted either was near as mean. When pushed I knew what I could do.

"I said not in here!" It was the doctor sensing big trouble. There was resolution in his tone. "And that will be one dollar for my services."

"A dollar."

"Yes, one dollar, unless you want me to take my stitches back out."

"And if I don't pay?"

"It will be a long run to Mankato."

I didn't know who was going to do the chasing, but I suspect that Matthews did. With some grumbling the fee was paid and the duo left. I also suspected that they would not go too far. What they wanted with me was a mystery, but I sure didn't like the man and was all for showing him just how much.

"You make great friends Daggit," the doctor said, "Now drop your pants and bend over."

Chapter 7

▼

I had not known what the doctor had poured on my butt but it caused quite a "yowl" out of me.

The doctor had been most astute. As he had given inspection to my second butt hole, he noted a lack of deep penetration.

"You are a lucky fellow," he had said. "The Injun who stuck the arrow in your butt surely lacked strength or purpose. I've seen many arrow holes; this one hardly made it two inches deep into your buttock. A little arrow it was too, one of those bird points I am thinking.

I never answered. I thought the "yowl" had been sufficient. Glad I was to now have my pants up; my dignity restored, and to be heading out the door.

I needed to get home. Helga would be worried as I was now a full day overdue. I had left little that needed her attention; Hans was enough for her to take care of. My boy would be walking soon. Oh the times we would have. A full year now Helga and I had been married. We had met, taken a few walks together, talked, perhaps more earnestly than appropriate, then married.

"Hi, my name is Brewster." was all I had said. Presto, fourteen months later my son was almost a toddler. I missed them both and wanted to make tracks for home.

As I exited the front door I was greeted by more than the warm morning sun. Standing before me in the street, still glaring, was the bandaged Richards and the Sergeant. They had no doubt tarried. Their purpose involved me though their reason was a growing mystery. I had caused them no harm.

There were townsmen about but none had taken an interest in these soldiers. It seemed that the entire morning bustle was in response to the pending Dakota dangers.

"You there," it was Matthews.

As my mathematical ability was still intact I quickly made the comparison. My butt now had two holes and I was looking at two of the same. Both men were big, pistol totting, and intent on causing me harm. Irving was over at Svenson's house, but my blade was comfortably sheathed. It was close to hand.

"We want a word with you," ordered the Sergeant.

I walked straight at them, not a stride did I miss, and not a word did I say. I saw Matthews clench his fist and brace his leg. The sergeant was already set. Not three steps closed the distance.

"I," began the sergeant.

"Whomp," my right foot was embedded deep in his crouch. He went down in a crumpled pile. As his knees hit the ground my round house right caught Matthews dead center on his recently stitched forehead.

Matthews came around with his own right hand that took me hard to the shoulder. I was bowled back but recovered and began pounding him with lefts, rights, and lefts. He was swinging wildly as blood flowing from his reopened wound filled his eyes. He could not see me, but I could clearly see him. Each punch I made was hard placed with great effect. Matthews was taking a beating.

A crowd had gathered but no one made any effort to intervene. It was either none of their business or they wanted no part of me.

I hit Matthews one last time; a right to the jaw and down he went to his knee. A boot to his head laid him along side the now vomiting Sergeant.

"Brewster, Brewster, what is this?" Svenson asked as he came to my side. He had just pulled up with his horse and wagon.

"Damn you Daggit," the doctor was coming up from behind me. "I just sewed that man up."

"Well I just hope he has got another dollar in his pocket." I said as I climbed into Svenson's wagon. "Take me home Sven."

Svenson took his place on the seat, and then gave the reins a snap.

"Giddy up." He said to his horse.

I was on my way home.

Chapter 8

▼

Svenson had a nice wagon, best around they said. He also had a decent horse to pull it. What we lacked was a real road to pull it over. What we traveled was a four hour bumpy trace through the piney wood. Little relief was there for my sore butt. I found some padding to sit on and did the best I could with it.

I had not slept for more than a day now and was quite tired. Occasionally my head would drop but the next rut or dead fall would jar me awake. Futile were my efforts.

"What caused you to beat up those two soldiers?" Svenson finally asked. He was just dying, I was sure, to know the rest of the story. "You really put it to them."

"They were waiting for me in the street. They wanted to fight, not me."

"I wonder what for?"

"I just don't know. I've tried to reason it out. Matthews knew that the table falling on his head was an accident. I only know that I was a little testy with that red headed uppity Lieutenant of theirs. Who knows, maybe he set them on me."

"I saw him ride off; he didn't say a word to them as far as I heard." said Svenson.

"Me either."

"Tell me abut those Indian attacks again. Do you think they will come this far north?

"It is hard to say Sven; we don't see many Dakota this far back in the forest."

"You are right; they stay mostly out on the prairie. I wonder what caused them to attack you in the first place; we have not had real trouble with them for years."

"I can't say. I was bending over to fill my coffee pot and an arrow got stuck in my butt."

"Damn, I bet that hurt."

"It surely did, but it hurt a lot more when I pulled it out."

Sven went to laughing, "I just bet it did."

When he regained his composure he asked, "Well how did you get away?"

"I out ran them, simple as that."

That is where I left the conversation. I changed the subject when ever Sven came back to it. I had no desire to tell him about the ten little Indian boys.

We talked the rest of the trip about family, friends, horses, and dogs: just this and that to pass the time. He made mention of the young niece who was staying with them.

Lydia Layton was her name. She had arrived a few weeks prior for a summer visit. Nice girl he said, adding a disclaimer, as far as in-laws went.

"You know Brewster, you can pick your nose, pick your friends, but you can't pick your relatives."

It was my turn to chuckle.

By and by old Sven remembered that he had a bottle of whiskey stashed under the wagon seat. To my delight it was almost full. Its shared consumption did much to loosen the tongue and ease our ride. Svenson must have known a hundred jokes and he told them all. We were still laughing as we crested the knoll that led down into my little valley. Glad I was to see my sign at the entrance to my lane.

"Daggit" it read. As I could not read or write, I was quite proud of the sign. I had made it myself. Helga had got me started, but I did most of it.

As I looked further down my lane, the joy I usually felt was changed to confusion. Nothing in my brain could comprehend what my eyes were seeing.

Instead of Helga and Hans in the lane I saw wagons, teams, horses and people. They were everywhere, all of them just milling about. These people were dressed to the nines in their Sunday finest, all except the two men leaning against a wagon. Both of these men held shovels.

Shovels, why did these men have shovels. There was nothing to dig at my home. I had my house built; my well was dug.

"Sven, where is my house?"

My house was gone. I knew where it was. It wasn't there anymore. Someone had replaced my house with charred pieces of wood and blackened stones.

"Helga!" I yelled. "Where is Helga? Where is Hans?"

I searched the grim sullen faces for her pretty blue eyes but they were not there. Tears aplenty I saw in their eyes, but there was no Helga.

Two ladies moved to their left. Behind them, in the glen down by Crow Creek was a new grave; a grave with two crosses on it, a big cross and a little cross.

Chapter 9

▼

"We are so sorry Brewster," it was Carol Short, my neighbor to the west that broke the silence. John saw the smoke and went a running but the house was totally aflame. There was no putting it out, no saving them.

John had been one of the men with a shovel. He now stood next to Carol but said nothing. He made no eye contact.

I knew he had dug a deep hole, he was a good man.

"After the fire died out John found them both." Carol said.

I started walking out to the grave and the throng followed. Carol kept her arms around me for most of the way. She kept saying consoling things that I neither heard or cared about.

When we arrived at the freshly filled grave I just stood and stared. I was looking at the two crosses but what I saw was my pretty wife. I saw her sparkling eyes and her blond hair. I saw that boy of mine in her arms.

"We just had a funeral for them but we can do it again." It was Reverend Baylor putting his arms over my shoulder.

Not a word could I muster, nothing at all. My throat and chest were tight as if both had been somehow stretched. A strange fluid filled my eyes.

Finally after several minutes I said, "I would have liked to have seen them."

"No, you wouldn't have," uttered John a bit under his breath.

"Blessed are the good," began the Reverend.

I heard only bits and pieces from that point on. I just stood there in my newly acquired calf length pants and oversized shirt. At least I had sleeves aplenty to wipe away that strange fluid that rolled down my face.

The reality of their deaths was setting in. I had only been gone a week; a week to sell some cattle and better our lives. And now they were gone; gone forever.

On and on Baylor went about the opening of heaven's gate and the goodness of God. He threw in some Joshua stuff, and some Jesus this and Jesus that. Then the Reverend began quoting biblical scripture which had no relevance at all. He had totally lost me.

I was not following his sermon. He was just babbling words. At this moment in time I saw no goodness, no love of man. I saw only a grave. I felt violated. I felt alone. Here I stood with friends and neighbors and I felt alone.

Baylor came to the ashes to ashes part and most of the women went to wailing. I wanted to cry. I wanted to throw myself on the freshly dug earth and weep for my loved ones but I wouldn't let myself. I had never cried before; I kept telling myself that I wouldn't cry now.

As the congregation regained its composure they began to sing.

"As we gather at the river,"

I knew most of the words but I did not join in. I just stood and looked at the new grave which held my wife and child. No comfort did the service bring.

I found no solace in the words of bereavement the individual mourners gave to me as they parted our new family pot.

The last to take his leave was old Sven. As he extended his hand I found therein a gift. It was the bottle we had worked on most of the morning.

I took a swallow; then another.

That night, alone in the dark, I cried; that night and many others.

Chapter 10

▼

My grief was so real, so painful; little could I do for months on end. Our, now empty, one horse stable became my home. Little if any improvements did I make to it.

From the door of the stable I could see the glen that held those that I could hold no longer. I left my vantage only to find something to eat or more often, something to drink. I became much accustomed to the taste of whiskey.

As the days grew shorter and colder my now well pickled brain sensed just barely its own eminent demise. Should I fail to amend my ways, I would either drown in my own sorrow or freeze to death in the doorway to the stable. These things I well knew; yet I did nothing but sit, imbibe, and think.

No reason could be given for the fire that claimed my family. Accidentally caused was what people said. It was hard for me to believe such reasoning as Helga had always been very careful with tallow and fire. It had been summer and we cooked outside to keep the interior of the house cool. She never burned more than one candle at a time and was always attentive to it. It just did not seem possible.

John had seen no other people about when he ran to the flame, no one at all. He said that it was well after dark when he noticed the glow in the sky. John knew there was big trouble at the Daggit place.

"When I crested the knoll, just past your sign, I knew all was lost." John had told me this same story more than once.

He was so right; all I had now was my cold stable, my one grave cemetery, and my "Daggit" sign which proclaimed it all.

John had heard stories about my problems with the Lakota and the fight with the soldiers down in Hutchinson. He often brought these incidents up in conversation; little else exciting was there to talk about. He always wanted the specifics; the blow by blow details. Short wondered if the men I fought in Hutchinson were some of the same soldiers that had ridden through Crow Creek the day before the fire. Minnesota, he said, was sending more than its share of soldiers off to fight the War of Succession. John's personal view was much like my own; so what. Neither of us cared if Alabama was part of the Union or not. Neither of us cared if there were slaves in Virginia. If those black men didn't want to have task masters they should do something about it. We talked about this whenever John came to check on me. Carol sent him often.

Other neighbors and friends took notice of my depression, each in their own way tried to help. They brought food and occasionally some more liquor. Carol rarely allowed John to consume alcoholic beverage. If I had a bottle he would always stick around and have a spot or seven. John was just so considerate; he never wanted me to drink the whole bottle. He was there to help.

Never once did John verbally harangue me. Carol was quite the opposite. If she had an opinion she made sure I knew exactly what it was. What was most obvious was her desire for my well healed butt to move from the stable back to the real world. I think too that she was tired of sending over meals and having John come back home half drunk.

Svenson would drive his wagon up to Crow Creek from time to time. I enjoyed his visits. Unlike John, Sven always brought a bottle or two with him. He also brought news from down South. He lived only thirty miles away; he would always refer to home as down South. I lived up North. It seemed that Minnesota had spent the entire summer engaged in hostilities with the Lakota. No one was certain as to what had caused the uprising, but there had been some speculation that a lone white man had shot and killed several Lakota children. This lone rider had beat up some others. It was said that he had blinded yet another, a chief's son at that.

"Who would ever make up a story like that?" I asked reaching for the bottle.

"Well some of those Injuns they're fixing to hang said it."

"Hanging?"

"You don't hear a thing this far north do you boy? There is going to be a real hanging Brewster; the biggest hanging in the history of the United States. Maybe it will be the biggest hanging ever. Yes sir, right down in Mankato they are going to swing 35 Lakota braves at the same time. I hear it will be one lever, one drop. It should be something to see, I can tell you this; I won't be missing it.

"Thirty-five?"

You heard me. If these hangings don't send a message to those heathen savages nothing will. You know darn well those Sioux killed and scalped over 400 whites this past summer. A goodly many of them were women and kids too. These hangings should put an end to it once and for all.

"You think that will do it?" I asked reluctantly passing him back the bottle.

"Those hangings and the bounty will do the trick." he said taking a pull on the bottle.

"Bounty?" I was surprised.

"You don't hear spit this far north, do you; especially sitting out here in this barn by your lonesome."

He passed me back the bottle and went on talking.

"It seems the State of Minnesota has given warning for all Injuns, excepting just a few friendly tamed ones, to clear out. Any savage; man, woman, or child caught this side of Lake Brownstone is to be shot and scalped. The State is going to pay $25 for each scalp. Believe it or not, they are even paying the full price for the little papooses."

I didn't have much comment on the matter, but I was sure as to the cause of the whole shebang. Svenson might have made some of his own deductions, but if he did he kept it to himself.

"Oh, I forgot, I got two letters for you from my niece, Lydia, you remember her."

Well, I did.

"I totally forgot to give you the first one. It has been under the wagon seat for weeks."

"You know I can't read," I was reaching over for the bottle he had left unattended as he went to his wagon for the letter.

"Well, I'll just read them to you. One is very short and I already answered it for you."

"You what?"

"Not a worry, I knew what you would say so I just wrote her back. That way she would not know I forgot and left the letter under the wagon seat for most of the summer."

As Sven was handing me the letters his eyes went to the vacant spot where he had placed the bottle. I could detect a hint of disappointment. One of the letters was just a blur. The paper had gotten wet, the ink had smeared. Even if I cold have read I would not have known what it had said. I must have looked puzzled as I gave inspection to it.

"All it said," Sven addressing my befuddlement, "was her extending her condolences on your loss. She wished she could have been here to someway comfort you, but she needed to go home, her own mother was gravely ill."

"You answered her note?"

"Yup, I wrote and told her you wished she could have been with you as her presence would have in itself been most comforting. Then I wished, no you wished, her a safe speedy journey home."

"And the second letter?"

"It is from her too. She says that."

I cut him short, "You already read it?"

"Well you can't read it; how is a man supposed to know what it says.

"I guess."

I took another sip from the bottle. He took it back.

"It says," he began, "Dear Brewster, I hope this letter finds you in good health and somewhat recovered from the grief you must feel. Though I never met Helga face to face we had corresponded for many years. Through these letters I grew to love her very much. Your loss touched me too. Only time and God can heal. I came to appreciate your grief as I arrived home to find my own mother two weeks gone. Death comes to us all. Once I have my affairs in order; it is my plan to return to the Svenson home. They are the only family I have left. I am too young to marry and a lady should not live alone. Perhaps we may soon visit in earnest. Our bathtub meeting was far too short."

I was giving thought to the "earnest." Helga and I had talked in earnest.

Sven on the other hand was focused on the "short" encounter.

"Short, too short," Sven was rolling on the ground. I had never seen him laugh so hard. "Too short she says."

He either couldn't or wouldn't stop laughing.

"Pass me back that bottle," I demanded, trying to change the subject.

"Then she says," Sven was laughing so hard words were not coming, "I'm so looking foreword to seeing you again. I just bet she is, Shorty."

Sven was still laughing, that contagious infectious laughter that soon had me joining him.

When our hysteria had run its course and we could again breathe I asked, "Do you think I should write her back?"

"I already did," he replied, "I made it short."

Laugh again we did. We laughed and laughed. Old Sven was good people.

Chapter 11

▼

That Mankato Hanging was to be the gala of the century. Just about everyone was going; John and Carol included.

"Won't ever see the like again," justified John. "They are going to swing them all at the same time. Good riddance too. What we need here in Minnesota is progress. These backward ignorant savages just have to go. Why Brewster, it just isn't safe to leave a single one of them alive."

John did have his opinions.

Carol wasn't near as anxious to see the actual killings. What she wanted was to make sure John did not dally. Besides, who wanted to be left alone with all the men folk going to Mankato. If the Lakota weren't already mad enough; they certainly would be after the hangings.

I wasn't sure if it was Carol's insistence that I move on with my life, Svenson's humor, Lydia's letters, or the dusting of snow that covered my new day, which caused me to mentally say goodbye to Helga and Hans. It might have been a combination of all four; it just might have been. It could have also been the crash of the empty whiskey bottle that I had just flipped onto the pile of previously broken glass just outside the barn door. Who was to say?

I was out of liquor; I was bone cold, and unfortunately dead sober. I had no future prospects and I wanted to forget my past.

There was a faint flicker of the morning sun through the snow blowing flurries. I just faced that orb which hid somewhere overhead and just walked in its general direction. I did not look back. I just kept walking.

Two days I walked with neither food nor beverage. Early that second afternoon I reached Minneapolis. I was able to procure a meal with the

Hiram Layman family. They asked no questions and seemed eager to help a man of the road. I was even given directions to an inn that might trade work for lodging. Nice folks they were. Theirs was a nice place, something to strive for.

It was a bit of a walk to the inn. Late was the day when I arrived. It was a small eatery with some rooms to the rear. I was cold, hungry again, and broke. No stranger was I to the line, much of my younger years I had spent on the move. I had never had a liking for the Minnesota winters. After my mother passed away I had returned home to help my old man. Five years now I had spent with ax and plow helping him. Then he died. One morning he just did not get up.

I was dragging up; I had had enough Minnesota for two life times. Not a full mile did I walk down that road when Helga caught my eye and then my heart.

Another year I spent with that ax and plow. I built on to my father's house and added to the fields. With Helga by my side the toil was much different. Work I did, but I found comfort aplenty in Helga's arms. We were building a new life together, nothing seemed too hard or impossible. Now it was gone. All I had left was the pain in my heart, brawn in my back and shoulders, and a thirst. I wanted a drink.

It was warm inside the inn. Lanterns had been lit. There were two long tables that both led to a stone fireplace at the far end. The right side table had men seated at it who all seemed busy with their forks. A group of soldiers laughed and cajoled at the other table. Drink they had and it was drink I was in need of.

She came from a room to the right; striking of figure she was, just striking. She was my age, maybe older. It was hard to say, but every eye in the room was on her. These eyes followed her every move, and well she knew it.

Apparently my ogling went noticed; as her eyes noticed my eyes taking in her every feature.

"You there; are you going to sit and order or whistle Dixie." I liked the sound of her voice.

"Me?" I answered.

"Yes, you," she said, "And let me guess, you have a hunger as big as all of Wisconsin and nary a nickel or window to throw it out."

"It shows?" I said, but for the first time I was actually concerned about my appearance. What a sight I must have been. Standing before this woman was a tall, dirty, bearded man dressed in little more than rags.

"It shows. Now sit, no man goes away hungry. We have work and you will earn your meal I'm sure."

"Don't you want me to work first?"

"No, do I look stupid? A man with a full belly can out work a starving man any day of the week. Besides, once you have tasted our cooking you won't be in a hurry to go anywhere."

How right she was. I could smell the mulligan as someone in the back dipped it from a pot. Drool, I was sure, was filling my beard as she placed a heaping plate of the gruel in front of me. It was both hot and delicious. I ate with purpose. The lady left and returned with both coffee and biscuits. These too were polished off.

"Hungry were you?" asked the soldier seated closest to me.

I could see he was a three striper, a sergeant I thought.

"Pretty isn't she?" He asked without even allowing me to respond to the first inquiry.

The sergeant was watching the lady disappear into the kitchen.

"I had me one like that once but she ran off. I sure would like to have me another."

"Ya, me too." was my reply.

I drank more of the coffee; it was hot and black. I didn't need this conversation, it reminded me too much of Crow Creek.

"Yes sir, that old lady of mine was a looker, and cook, damn that woman could do wonders with a pot of beans."

He took another drink of his liquor. It was both wet and brown; just the way I liked it.

"Recruiting, that is what we are doing, looking for a few good men; men dumb enough to march south and stick their nose into someone else's business, men who want to face up to those Johnnie Rebs."

He swept right with his arm, "I got these four prospects up North. Willow River is where I found them. A recruiter has to look long and hard to find replacements."

Four young boys sat the other end of the table. Not a one of them could have been over 16 if he was a day.

"Ya, is that right," I replied.

His conversation was becoming annoying. I wanted my coffee and just maybe a sip of his whiskey.

"Yup, I am just looking for a few more dumb asses to meet my quota."

"What does it pay?" I asked shocking myself as much as the sergeant.

"Fourteen dollars a month, Yankee Greenbacks; feed and found. Interested are you?"

The sergeant was looking me over.

"Here," he said passing me his bottle. "Have a spot."

I poured some of the whiskey into my cup; then drank it down. It burned so good.

"Have another," suggested the sergeant.

I did just that and felt much better for it.

"We march tomorrow. We will be south of the Mason Dixon by November."

I poured myself another glass before he offered.

"Have another," he said.

As I already did, I had a third, then a fourth.

"Mary," he yelled, "Mary, bring me the bill for this fellow."

Morning brought with it a warm wind from the south, a headache, and induction. I was now a private in the Second Minnesota Volunteer Infantry.

Chapter 12

▼

From Mary's eatery to the assembly building at Fort Snelling was a long heckling walk. Those young recruits made it their special purpose to harangue and harass me.

"I didn't know the sergeant needed a few old men, I thought he said he wanted a few good men." teased a teenager with not a single whisker on his face.

"He said that he wanted some good old boys." said another recruit.

Someone responded with, "Well he got what he wished for."

They all began laughing again.

"He said that he needed another dumb ass." laughed another youth trying to not be out done. This boy was a little bigger and looked at me as he made his comments.

I had never considered myself old or stupid, yet as I marched along I now felt both. For a taste of his whiskey I had committed my twenty eight years of life experiences to my country's new cause. Marching off we were, to shoot other country men because they thought a little different. It just did not make much sense to me. In my wanderings before I came back to the farm I had spent some time south of the Ohio River. I had met many nice people, men with character, men who knew how to fight.

"Wonder if they can find the rag man a uniform to where; he surely needs something to wear. The cheeks of his ass are showing." These boys were giving it to me.

Yet, I chuckled a little from time to time; the boys were doing little more than telling the truth. Trouble I did not need.

"I suspect he won't up and run when we take it to those Johnnie Rebs. He will be too busy trying to lift his walker and cane."

There was a roll of laughter, laughter which was ignored by the sergeant's order to knock it off.

Despite his efforts, many were the insults and jokes, all of which were aimed at me. Once at the induction center their incessant haranguing stopped only briefly when we were lined up with about a dozen other recruits, most of which matched up well with our boys; young and disrespectful.

As we stood the line there was snickering aplenty, starting first with my original hecklers then in extended up and down the line, then other men started to get involved.

Twice the induction sergeant attempted to gain some order but he was for the most part ignored.

"I have never seen such a group of inductees." he said, over and over.

"Atten hut!" was the order. An officer entered the room. He was about my age, shorter, with a peculiar mustache. A gold bar sat on each soldier.

"Gentlemen, welcome to the Second Minnesota Volunteer Infantry, a branch of the United States Army. You will be sworn in, outfitted, fed, and marched; all of it today. We are on our way to join up with the rest of this unit now camped outside of Red Wing. You are replacement soldiers for men already fallen in the service of their country and its great cause. We expect each man to do his share."

"Even grandpa there," was the hushed mouth comment from the rear.

The entire rank went to laughing again.

"Atten hut!" was the silencing order from the sergeant.

Most obeyed, though some subdued snickering could still be heard.

"Sergeant," said the Lieutenant, "you have certainly reached the bottom of the barrel with this bunch."

"Sir?" questioned the sergeant.

"What we have here are twenty-three disrespectful smart asses and a dirty old man." He was looking at me as he made his comment.

"There was not much left out there to recruit," justified the sergeant, "the rest had already been taken. We did the best that we could."

"Damn," was all the lieutenant said as he surveyed the two lines of men. Then he said, "Lord help the Union. Recruits, repeat after me. I, state your name."

I complied, "I, Brewster Daggit,"

At the same time, behind me, I heard some kid say, "I, state your name,"

The whole assembly broke into laughter. Many were the orders to quiet down by both the sergeant and the lieutenant before order was finally restored.

When finally the oath was taken; I and the others were officially inducted into the army. Next there was the processing line where pertinent information was being recorded.

"Name," the clerk requested.

"Brewster Daggit," I replied.

My hecklers broke up again, "Brewster, Brewster," they were all laughing.

"Brewster the rooster," someone yelled.

"That will be enough," ordered the clerk, though little good it was doing. These boys could not contain themselves.

"Your whole name, sir" asked the clerk.

Someone yelled out, "butt."

The unit exploded with laughter.

When finally the exasperated clerk had my attention again, he asked my address.

"My address?" I asked. I had never been asked for an address before. I was stalling for time.

"Your address?" he asked again.

"Crow Creek," I replied.

"Crow Creek Brewster the rooster," one of the hecklers blurted out.

"Erka, erka, caw!" some kid was just hooting.

Again the whole place was up for grabs.

"Enough!" it was the sergeant now walking the line. "That will be enough."

"Your date of birth sir?" asked the clerk.

Again I was stumped. I paused a few seconds, gave it some thought, and then replied, "November, 1835."

Again there were some who snickered; snide comments, but most were very hushed of mouth. The sergeant continued to stare at the line of recruits. He was doing his best to control them.

"What day was it?" persisted the clerk.

I could only honestly respond with, "I don't know."

The clerk seemed vexed as he said, "Well, just pick one."

"Sunday," I answered without even thinking.

The entire unit burst out laughing again, even the clerk and the sergeant.

When the laughter finally subsided he asked, "Next of kin?"

"None, sir"

"Then who if anyone should we notify if you are killed or wounded."

"Elif Svensen, Hutchinson, Minnesota," was my answer.

Even the best of men, men with long fuses and lots of never mind will tire of constant haranguing. As the day progressed the lack of internal fortification was taking its toll. I was sick and tired of the constant teasing. Even more I wanted a drink of whiskey. I was not in the best of spirits.

We were issued uniforms. Despite the ceaseless verbal jabs on the part of the young soldiers I was able to cloth myself in my new attire; long underwear, a heavy blue shirt, and winter pants with a stripe down the side. Although itchy, I was quite warm. The boots, complete with new socks, were a good fit. I tried to remember when I had owned socks without holes. Then I tried to remember when I had a pair of socks.

My wondering mind was quickly brought back to Fort Snelling.

"Well look here," it was one of my constant hecklers. He was a young lad, maybe not yet sixteen. He was as tall as me and carried come weight. "Grandpa Brewster Rooster thinks he is a soldier."

The sergeants had left the room; I saw none of them.

"I have had enough, boy." I replied emphasizing the word boy. "It's over."

"Is that so Gramps," one of the other boys had stepped forward.

It is hard to say what the uniforms did for these new soldiers, but they had their courage up and they were looking for a fight. No less than seven of these new soldiers were crowding forward.

That first kid never knew what hit him; hard was my right hand. I caught him solid to his cheek. Down he went; as his knees hit the floor I kicked him square to the chest, the force of which flipped him onto his back.

There was a lad, not near so tall, who had his fist cocked but his eyes were diverted to the kid on the floor. I blindsided him with my recovering left fist and spun him to the floor next to the first kid.

Now I was among them, knuckle and skull; I hit or kicked every target I found. I gave much more than I received. So many were they that what punches they threw were for the most part without effect. They just could not get a clear shot at me as their buddy would be in the way. I on the other hand had faces aplenty and I was scoring hits.

"Wack, wack," I would punch one, he would fall back and I would have another taking his place. To each I gave full measure. Blood covered my hands, none of it was mine.

In less than a minutes time I had five down on the floor and two hurt one retreating into the circle of young gaped faces.

"Now, its over," I roared, "I have had enough." I was trying not to gasp for breath. "You will leave me alone. Do you understand me?"

Not a sound did they make; not a sound.

"Now line up on that wall and sit your asses on the floor. Keep your mouths shut, not a word. Do you hear me?"

I was really mad now. "Move!"

Twenty young soldiers helped five fallen hecklers to the wall where they all silently sat. Not a word was uttered. There were a few near sobs from the five, but no other sound could be heard.

I sat the opposite wall and stared at them. Twenty three kids who couldn't fight their way out of a gunny sack looked back at me. Not a one dared to glare; most would not make eye contact. All I could do was shake my head. The state of Minnesota was sending these boys off to die.

These boys did not glare, but I did, not a one took the challenge. I knew I could not lick the whole lot of them, but they didn't. I for sure had their attention.

Bye and bye the sergeant and lieutenant walked back into the room. Both were dumb founded. The unruly disrespectful platoon silently sat the wall looking straight ahead. Five of them were still bleeding; two of those looked ahead with one eye, the other now swollen shut.

The lieutenant assessed, and then looked over at me again.

"Sergeant," he said, "promote this man to corporal."

He was looking at me. "What is your name?"

"Daggit, Sir." I replied.

"It is Corporal Daggit." he said as he left the room.

Three weeks later as we camped near Galena, Illinois, I was promoted again. They now called me, Sergeant Daggit. These boys were poor students at best, but they did learn.

Chapter 13

▼

Training, what little there was took place as we traveled. We had been issued uniforms, boots, infantry equipment, a musket, and a bayonet while at Fort Snelling. Not an hour later we were on the march.

Our rifles were not shot over a dozen times throughout our travels. The weapon was my first experience with the percussion cap. Although heavy, I found its loading easier and faster than old Irving's. We practiced actually firing the weapon very few times as ammunition was just not available.

"Just look down the barrel and fire low." was what the quartermaster had said. "Aim for the belly and you will take them where they live."

I knew I would hit what I shot at with Irving; it was always loaded with buck shot. I was not so sure with this new musket.

We arrived in Lebanon Junction, Tennessee as raw, untested, replacements. The Second Minnesota had itself not yet been battle tested but there had been many fatalities thus far, men who we were replacing. Disease, I was told, took men by the scores, more than the rebels ever did. As we marched into the encampment we were heckled by many. What I saw were gaunt, sickly looking men, filthy of uniform and person.

Chuckle to myself I did, in camp were men who were dirtier than me. Although I had cleaned up some since I left Crow Creek, I still carried crud aplenty. Sure I was the smell of my person would keep the Rebs out of range. The combined smell of this Army of the Cumberland should probably keep the Rebs clear out of the state.

As I and my squad followed the Lieutenant I could see many of the odiferous sources. Open fly filled latrines were scattered among the hundreds of tents. Not a one of these pits was without users. Bare butts hung out over the latrines, the corresponding bodies counterbalanced without regard on the other side of the rail. Men squatted, smoked, chatted, and grimaced, shoulder to shoulder. If the smell wasn't offensive enough, the causal indifference certainly was.

"Welcome to Lebanon." A Captain greeted us at the big tent. He had a sly look about him. He carried more weight than he needed. "Lieutenant," he said, "Present your replacements."

"Sergeants," Lieutenant Preston yelled out. "Bring your squads to the line."

"Right face," I answered.

Twenty three of my squad turned right, one turned left, one did a complete circle.

"Form two lines to my right. Now!" was my next command.

The squad fell in without too much further confusion.

"Attention!" I ordered as did the Sergeants from the other squads.

My squad complied.

The Captain gimped along the line and took survey of his replacements. He favored his right leg.

"Well done Lieutenant." he said addressing our contingency. "My name is Captain Richard Jordan. I am your worst nightmare. I am the asshole of assholes."

I had not yet spent an hour in this camp, and not six minutes with the Captain; far be it for me to dispute the man. In fact, as I listened, I concurred with his comparison.

"You will be soldiers here. You will obey all orders. No exceptions will be tolerated. Punishment for infractions will be severe. All dereliction of duty will result in court martial. Those found guilty will not be mustered out. You will be shot. That is all."

He turned to Lieutenant Preston.

"Your squads will pitch their tents on the east end of camp, just west of the creek. The spot has been flagged. Sergeant Murphy here will show you the exact spot. You will report within the hour for further assignment."

He turned and walked into the command tent.

"Left face," was the order from Preston.

"Left face," responded the squad sergeants.

"Forward march," was the command.

We then marched to the east end of the encampment, this Sergeant Murphy leading the way. A flag marked the designated spot where we were to camp. Murphy pointed out the obvious before he left. I gave out our squad assignments. The men responded as they had since Galena. My word was law. I didn't know if they respected the new Captain, but well I knew they still feared me.

My job was to see that the work got done, not to do it. Tents were pitched; gear was secured. My charge did as directed.

I knew all of them by name; I was friends with few. Most were just too young and immature to associate with. Their all too consuming goals in life had much more to do with their carnal appetites than anything else. Doubt I had as to whether any had actually ever consummated a relationship, but their constant braggadocios conversation might lend some validation to their claims of lustful conquests. Simply put, tell a lie big enough and often enough even a prevaricator will start to believe it himself. So intent was the squad in these types of conversations little or nothing could or would divert them. Unfortunately many of my squad would experience death before the carnal pleasure they desired.

Me, I just wanted a drink. It had been days since I last had a taste of whiskey.

Our evening mess was far from palatable but we ate it anyway; beans and some type of stringy meat. They boys had a lottery as to what type of meat it had been; dog, cat, horse or mule. They ran the gamete of possibilities with no definite winner. No one could make it past the latrine to ask the cooks.

It was not yet dark when we were summoned for a camp inspection. Captain Jordan along with his entourage stood us at the line.

I was quite proud of our layout; it looked good to me. Shipshape was the term that came to mind.

"Lieutenant Preston, who is in charge of this squad?" asked Jordan. His voice was not at all pleasant.

"Sergeant Daggit, Sir," answered Preston.

"Sergeant Daggit!" bellowed out the Captain.

"Sir," I responded.

"Daggit, move your tents back twenty paces. Dig your latrine over there." He was pointing at a spot on the ground that was not ten feet from the latrine we had already dug. "Move your stores over there. Put your water barrel over there."

On and on he went. There was no reason for any of his changes. Fifty feet back was no different than fifty feet right left or where we were. We were in a huge hay field. And to top it all, no matter where we moved, our existing recently dug latrine would still suffice.

"And do it now!"

He then walked off admonishing Lieutenant Preston who trailed along.

I was mad; mad to the bone. There was no reason at all for any of it. Our camp was at the designated flag, the flag pointed out by his personal sergeant.

It had taken several hours to set up camp, it would now take the same to take it down, move it fifty paces, and set it up again. Then to make it worse, it was now dark and we were tired.

I took a deep breathe, then another.

"Squad, break camp. We move fifty paces to the rear," was my order.

Move we did; fifty paces arrear. My exhausted men hit the blanket well past midnight.

Reveille announced the new day. My untimely awakening came with two affirmations. First, Jordan was indeed an asshole; and two, he was my worst nightmare, at least that night he was.

Chapter 14

▼

I had a dislike for Captain Jordan and I was not alone. It seemed he gave annoying burdensome orders for the sake of giving orders. We were not singled out; he was not particular with whom he trifled. He couldn't help himself. He was who he said he was; no one could have described him better. He was an incredible blemish on the Army of the Cumberland.

His order to move our camp the previous night had been especially disheartening. His next order to Lieutenant Preston was to break camp and prepare to march; and we had not yet finished our wet breakfast. Steady was the mornings drizzle. Our world was turning to mud.

Just six hours previous we were a few feet affront; now we were dragging up again.

"Pack it up," I ordered, "we are moving camp."

"Again?" questioned Corporal James.

"Again," I answered.

"In the rain," he moaned.

"In the rain."

Many were the grumblings but the boys began their tasks. I could see up and down the line. Everyone was breaking down their quarters. As we fell to our work the rumor mill made its way through our rank.

"Yippee, we're going to the big show," yelled Knoll. Dirksen Knoll had for sure lied about his age to enlist; he could not have been a day over thirteen. He thought this was a game as did the Carpenter twins, Jonathan and Bernard.

The twins were from Willow River. They were tall, big of bone and well muscled. Both had however been put in their place that first day at induction. Big they might be; neither could fight for spit. Bernard still carried my mark on his cheek.

A few of the other men chimed in with hurrahs and bravados.

"We're going to show those Johnnie Rebs who we are!"

"We're going to run them all the way to the ocean."

Some of the others were of the opposite emotion. Erik Miller and Christian Pauli said not a word. Emerson Blankenship, the oldest of the squad, had never said a word; not this day or any other. Many times I felt sure he was devoid of all mental process, and then he would surprise me and successfully tie one of his boots.

"Stack your gear on the mark," Corporal James was most diligent. He and I talked from time to time, that was about it.

Corporal McCormick and I were closer. We shared a tent and conversation. McCormick was from New Ulm. He was the oldest of five children in a strongly Methodist family; the other four were sisters. He said that they were all blond, much prettier, and a lot tougher than he was.

"Where do you think we are going?" McCormick asked.

"I'm not sure, but where ever it is we will be the last to know. We just do as we are told. If we knew, we would turn and run for sure. Who wants to die?"

"Not me," McCormick was most emphatic.

Within the hour, we, the now well practiced decampers, were prepared to march. Our wet gear was neatly stacked and waiting for the teamsters to arrive.

"Sergeant Daggit," it was Lieutenant Preston. "Call your squad to attention. Call roll. See that they are prepared to march."

I did as directed.

Before me stood two soaked corporals and twenty some soldiers, boys each and every one of them.

"Corporal McCormick, call the roll."

I would have done it had I been able to read the roster. Try as I might, the letters just never fell in to place for me. Good thing the army never tested literacy; I would have been a buck private forever.

"Anderson, Steve," began McCormick.

"Here," here came the high pitched response I had become accustomed to.

"Blankenship, Emerson," called out the Corporal.

There was no response.

"Blankenship!"

There was still no response. The Corporal was standing directly in front of the man not three feet from his face. Still Blankenship ignored him.

Looking at Emerson I swore the lamp in his head was lit but no one was home. McCormick had been telling me his bucket never reached the bottom of the well.

"Emerson!" shouted the Corporal.

"Yes," he finally responded.

"Say here," ordered McCormick.

"Where?" questioned Blankenship.

"Never mind," replied the exasperated Corporal. "I swear you are the dumbest son a bitch in this entire Union Army."

There was no response from Blankenship. Nor was there a second doubt in the rest of us. McCormick had hit the nail on the head.

"Black, Vincent."

"Here."

"Butts, Joseph"

"Here."

On he went through the roster. I took note as to each man's equipment and armament. A motley crew of young misfits stood before me. Most were terribly naïve. Little did they know what lay before them, but such was the way of young men and war. Only the most stupid of men would volunteer to face death. If the politicians and generals had to stand the line there would be no war. As I saw it, I was the dumbest of the dumb; even dumber than Blankenship. I had joined this fight for a drink of their whiskey. Here it was, not two hours into the new day and it was a drink of whiskey I dearly wanted.

"Smith, David" called out the Corporal.

I knew he was the last name though not why. I certainly wished I knew the order the letters came in. My twenty-eight years had been spent doing everything but the alphabet. I thus far had the first three letters down pat, but after that I could easily get confused.

"Smith," called out McCormick.

"He has his butt over the rail," responded Dowell. "He has been there off and on all morning."

"Permission to join him," requested McMickle.

"By all means," answered McCormick. "Be ready to march within the hour."

I watched as McMickle, Dowell, and four others joined Smith at the rail. I briefly considered the same but saw right off there was a lack of space. I could wait; at least I hoped I could.

Chapter 15

▼

I had heard somewhere that an army marches on its stomach. Mine was empty. My entire system was void of substance. Everything that I ate went right through me. I was miserable. My only consolation was that everyone else was just as miserable.

My legs were almost numb from their hour upon hour labors. Deep was the mud on the road we followed. Lucky we were if we made ten miles progress each day.

North by northeast was our trek. Our destination was unknown. Seven days now we moved. The persistent winter rains so common to Tennessee had abated. Little help was there from the weak winter sun. The road did not seem to improve.

As we plodded along I learned why they called our plague the trots. Men by the score would fall out along the side of the road to relieve themselves. Then they would have to jog or trot to catch up to their respective unit which never stopped moving.

The farther off the road one went in search of privacy, the farther he had to run to catch up. Hence, none moved more than a few paces from the road. Now add to the scene the sheer number of soldiers, over five thousand of us they said, most in a state of constant diarrhea, one begins to understand the endless line of butts along the road. We thought we were in Kentucky, a beautiful state it might have been, if it were not for the butts of the Army of the Cumberland which were never out of sight. Look here, look there, there was no escaping the view. I became numb to it. I could look, but I got so I did not see. I just marched, one foot in front of the other, hoping to avoid the view, the stench, and the pile.

My boys grew less and less enthused with their life in the army. I had grown totally indifferent. I only wished someone would offer me a dram of whiskey to help me take my leave of this intolerable situation. I would surely be homeward bound.

"Home," it hit me again, I had no home. Once I did, now all that was left were some charred boards and a lonely grave. Yet inside me there was a longing. I could not explain the feeling.

Plod on we did. Plod and plop; plod and plop.

Two days later we were well up into Kentucky. Little had the scenery changed. There were still hills, trees, mud, and butts. For reasons unknown to me we were told to halt and prepare a camp of consequence in a huge meadow that ran parallel to what the Lieutenant called Mill Creek. He said we were near a town called Logan's Crossing. Neither geographic name meant much to me. What did grab my attention was news that the Confederate troops were amassing to the east. How the name General Zollicoffer made it from their side to ours was a mystery for sure, but it was he and his army we were about to engage. General Thomas was said to be in charge of our army. Thus far I had not even caught a glimpse of him.

We were said to be near five thousand in strength, more men than I could count, but I was sure I had seen every one of them squatted along the road. Few were the faces I knew; I could not say the same for the other ends. I had no idea how many Rebs we would face or when. My task was simple; make camp.

Within but an hours time my squad was near finished with our tasks. Hopeful we were that Captain Jordan would not drop in.

"Daggit," yelled the Lieutenant. "Mail call."

"Squad to the line," I ordered.

The boys, now well practiced, toed an imaginary line.

"Sergeant, call the roll"

"Corporal," I called out, "the roll."

"Anderson, Steve."

"Here," came that squeaky voice.

"Blankenship, Emerson."

There was no response.

"Blankenship!"

Still there was no response.

"Emerson!" shouted the Corporal.

"Yes."

"Say here, you dumb ass!" shouted McCormick.

"Here you dumb ass," replied Blankenship.

The laughter from our squad could have been heard clear back in Minnesota. The boys were falling all over themselves; Lieutenant Preston and I included. Even McCormick, the dumb ass, was rolling.

By and by order was restored and the roll call resumed.

"Smith, David."

There was no response.

"Smith, David," yelled out the Corporal.

"He fell behind this morning. He stopped to stoop and just never caught up." was the reply from one of the Carpenter twins.

"Missing one, Lieutenant," was my report. "David Smith fell behind. I will have the infirmaries checked."

"Very good, Sergeant," he said. "Here," he handed me a package. "Your squad's mail has caught up with us."

I naturally handed the package to McCormick who read off the names of the boys who had mail.

"Blanc."

"Knoll."

"Reed."

"Sergeant Brewster Ulysses Daggit."

"Who," was the response from the twenty odd soldiers present, me included.

"Yes, you have a letter, Sir,"

I took the letter in hand and looked it up and down. As I did many were the comments and snickers

"Sergeant Brewster Ulysses Who," was the general gist of their humor.

It took but an evil eye to remind the boys what had happened at their induction. The squad took their mail and their leave. Many were the muffled chuckles as they walked away. Reed and Miller seemed to be enjoying this moment the most, I sent them in search of Smith.

I was left with my letter, my first letter ever. I looked it up and down. There were letters and numbers covering most of the face of the envelop. I could make out my name. That much I could recognize. Helga had gotten letters, but not me, not ever.

I was going on twenty-nine or so and was holding my own letter. It was a real treasure. It was like money or something. Someone had sent me something. I just could not imagine who could have thought enough of me to actually write me a letter.

I carried this most important correspondence to my tent. There I sat trying ever so hard to make out the letter. There just had to be some clue as to who it was from. No one even knew where I was.

"Can I help you with that letter?" it was McCormick at the flap.

"You know?"

"Sure," he said. "If you will allow me."

I handed him the letter.

"To Sergeant Brewster Ulysses Daggit.," McCormick seemed to be having composure problems. "Ulysses?"

"And."

"Nothing Sergeant, he said, "it's a fine name."

"Well I did not pick it out."

"I bet not," he said, then continued with the letter. "It is from a Miss Lydia Layton."

"Who?"

"What did they call you back home when you were growing up, Little Bud?" McCormick was ignoring my question, still focused and still laughing about my name.

"Where did you come up with Bud?"

He was laughing, "Your initials spell Bud."

"Well that is news to me, now will you read the letter before I bust your head."

McCormick seemed to gain some composure.

"Your letter is from a Lydia Layton," he said, repeating himself.

"Who?"

"Lydia Layton."

"It must have been sent to someone else, I never knew a Layton."

McCormick said, "Well, it says it's to Sergeant Brewster Ulysses Daggit, Second Minnesota Volunteer Infantry. I don't suppose there are any other Brewster Ulysses Daggits in the whole Union Army." He had emphasized Ulysses as he made his point.

I clenched my fist and made mine.

McCormick was laughing again. I wasn't. No humor did I see in the situation. Finally he opened the letter and began, "Dear Brewster, So worried we were when Papa Svenson went to Crow Creek to visit and you were not to be found. We thought the Dakota must have taken you captive. Through our investigations we learned that you so nobly became a Union soldier. We are very proud. I must say you made quite an impression when last we visited. You were the first full grown man I had ever seen in a bathtub."

McCormick was laughing so hard he had to stop reading. "Full grown." He said it over and over. I had to smack him a lick to get him to read on.

"Helga had written me many times singing your praises. She said that you were strong, kind, and gentle."

McCormick went to laughing again, "Strong, maybe, but kind and gentle; not in a million years."

Finally after several more smacks to his arm he quit laughing and continued.

"Perhaps when this conflicts ends you and I can finish the bathtub visit we started. I have returned to the Svenson's. My visit home was most saddening as my mother passed away. The Svenson's are my only relatives so I shall reside with them. Be safe, your friend, Lydia Layton"

McCormick handed me back the letter.

"You must have made an impression is all I can say. Yes, Sir, a really big impression. Buddy Boy is it, a full grown man." He was laughing again, but I suppose I was too.

Yet this letter had set me to thinking.

Chapter 16

▼

Where he got it I did not ask, but Bob Reed had an almost full bottle of whiskey to trade. Bob was twenty, not to tall, and not too thin.

"What will you take?" I asked, much in the bartering mood. I would have given my first born son if I still had him. Many days had passed without a drink.

"Here you go Sarge," he said, "what I want is a chance to go home if ever you can make it happen. I am not afraid to tell you either. It is this dying that troubles me so; I am scared to death already. It is sure to be a short trip for me."

"Me too," I confided, as I took his bottle. I uncorked it and took a pull. The contents felt warm as the fluid moved down my throat. "If ever I can oblige you I will, I certainly will."

Busy was the camp with most engaged in some endeavor. The bottle I put to my lips and in front of God and everyone I let its contents warm my soul again.

"Much appreciated Bob, I won't forget the favor."

When I corked that bottle its volume had been substantially reduced. It was not the liquor that put a man's butt to the rail; it was the food, I was sure of it. The food, its poor preparation, and the flies were making men sick, me included.

Here I was again, for the third time today perched with my butt over the pit. Smith we had learned had died of the diarrhea. He, according to reports, just dropped his trousers and fell back dead. I looked down, much disgusted with the view, and rued the same fate. At least I had a bottle in my pocket to look forward to.

"Hey, is this the Minnesota Second?" someone from a cavalry unit riding by yelled out.

"It sure is," yelled back one of our boys.

"Where are you from?"

"Hutchinson," yelled Miller, "I am from Hutchinson."

As I was busy at the rail I could not see nor did I wish to make eye contact with the mounted soldiers. The only privacy in such situations is the lack of eye contact. The contention is that if I am not looking at you, you must not be looking at me.

The mounted soldiers had reined up and were visiting with our boys, this I could hear from the conversations. The men were talking of home and who knew who.

"You there," came a remotely familiar voice.

I looked up from my task to see a big blond headed soldier with a deep scar to his face. He was looking down at me from atop a huge brown horse.

"Remember me?" was all he said as he gave the horse the boot, spinning the animal hard left. That horse's rump caught me square in the face and forced me backwards off the rail into the stinking excrement below. I hit hard and sunk deep. With my trousers down like they were recovery was impossible. I was covered head to toe with a substance so vile I began to retch uncontrollably. Great was my efforts, but I reached the edge of the pit to see the man ride off and join up with others of their outfit. Look at me they did, they looked and laughed; then rode off.

By the time I got my trousers up and retrieved my rifle they were out of range.

My boys dared not laugh, no one in our camp did. No one wanted their ears boxed or worse. I could not remember ever being madder.

God the water was cold. There I was waist deep in the middle of January in the middle of Mill Creek. I was buck naked and trying hard to remove the excrement from my body. My boys had found me some soap; several were at the shore line scrubbing my uniform. Not a soul dared a snicker. They appeared to take my indignation as seriously as I did.

Men camped nearby, however, were not near so kind. They out and out laughed. A man covered in excrement really does not have the will to rebuff. A man naked, freezing his arse off, is even less inclined to engage his hecklers.

Reed's whiskey did much to warm my inners; it did even more to stoke the rage within. As I saw it; it was me one, and Blondie one, but even Steven was not my manner. I had a score to settle and it would not be pretty. No one, but no one, dumps me into a latrine. Finally, I had found a reason to get involved in this war, I just happened to now be on the wrong side.

Chapter 17

▼

With the help of warm clean clothing, a big fire, an evening without rain, and the rest of Reed's whiskey I survived the night. I woke relatively warm and fairly rested. If it were not for my pounding headache I might have called this a good morning.

Lieutenant Preston, however, took exception. "Good morning men," he said.

McCormick said something back to him.

Preston continued, "It seems the Rebs are massing up for a fight, a least that is what the scouts are reporting. They are a day out, but they are coming. We are in for it boys. Get your men ready Daggit, I do not think we will move until tomorrow but get the lads ready."

Preston was obviously nervous, I thought he was repeating himself.

"Have your boys write their letters home," he said. "There is a whole army of Rebs coming this way and I'm afraid some of our men will not be with us tomorrow night."

Preston walked away leaving me little in the way of encouragement.

As I looked out over our little part of the encampment I saw before me twenty-three men, all young and naïve; not a one of which had a mean bone in his body. I tried not to imagine which of the boys were going to die. I tried not to mentally name them but I could not help myself.

Blankenship was for sure in big trouble. He was little more than cannon fodder. Young Dirk Knoll probably would not see his fourteenth birthday. Louis Blanc, Whiteboy they called him, always wanted to go first; no matter what we did. Pauli, the Carpenter twins, McCormick, all might fall, who was to say for sure.

It might even be me. You just never knew for whom the owl called.

"What are you thinking about, Sarge?" It was McCormick taking a seat next to me at the fire.

"Tomorrow."

"Me too," he said. "Someone famous once said something about for whom the bell tolls. I never was real sure about the saying until just now."

I did not respond.

"You just never know," he said.

We sat for a while in silence. I just looked at the fire. It would have been an out and out lie to say I was not concerned.

"Want to write home?" McCormick asked.

"I don't have one anymore, they are all gone. My wife and son died in the fire. I am the last Daggit as far as I know."

"Well how about a letter to that girl?"

"Who?"

"Lydia Layton, you idiot, she seems to be interested in you."

"I only met her once in my life."

"And you were naked."

"So."

"You made an impression."

"I hardly know her."

"Well, you will probably get your head blown off tomorrow," McCormick said most unreassuringly. "You might as well write and tell someone something, you may never get another chance. At least give her the courtesy of a return letter. Return letters are only polite, the right thing to do.

"Polite?"

"Forget it Sarge," he said. "I have a pen, paper and ink. You talk, I will write it down for you."

"I have never written a letter before; I don't know what to say. I don't even know how to start one."

"Its easy, let me start for you. Dear Lydia," he said.

McCormick put his pen to the paper and wrote, {my dearest Lydia,}

"Now what he asked?"

"Ah, I hope you are well and in good health."

McCormick wrote, {I pray this letter, possibly my last, finds you in good health and recovered from the deep loss of your wonderful loving mother. I am so sorry to hear of her passing, but rest assured she is comfortably waiting at the side of our lord for you and yours. It is not our place to judge his wisdom. She watches over you and waits your coming.}

As I was watching him write I said, "Hey that is a lot of letters to say I hope you are well."

"I took the liberty," he said, "and gave condolences on the passing of her mother. It is always proper."

"Oh," was all I could say.

"What more?" he asked.

"Have her tell old man Svenson that if I don't make it home my holdings at Crow Creek are his to sell."

"Ok, that is very important."

He wrote again, {Lydia, I have no family, no one to leave my farm to; consider this letter, penned this date, 18 January 1862, written by Corporal Jason McCormick, to be my last will and testament. Should I die, this letter is your legal right to possession of my Crow Creek Property.}

"What next?" he asked.

"Thank her for writing me; hers was the only letter I ever received."

"That's good."

He wrote, {upon receiving your letter there came a great joy to my heart. That there was someone left in this world who even thought or cared about me was morally uplifting.}

"I think you should put a line or two in the letter about wishing to see her after the war. That way she knows you are serious."

"Serious about what?" I asked.

"Forget it, I will just say what everyone does, yours truly, then your name. You will probably get killed anyway."

"I hope not."

"Me too," said Jason.

Somehow in the past ten minutes, McCormick had changed his name to Jason. He was no longer my Corporal, he was my friend.

"How should we close this letter?"

"Close it?" I asked, this writing was beyond me.

"Yes, he said, "it is proper to close a letter with something like yours truly or respectfully written; then your name."

"Yours truly sounds good, that is what she said."

The good corporal, my new best friend, wrote; {lovingly yours,}

"Make your mark right here he said handing me his pen. Right here, he put his finger at a special spot on the paper. I looked over my first letter and ever so carefully scratched my name. {Brewster Daggit}

The corporal said that he remembered the address and would get the letter posted. He walked away just whistling. He said, "Buddy boy, you should always remember that the pen is mightier than the sword."

I did not have a sword, but my bayonet needed attention.

Chapter 18

▼

"To arms, to arms!" yelled the voice.

I had not yet fallen asleep.

"To arms, Rebs are coming!" It was the same voice coming from the darkness beyond our fires. I could hear the pounding of hooves from the messenger's horse as he raced by our camp and on to another.

"Lieutenants report!" he yelled.

The messenger was riding the line of tents spreading the alarm. I heard his voice diminish as he moved along the face of the camp. His voice was soon drowned by the blare of trumpets. In his wake lanterns and torches were being lit. The camp was coming to life. Men were moving, preparing themselves for the inevitable horrors to come. I was one of them.

It was a cold night, a night with no stars or moon. I fumbled some in my efforts to dress; perhaps the refreshment of the earlier evening had not yet vanquished itself from my brain. In due course, however, I found myself uniformed, booted, and armed.

Our squads were put at attention and I did a torch light inspection. No sooner had I walked the line than we were falling in line with other troops. Within no less than thirty minutes our whole army was up, dressed, and marching. Our squads were in columns of two behind other squads in their respective columns of two. As we marched; cavalry raced past us. Horse drawn cannons and war wagons were moving to the head of the column. Teamsters were yelling, cursing their teams. Whips cracked over the heads of the animals as they dragged their loads forward.

Ahead I could see bright flashes of light followed by the blast of cannon. So many were the blasts they became one continuous roar. So many were the explosions the entire horizon was aglow with pulsating red, white, and yellow light.

"Giving them hell aren't we Sarge," it was Quincy behind me.

"I hope so," I replied. There was no way to know if the cannon fire was their side or ours. Maybe it was both.

As we marched louder grew the bombasts, brighter were the lights. Forward moved the columns.

A man ran past me, he was going the opposite direction. Then another flashed by.

"Hold to your step." I shouted.

"Hold." yelled the corporals.

Louder still were the blasts, I could feel their heat in the air. I was no longer cold. I was sweating, but not from exertion. My heart was pounding in my chest, its beating as loud as the cannon blasts. I knew for sure everyone around me could hear it too.

To my right a horsed officer appeared. In the dim light from the far off cannon blasts I could see it was our own Captain Jordan. He had his saber drawn and was waving it around in the air. What the man was shouting I had not a clue. Nothing could be heard over the deafening noise of the cannons. Ours were firing, theirs were firing back.

We were lead to my left behind a long line of Union cannon. Their respective crews were well practiced. Not a move was wasted as each man did his job. Occasionally I saw spaces in their rank, spaces only occupied by pieces of metal and clothing. Chunks of dark sweet smelling meats lay randomly about the ground.

Ahead I saw a terrific blast of light. The explosion raised a cannon crew from the ground. They flew like rag dolls up into the sky, their bodies clearly visible in that split second of light. Then eternal darkness became their world. Still we marched a line along the rear of the cannons. I saw more blasts, but most fell short in the field in front of our artillery.

Two more men ran past towards the rear.

"Hold," it was McCormick. "Steady with your pace."

The line was soon stopped and I heard the order to right face which I repeated.

"Advance to the wall," it was Preston giving the order.

"Forward," I repeated.

The cannon fire was still deafening, and we were walking towards it. We moved not more than a hundred paces finding ourselves behind the ranks of other soldiers. These men had apparently been at this station the entire night. In the early predawn dawn I could see they were well haggard yet wide of eye. These men were as afraid as I.

To my relief we were behind a breastwork of earth and log.

"Fill in, fill in your rank," it was Jordan coming by on his horse.

"Fill in boys," it was Preston this time.

I could hear Jordan over everyone, "You men, fill that gap. Move that log. Bring up that wagon."

The man just never shut up. He rode up and down the line giving commands to anyone who would listen. Most men just hunkered down as the cannonade was now starting to fall just ahead of us.

I had no idea what time it was or what was going to happen. I wanted a drink of water. No I wanted a drink of whiskey; no wanted the whole bottle. Never had I felt so frightened, so hopelessly not in control.

The cannonade for the most part kept falling in front of our position, causing little or no damage to no more than our ears and senses. Occasionally a shot fell in behind us, but it was the exception. Despite the chaos just a piece of rational thought flashed through my mind.

The Rebel cannon fire was just a few feet short of our position. Our cannon fire was no doubt a few feet short of theirs. All through the night neither side could have known if their firing was with effect. They only knew they were not being hit with fire from the other side. It was a mutual draw. To get closer meant to be subject to a hit from the other side. In the darkness, scouts could not make their reports to the generals who were naturally well back. Now with the coming daylight and visibility things would be changing.

To huddle against the breastwork seemed our only defense against the constant cannon fire. Blast after blast shook the ground and pounded hard our internal senses. With the light of day their artillery began to take effect now. I could see in the light of a near miss, hundreds if not thousands of men, pressed for the safety of the logs.

Never before had I feared the sun, yet I did today. With the rising of this sun would begin the assault, and with the assault would come the horror of battle. Men were going to die; their men, our men, me, who was to say. So loud was the cannon fire I doubted I could hear any owl that might be calling out my name. I could not even hear Jason who was crouched right next to me. I wasn't sure but I thought he was praying. I hoped he was including me.

Chapter 19

▼

As the sun peeked over the horizon to the east, I peeked over the breastwork from the west. Before me sloping away was a huge field filled with holes.

Five minutes now the artillery had been silent. Napoleons, they called them, had fairly well covered the field. These twelve pound cannon balls did much to disrupt the landscape. I saw literally thousands of blast craters; the whole field was pitted. Initially my fear was twisting or breaking an ankle as we went through the pitted earth. Then I realized that the cannonade that had caused this damage was still zeroed in to do it again, this time while we were in it. To say I was even more disheartened than I was would have been an understatement. I just hoped the plan was for us to defend rather than attack.

Off in the distance I cold hear the blare of trumpets. The sun had almost quartered itself over the horizon. This light of day was coming much, much too fast. I was even thirstier.

I could now see the fortifications behind which we hid. We were on the crest of a hill that was a half mile long. The trench we were in had been hastily dug by men with shovels, the dirt was all banked to the east. There were gaps every few hundred feet that were left flat and open. I could see these breeches offered access to cavalry or cannon.

This was not a defensive position. We were not going to wait for them to come to us. We were for sure crossing that pitted hell.

Thousands of men waited behind the wall for the order to move forward. Thousands of men, me included, did not know for sure what was going to happen. Whatever it was each and every man was praying that it was not going to happen to him.

Behind us, lower down the ridge I saw cavalry troops getting organized.

"Daggit!" it was Preston returning from his last report call. "Prepare your squad to defend this section. We will not be advancing, at least not yet. Plant our flag on top of the wall."

This news caused me great relief; I liked it just fine behind the wall. I would have liked a higher wall but this would do, yes all things considered, it was a great wall. It would do just fine.

Many things were happening at the same time; too many to dwell upon a single aspect. Men, horses, cannon were again on the move. There was shouting, cursing, and a general hysteria. We, however, were the lucky ones; our assignment was to defend this small section of a long, long line of dirt and log. I put our squad along the crest of our breastwork. After the squad and flag were in position I looked up and down our rank. I saw them as they were, twenty some wide eyed terrified boys. They each held a rifle they hoped never to fire. The bravado I saw and heard earlier was gone.

To our left and right were squads of seemingly more seasoned veterans. Most of them had beards, something my boys may never acquire. These men sat back and smoked. They talked among themselves. Outwardly they seemed to have no regard to the pending fight. I took note of their sergeants and emulated them as best I could in my orders and actions.

I saw mounted scouts racing in and out of the breaks in the breastwork. Messengers galloped their horses along the line. Now the empty wagons moved steadily along line. They had delivered their respective loads and now stood by for the dead and wounded.

"Blammm"

An exploding cannon ball had hit with effect. Men were screaming. Men were down; bleeding, hurt, and dead.

They had the range and let go with volley after volley of cannonade. More men fell; more men died.

Cannon fire was returned from our side much diminishing the cannon fire from theirs; but fire still they did. The smoke from the blasts made visibility near impossible. No more than a hundred paces could I see. Within that hundred paces not less than a dozen men lay dead, scores of men were injured. Their cries for the most part brought no help.

As I looked out towards the Rebel lines I saw our own Captain Jordan riding his horse back and forth in front of our breastwork. He was still waving his sword in the air and yelling something, which no one could hear, if ever they cared.

"Hold men," it was Corporal James to my right. "Hold."

"They are coming, I can see them," someone yelled.

"Hold," McCormick was yelling.

All eyes were to the far edge of the smoke. We could hear the Rebel yells but no target yet presented itself.

"Ready," I yelled. "Ready your rifles."

"Ready," yelled the corporals.

Still the only thing we saw was Jordan in front of us waving his sword in the air.

There came next a blinding explosion and horrific blast in front of our position, the result of which removed Jordan and his horse from the field. They were there; they were gone. All I saw was a sword come falling back to earth from some place up in the sky. It landed on the ground just few feet away.

"Damn," was all I could say. "Damn that was one fine horse."

If anyone heard me I never knew as the field in front of us was now gray with advancing men; advancing Rebel soldiers with their rifles at the ready.

"Squad one," I screamed, "fire!"

The report from their rifles shook my world. At that very moment what fear I had was gone. I had in an instant gone from a man to a soldier.

"Squad two," I screamed, "fire!"

So loud was the noise I didn't know if my orders were being heard, acknowledged or followed. It was now every man for himself; aim, fire, load, aim, fire, load, over and over. So heavy was the smoke I was never sure if I hit my targets. Men yelled, screamed, cried and died. Some ran for their lives, most stood aimed, fired, and loaded.

The Rebels advanced over their fallen. They kept coming up the breastwork where we met them barrel and butt.

I bashed them good, dropping several at my feet. Our boys held. Reinforcements came up from behind us, muskets loaded at the ready. Their face to face volley with the Rebs broke their back and they fell back, some still firing as they would manage a reload but most just ran for their lives. As these men withdrew, cannon fire resumed from both sides. We hid again, tight to the wall. There were fewer of us; it wasn't so crowded this time. Christian Pauli, a Carpenter, Anderson, and Corporal James were down and not moving. Dirksen Knoll was hurt as was McMickle. Knoll had a bad wound to the arm. McMickle had a bloody groin. He wasn't yet dead but probably wished he was. Those wagons behind the line began to take away the wounded. The dead were left as they fell.

There were two dead Johnnie's at the crest of the wall. One had a pistol in his hand. The other, just a boy, had a revolver still holstered. I reached up and took both the weapons. I stuck them in my belt.

Chapter 20

▼

"Close ranks!" was the order.

Forward we marched, weapons loaded at the ready. The bomb blasts and rifle fire grew louder as we walked. We were a line of soldiers perhaps a thousand strong spread across a huge rolling field. Through the now clearing smoke, a quarter mile ahead, I could see our objective. On the hill ahead of us were the remnants of the Confederate army we had earlier repelled. Then, as if God was on our side, the now defenders of the hill, were being hit with heavy Union cannon fire. So heavy was bombardment that the resulting smoke once again hid our objective from view.

The fact that I could not see them did not mean they were gone. They were ahead and waiting.

From the north came another detachment of Union soldiers, flankers they were called. This column of blue was not near as strong in numbers as ours, but a goodly number it was. The flankers began to take cannon fire from the Rebel line. Then exploding cannon balls began to rake through our lines.

"Kablammm!"

Men to my right fell, men that I did not know.

From the wall of smoke directly ahead of us came the cavalry, our cavalry. At least fifty mounted men, all with blue shirts, were coming right at us; cannon fire chasing them as they fled. They were retreating towards us and we were still marching towards them.

"Ready!" was the order followed by a quick change. "They are ours, Yanks are coming."

The cavalry had closed faster than anyone expected.

Someone yelled, "Spread ranks, let them through!" Little good was the order as men had done just that on their own.

Right behind the fleeing cavalry appeared a line of gray soldiers. There were more than I could count. A Rebel yell, a battle cry, near drowned out the roar of cannon and rifle as these men broke from their double time march into a run. More men than I ever imagined were even in the Confederacy were coming at me with rifle, bayonet, pistol, and sword.

"Forward!" some Union officer yelled.

Cannon blasts fell behind us, on us. Cannon fire raked the Rebel assault, yet they came, and still we advanced. Men seemed to fall by the score, both gray and blue.

And we, the infantry, Gray and Blue, advanced on each other.

"Ready!" was the order again, followed quickly by, "Fire! Fire! Fire!"

The Rebs were less than one hundred yards off and coming fast. They were shooting at us, we were shooting at them. Now cannon fire from both sides was hitting heavy with great effect.

Men fell to the ground, writhing in their agonies.

Still we raced towards our enemy.

At twenty yards both advances stalled. Men just stood and fired. Heavy were the losses, blue and gray. Few were the misses from such short range. As a man fell, another took his place. The noise of battle, the screams of terror and death, the smell of it overwhelmed my senses.

"Fire, load, aim, fire!" I repeated to myself over and over. My targets were many, my targets fell.

Despite our efforts we were forced back, stumbling over our dead and wounded as we did. We regrouped, quickly formed new squads, and then advanced again. We were forced back again.

I was hit; something hot spun me in a circle. I fell to the ground and took cover behind a dead horse, the space mostly taken by its former rider. The trooper sat motionless, his back to the belly of the horse, holding his blood soaked chest.

The Rebs were advancing again through the heavy smoke from battle. It was hard to see just how many there were. I saw no Union soldier still standing. There could have been a hundred ten feet away, but not a one I could see. Rebs were just feet away when I remembered the pistols stuck in my belt. Quickly they filled my hands, left and right. I did not even know if these weapons were loaded. I had never even fired a revolver before, but I knew the principle.

Cock, aim, fire. Cock, aim fire. The gun in my right hand cracked and spit out fire and death. A Johnnie fell at my feet. My left hand took another at three feet; then another, and another. My shots were from no more than a few paces and I was making hits. Men fell, men died.

"Click, click," my revolvers both fell on empty chambers.

As I looked for another weapon, something to at least throw; blue shirted soldiers were again advancing. The Rebs were again falling back.

As our line moved past me I just turned around and sat down behind the dead horse next to the wounded trooper. I just closed my eyes. I was hurt. I didn't know how badly, I didn't care. I just sat with my eyes shut and hoped the world would just go away.

When at last I opened my eyes I expected to see the Pearly Gates of Heaven or worse. What I saw, however, was the bloody bearded face of the man who shared my equine fortress.

"You're Daggit, aint ya?" he choked. Blood was coming from his lips. He was still leaning his back against the belly of the horse, he had the rear quarter, I the front.

I just looked over at him. There was familiarity but I could not place him. I could see that he was not Saint Peter, nor was he Satan. He was merely a sergeant, and probably in limbo just like me.

"Daggit?" he questioned again.

"Yes," I answered.

"Well you whipped me once fair and square and you just now gave me a few more minutes to live."

He made a few more moaning and coughing sounds, weak though they were.

"I am hit hard and not long lived." He was coughing again. I could see that the blood stain on the front of his shirt was growing.

"Who," I started to ask.

"It's me, Big Johnson Maher," he coughed. "You whipped the bejesus out of me and Clayton Matthews back up in Hutchinson."

Slow was the recognition but it came.

"I'm dying, Daggit. I've been dying for most of an hour. It's just," he coughed again, a little more blood spewing down his chin, "well, I have been waiting for the angel of death to carry me off. Damn if it isn't Brewster Daggit they send to get me."

"I'm no angel."

"No, but you was sent as sure as I'm dying.

He moaned then coughed again.

"I'm not going to cross over unless I come clean. I'm coming clean. It wasn't me. God knows it was not me. It was Clayton and Lieutenant Boland that done it. I just stood at the end of the road looking at a stupid sign."

"Sign?" I questioned, moaning some myself. There seemed to be a huge hole over my left hip. A chunk of me was gone.

"Your sign, the Daggit sign," he said, his voice now much softer, much more raspy.

"Did what?" my brain finally catching on. Maher was trying to tell me something.

"Your, Mrs. Daggit."

"Who?"

"Your Mrs. and boy, they died hard, real hard."

"What?" I asked, getting to my knees. I grabbed him by his shirt. "What did they do to her?" I demanded.

"What," I was yelling, "What did they do to her? What?"

I was shaking him, banging his head against the dead horse; but neither responded or ever would.

Chapter 21

▼

One week; two; three full weeks I endured the screams and smells of the infirmary. Many were the wounded and sick. Death was all too common.

I witnessed the horrors of both the mutations and amputations. They surpassed the battlefield terrors that I had somehow survived.

I had been forced abed many days as we waited for my new hole to mend. As I did I saw arms and legs forcibly removed from screaming men who were still intending to use them. The smell of gangrene and death permeated my nostrils.

For days on end as I listened to the screams and moans I thought of Helga and my boy. I could mentally hear their screams. I loathed the men who had caused her death. The men who killed my son would pay with their lives.

I knew them both, I would find them.

I made vow after vow to myself; vengeance would be mine, mine alone.

I seethed in my anger. Incapacitated as I was, little else had I to do.

Pained though I was, my slow healing wound had an upside. At least I did not have to bury the dead. The word was, at least three hundred Union and six hundred Reds had perished. At least twice that many men were receiving treatment in this butcher shop. I hoped they had dug a few extra holes. More men were sure to join their comrades in the ground, if their wounds and treatment didn't get them, disease surely would. Everyone was sick.

Yet, I was spared. Week three, day four, I was given my leave and sent back to my unit. I had with me a letter to present limiting my physical exertion until I was fit for duty.

The hole over my hip was healing, my heart was not.

As I walked through the encampment looking for the Minnesota Second, I searched the faces of the men I passed. I looked at the flags. Actively I sought out Matthews and Boland. No luck did I have.

"Hey Bud," I heard a man yell. "Sergeant Bud is back."

I hoped the hale was for someone else but well I knew the voice; it was Private Reed.

"Bud's back," became a chorus as men of my unit came from their tents and duties.

My men were calling me, Bud. They were accenting the Bud as they yelled out. No one had ever called me Bud, no one but Lydia in her letter. There was for certain a snake in the old wood pile.

"See you made it, Bud."

"Welcome back."

"Hurt were you?"

Many were the questions and comments as men of my squad gathered around. I was being squeezed, shook, patted and cajoled. It was Buddy this and Bud that.

When once I could speak the only vocal response I had was simply, "Where is McCormick?"

"There he goes," someone yelled. "He's running for the high ground."

He was too. Jason McCormick was running away from camp. He could have run faster had he not been laughing so hard.

Few were my physical labors for many more weeks as my wound was allowed to heal. Twice we moved camp; I contributed little to the labors. It was all I could do to just march along. As we marched I searched the faces of the men we encountered.

My plan was simple. Find them, walk up to them and shoot them both dead with my pistols. I had confided Maher's dying declaration to McCormick; that and my plan. McCormick said that he knew Matthews would die anyway for the latrine incident, now there was even more reason; but he cautioned me to use some logic in this endeavor.

"You know Sarge, as justified as you are you have got to think this thing through. You probably won't find them both together; life is just not like that. If you kill one the army will surely hang you, especially since you aren't even an officer. The one you don't shoot gets off free and clear. You can not prove the Crow Creek case; no witnesses, no evidence. You can't even verify what Maher told you. Everyone will think you killed a man because his horse knocked you into the latrine."

"And," I retorted with some indignity.

"Most thought it was the funniest thing they had seen in months."

"Who laughed?"

"About everyone, except me," smiled Jason. "But if you shoot one, you will for sure never get the other. You will be hanging from some cottonwood tree."

Jason then went to his pocket, "Oh, I almost forgot, I've got a letter for you, it came just today."

He looked it over, "It says to Sergeant Brewster Ulysses Daggit; would you like for me to read it to you?"

"Sure, who else could I possibly trust," I said with as much sarcasm as I could muster.

He opened it with an, "Oh my."

"What is it?"

"It says," He paused, "now don't get mad at me, I'm only the messenger."

"Read it."

"Dear Buddy," he began, trying hard not to snicker.

"What!"

"I'm just reading what it says," he interjected. "If you will let me continue, I will."

I did not say a word.

Jason read, "Thank you so much for your timely response to my last letter. I can only imagine how busy you must be. War is so unmerciful. I pray you will come home to us safe and sound. You are a man of such great character; of this I am very sure. Both Svenson and your late wife had confided in me often about the wonderful man you are. Both said that you were one in a million. You certainly seem to be. Your interest in me is very flattering but perhaps you are just a lonely soldier. Irrespective, do keep writing, my interest in you is most genuine and grows with each letter. Your new friend, Lydia."

I was speechless.

"Wow," Corporal McCormick was obviously much taken back as was I. I thought right off it was the near provocative content of the letter which brought on his response. Little did I know it was his own handiwork which caused his awe.

"We are going to answer her, aren't we, Sarge?"

"I suspect we can but I don't know what to say."

"I have always thought the truth made the best of letters."

"The truth always works for me." I said.

"Let's write her back," he said, "I have a pen and some paper. The army has plenty of ink."

"Right now?" I asked.

"What else do we have to do?" "Ok," I said, "how about, Dear Lydia."

He wrote, [My Dearest Lydia,]

"I want to tell her that I was wounded at Logan's Crossing but I have since recovered."

"That's good, she will want to know."

He wrote, [There was a terrible battle at Logan's Crossing, a small berg in southwestern Kentucky. I was hip shot and incurred a significant injury but have since recovered. The losses to my squad were many.]

"What next?" McCormick asked.

"Should I mention what Maher told me?"

"I think so; the more people that know what really happened back in Crow Creek the better off you will be when you exact your vengeance."

"Ok," I responded, temporarily lost in my own thoughts.

McCormick was busy with his pen. [A man known to you fell in battle. He was one of the two horse soldiers that I had trouble with in Hutchinson. His name was Johnson Maher. He perished at the Crossing, but not before making a dying declaration. Maher told me that his accomplice in Hutchinson assault on me, the scoundrel Clayton Matthews along with their red headed Lieutenant, James Boland, were responsible for the death of my wife and son.]

"What else?" It was Jason saving me from the internal screams I heard as I for the thousandth time, envisioned the Crow Creek assault on my family.

"I, ah, I don't care. Fill it in." I said as I walked away. "Say what you will."

McCormick did just that.

Chapter 22

▼

Life in the Union Army of the Cumberland changed little from day to day. Eat, practice maneuvers, eat, camp labors, eat, guard detail, all of which was rewarded with a miserable nights sleep on hard, rock packed ground. It was either god awful cold or hellishly hot. For the most part dry clothing never touched our bodies. We were soaked head to toe from either the snow, the rain, or the sweat from our labors.

Whiskey had been the bait that caused my enlistment into this madness. Once a soldier its procurement became a real problem. Rare were the times we had money to buy it if there were any to be had. Generally we stole it from civilians along our routes of march or if need be, from each other should someone else have been lucky enough to steal it first.

Women were harder yet to come by, especially if one had already wasted his money on the whiskey. As I saw it, it was a no win deal. The women were so ugly one needed to buy the whiskey first, then with a penniless pocket, the camp followers were but wishful thinking.

Never did we camp long in one spot or town. The war was like a game of chess. Our army would move to a place of advantage, and then the other army moved to take advantage of our place of advantage. Then we would pack up and move to still a different place hoping to upgrade our now disadvantaged position.

The eat, maneuvers, eat, work, guard routine was then mixed with eat, decamp, march, camp, eat, guard, and sleep. We moved as often as the Rebs moved, they moved as we moved. It seemed no one really wanted to fight, they just wanted to be in the better position if they were forced to actually do battle. Often times the moves themselves resulted in accidental hostilities.

We had skirmishes at Corinth and Tuscumbia, neither one I thought was planned.

At Tuscumbia we were marching along the north side of a pasture. On the opposite side of the same pasture marching in the opposite direction were the Rebs. Neither our scouts nor their scouts had spotted or reported the presence of the other faction. We were several thousand strong; I had no idea how many Rebs marched just 40 rods to the south. There was a bunch of them, of that I was sure.

As we saw them, they saw us.

They positioned a line of rifle men along the south pasture fence. We positioned men along the north rail.

"Daggit!" came the order. "Give us cover fire on command."

"Pick a target," I yelled, "ready; aim."

"Fire," came the command from Preston.

"Fire," I yelled.

The blasts from our rifles came at the same time as the reports from the Southern rifles. We may have had a hundred men on the rail, they the same.

The mini balls from their barrage smacked hard the rails and men behind them. We had men down all along the line.

"Daggit, I'm hit!" It was Lieutenant Preston behind me. He was down on the ground, blood poured from his thigh.

"Fire," I yelled. Then it was volley after volley. "Load, aim, fire. Load, aim, fire."

At least four times we did a volley fire. To what effect I did not know.

The Rebs did the same, their effect I could well see. Of the hundred at the rail, at least a dozen were down and were not moving. At least twice that many men cradled or nursed their wounds. Many were crying; screaming with their pain.

"Fire at will," I yelled. "Just keep their heads down."

For twenty minutes we fired at the south fence, they fired at the north rail. So thick was the smoke no assessment could be made as to what effect our rifle fire had upon their ranks. They too had problems with the smoke as their rifle fire was doing little damage. Gradually our army marched out of range as did theirs. Our fire diminished as did theirs. Eventually we vacated the fence row and I assumed they did too.

Lieutenant Preston, his leg now bandaged, Vincent Black, and Eric Miller were taken by ambulance to the infirmary wagons. Bradley Dowell was dead. A mini ball had entered his right eye and removed upon exit his left ear. We buried him along with 13 others at the rail where they fell.

The smoke of battle was just clearing as our men dug the graves along the fence row. Across the field I could see the Rebs busy with their shovels. All the diggers were well within range of each other but not a shot was fired by either side. We buried our dead then marched our separate ways. They went south and west; we went north and east.

Chapter 23

▼

When you are in the infantry and of low rank as was I, the plans of the generals are just as unfamiliar to you who carry out the details as they are for the enemy. I was always in the dark. I got used to it.

For months on end we moved, camped, and moved again. As we traveled, constant was my search for Boland and Matthews. I saw neither.

We joined up with other units, big and small, only to split up again. New recruits continuously replaced those who had previously fallen in battle, those whose injuries were beyond repair, or those who had succumbed to the many illnesses that plagued our camps. Illness I thought claimed more lives than the battles. This was just an observation that I had made. I was not a mathematician, just a soldier with his butt on the rail with naught to do but look around as he did his business.

Lieutenant Preston never returned. What became of him I never knew? He was replaced with Lieutenant Robert T. Haney. Haney was a nice enough kid. He was all of five feet tall, thin, and blond. If it were not for his whisk of a beard he might have passed for his sister. Haney caused no problems. He gave no orders other than those passed on to him by the Captain. When he was so obligated to do so, his squeaky high pitched voice caused many a smirk. As I frowned upon open cajolement at any officer's expense, never was the lieutenant embarrassed.

Haney and I developed an understanding. He gave no stupid I'm in charge orders and his charge gave him no grief. I was good with the arrangement as was my man of letters, Corporal Jason McCormick who just sat the fire circle with me.

"We got another letter, Bud."

"We?"

"Excuse me, you received a letter," he said. "I just happen to have it in my hand. Since I have written her back six times now I just assumed I was part of the we."

"Six times?" I questioned.

"Yes, sir, I just wrote a few extra ones here and there when I had some free time."

"What did I say?"

"Oh, not much, just some this and that's."

"This and that?"

"I only told her what came to mind. Do you want me to read this letter to you or not?"

As he spoke, he was already tearing open the envelop.

"Dearest Buddy," he began. "I so enjoy your letters, news from the war is important to those of us who wait for our loved ones at home."

"Wait," I interjected, "loved ones? Who is she waiting for?"

"Beats me," replied Jason. "Let me read this, will you?"

"Go ahead, you probably already read it."

Jason continued, "Your suspicions about Boland and Matthews were conveyed through Svenson to John Short. Short, in turn, told Svenson that he had leanings towards that very scenario but was without proof. Without basis he made no accusation. He was afraid of what you would do. I am afraid of the same; afraid that you will spend the rest of your life trying to avenge what the Lord will see to in due time. I'm afraid that you will not come home to me. Love, Lydia."

"What did she say?"

"She says that she is waiting for you."

"What is with this, I hardly know her."

"Well she certainly has an interest in you old Buddy Boy."

"She's nuts, I'm almost old enough to be her dad. I only talked to her face to face once, and that was just for a few minutes while I was in the bath tub."

"You were naked?"

"What to you think?"

Jason was now rolling on the ground, he was laughing so hard I thought he would near burst.

"She's nuts," was my only retort as I walked off into the camp looking for Reed. Reed almost always had a bottle of something hid close to hand. I was in need of a spot.

As I left the fire circle I did not see a more composed; smiling, whistling Corporal with a clean sheet of paper in front of him. There was no way I saw him pull the pen and ink from his jacket pocket.

Chapter 24

▼

August had been dry; September was worse. We were near twenty one thousand strong, or so it was said. We were, to a man, god awful thirsty. An army as large as ours requires an immense source of water for both man and horse. The Rebs also needed water.

Since the Battle of Mill Creek both sides had moved and postured, then moved again. So many times did we move, I had not even a clue as to which state we might now be in.

What I did know was my throat was parched and that my body cried for water.

The creeks we passed were either dry or polluted. Farm wells were of no use as their recovery rates were just too slow to sustain any real number of drinkers. Scouts were constantly on the move trying to locate water sources; scouts from both armies.

Rumors flew up and down the line as we marched. Up ahead they said was a place called Doctor's Creek. Doctor's Creek had two things; water and Rebs. The Rebs held it, we wanted it. I could hear gun fire just over the rise.

Things were happening. Too long I had been in this man's army not to know when a fight is upon us. Trumpets blared. Messengers galloped along the long column of thirsty men. Officers were receiving their orders, Haney included.

Haney drew his sword from its scabbard, raised it over his head and in his less than confident squeaky voice yelled out, "Sergeant Daggit, your squad, at a double pace, follow me!"

I had no idea where he was leading us but I gave the same order to my corporals who relayed it to their men. McCormick gave me that, "Ya right," look but did as directed. Recently promoted Corporal Carpenter also complied. Both squads were double timing behind Haney who was trying to position the men between other squads.

Haney looked ridiculous. His sword was nearly as long as he was. He was waving it around in the air yelling. He was acting like he knew what he was doing but I knew better. The Lieutenant who leads generally gets shot either by the enemy or his own men. Both sides wanted them dead. If the enemy gets them; there is no order to advance. If they get shot in the back, accidentally of course, there is no one to order the assault. Either way it's a win for the infantry soldier.

Seasoned officers stayed to the rear of their rank, well to the rear. They justified their position as being at a point where they might better direct. I always thought that being able to retreat ahead of the column was important too.

Below our advancing position, behind breastworks of wagons and timbers, were what looked to be a million Rebel soldiers. They were at least more of them than a man could count. Beyond the Rebs was a creek. It was a 10 feet wide fast flowing mountain stream. Our army wanted the water, the Rebs held it. A logical man might counter and say, okay, you guys can drink here, we will move a few miles upstream and drink there. That way everyone can just get along. Not in this world. Our generals thought we needed to drink where these other guys were drinking. We were thirsty, and we needed the water. If this was the only spot to get it; we were going to have it. This creek was the least tangible reason to fight I had thus far seen since enlisting. Who was I?

Buglers blew from both ends of the long slope. The trumpets announced the cannons that now lobbed their deadly volleys. The cannon fire came from both behind me and in front of me. Both sides began blasting the other. I would first hear the ignition blasts, then whistling missiles just before our world exploded.

Men and parts of men literally flew into the air. Those that survived screamed in their agonies.

"Charge!" was the order. "Charge!" screamed the Lieutenants. "Charge!" screamed the Sergeants.

Forward we moved, we were but a blue mass of terrified men; men who did not want to die. Our pace was much quickened. Each step was faster than the one before it. Heads were down, most tilted back to the side. Fools we were to even think not facing the enemy barrage might help one live a second longer. Each step was met with cannon fire and mini ball. Men fell by the score. As they fell we walked across their bodies, our rifles at the ready. The screams of men, cannonade, and thousand upon thousand of rifles stifled our senses. Forward still we moved. We could not have stopped if we wanted to. The men behind us by the shear weight of their number moved the columns ever forward.

At fifty yards our head down double time march became a trot. Our rank screamed as we attempted to scare the Rebs and booster our own bravado. As we screamed out our battle cries our trot broke into a run. Our run became a sprint. Thousands of screaming men raced towards the breastwork as a horde from hell itself. Not a Reb could I see for the smoke of their guns. As we ran men fell. So many were mowed down no distinction could I make as to their individuality. Men were there then they were gone. We ran at certain death, most men now resolved to just die and get it over with.

At ten yards, still at a run, I heard a voice yelling, "Fire! Fire!"

We leveled our rifles as best we could while yet on a run and let go with our first barrage. Not a target did I see for the density of the smoke. Three steps and we were in, over, or through their breastwork. It was barrel to stock, man to man. A thousand men were pushing and shoving trying to win the battle with the shear weight of their numbers.

I used my rifle to push and bash, it was knuckle and skull up close and personal. I stroked a kid, just a young boy in a gray shirt. Down he went. As I stepped over him my rifle was wrenched from my hands by a Reb to my right. He had it, and then he had no head. It just exploded. The weight and forward push by the men behind me prevented even attempting to retrieve the weapon. Within but a second we were many paces further into their lines, ever pushed from the rear. I was charging without my rifle. No choice did I have but to draw my pistols.

Cold was the water. I was now knee deep in the creek. I wanted desperately to drink but forward still I was shoved. Three, four paces we moved before I was again on dry land. I was on the opposite bank. No target could I see for the thick, acrid, choking smoke. Forward still was the push; the noise and madness was unmerciful. No step could be taken without crushing the now useless piece or appendage of a previously fallen soldier. Blue or Gray I could not tell, red was the color of the day, blood red.

We were moving uphill now. Our run was now a walk as men gasped for breath. So labored was my breathing I thought my lungs were about to burst. Yet forward still we moved, still pushed by men behind who were just as winded. The screams of men were deafening.

I was near blind, lost in a moving cloud of powder smoke. My eyes burned. Tears filled my face. I had no idea where we were. At maybe a hundred yards past the creek our assault had stopped. We were stopped dead.

No, we were being forced back toward the creek. The rifle fire had increased again. Their rifle fire was my assumption as we were the ones falling back. I was back stepping.

Suddenly there was a lifting of the smoke. There were no blue shirts ahead of me, only gray ones. A wall of gray shirted men was coming at me, me alone! I looked right, left, no blue shirts did I see. I was about to die.

Chapter 25

▼

The solid gray line of men was not three paces away. They were advancing at a walk, their rifles at the carry. I could barely see their faces through the acrid smoke. They no doubt could barely see mine.

I stepped back, preparatory to my pending flight and tripped over the feet of a lifeless soldier. Backwards I fell, my butt landing hard to the stomach of the recently perished. Hard was my impact, the force of which caused the dead man to expel his last remaining air. I heard not a sound from him, the roar of the battle what it was, but I strangely took notice of the warm gases he eliminated from his uncontrollable orifices.

At that very instance in time, my pistols, one in my right hand, one in my left, began to buck. It was as if they had a mind of their own. I sat my butt on a dead man's stomach and fired shot after shot.

My enemy was upon me, but their eyes were in the smoke. I sat below the cloud. Visibility was mine. I picked out my targets. Eyeball to belt buckle we were, and I was making hits.

Surprisingly I took care, aimed, and fired; first with one hand then the other, left, right, left, right.

Two, four, five men fell. I was actually keeping count.

Six, I hit him left. The bearded fellow went to his knee not a pace from me. Under the smoke our eyes met and he was taking aim with his rifle. As he did, the barrel of his weapon hit me right in the chest. He pulled his trigger and the hammer fell without effect. No shot was produced. He looked at me in horror as I shot him dead in his eye.

My shooting had produced a space in their line, the Rebs were marching around me, not because of my fearsome deadly fire, but because they did not want to walk across the bodies before me. I, under the smoke, was nearly still nearly invisible.

Under the canopy of the heavy smoke I could see a short fellow to my right. He wore a gray shirt and he had taken notice of me. I shot him as his rifle was coming to bear. The man fell at my feet. He was not dead; he wreathed yet in the agony of his wound. Blood flowed heavy from his chest. The man was game; he wanted me more than death. He got to his knees, then to his feet with amazing speed. He lunged at me with his bare hands. I shot him again and again. I shot him until he finally collapsed at my feet. As he went down his fingernails reached out and ripped flesh from my face as he fell.

The Rebel advance had stopped. The Rebs were now the ones falling back. They were passing me by again. They were being forced back the other way.

The ground began to vibrate; it trembled as if we were in an earthquake. The gray line of soldiers was retreating; no, they were running back up the hill.

Chasing them was the cavalry, our cavalry. I could not believe my good fortune. Right on cue, the cavalry was coming to my rescue. I was not the intention of their assault, but I did find their assault on the Rebel line most timely. In but a few seconds the running gray uniformed men were replaced with frothing beasts ridden by saber and lance waving horse soldiers wearing blue uniforms.

"Yeah!" I yelled though I knew not why. As I stood up the acrid smoke too began to rise. I full minute I stood my pile of corpses watching the cavalry race by. I was ever grateful I was not one of those whose body lay before me. I was thirsty. I was dry, ever so dry.

Through the now clearing smoke I could see the faces of our troopers as the spurred their mounts onward; each man no doubt searching for a place to stick his lance. I saw them all and mentally cheered them on as they chased the enemy away from me.

I saw a red headed man with Lieutenant bars race by. His was a fine horse. Befuddled was my mind, confused from battle it was, as it took too long for the recognition process to take place. He was almost out of pistol range when I let my hammers fall.

Left, "click."

Right, "click."

Both weapons were empty.

Next to me on the ground laid that short Reb's rifle. I grabbed it and took aim at the back of a red headed man who within but a second disappeared into the smoke of battle.

To my right came another target moving fast at a gallop. He too was in a blue uniform. He was big, blond, and scarred. He was Clayton Matthews. I leveled the rifle, took a deep breath, adjusted just a tad, and touched it off.

I actually saw the shot smack the horse in the rump. The shot crippled the animal which caused it to crumble to the ground. Matthews went flying off over the animals head. He hit the ground, rolled, and came up running.

I started for him, an empty rifle in hand. My intention at this point was to just beat the man to death. A few steps I took towards him, my assault hampered much by the other horsemen continuing to gallop by. Horsemen were all about me; I was lucky not to be bowled over. I began to make progress when I saw Matthews grab the reins of a rider less horse. He mounted and was off in the blink of an eye; none the wiser as to how he had lost his original mount, none the wiser as to just how close he had come to dying.

Chapter 26

▼

My disappointment with my marksmanship quickly waned as I took note of the carnage about me. The battle had moved up and over the hill; south into the pine trees beyond. I walked back to my pile of bodies, discarded the Reb's rifle and retrieved my empty pistols. Looking around I saw a field covered with bodies, hundreds of them. They were both blue and gray of uniform, but red seemed to be their common bond, blood red. Walking, crawling, wiggling among the dead bodies were the frames of men who would soon join them. They cried and wailed with their wounds and fears. Well they knew their own fates. Few would survive the day. The butchery of the infirmary would be their reward if they did. I could hear the battle raging yet somewhere to the south.

"Bud," it was McCormick making his way through the bodies, "We still live."

"Yes, but I don't know how."

I was still stricken by the horrors about us. The sight was unbelievable, ghastly. I wanted to cry. I wanted to vomit. I wanted to runaway, but didn't. I stood my ground as soldiers have done since the beginning of time. "Is anyone still with us?" I asked.

"Eight or nine, I think, we were forced back across the creek. I guess you got yourself separated," he said looking at the bodies of dead gray shirted soldiers who seemed to have walled off my position.

"Hot spot," was all he said.

"Ya, it was that," was all I could say. I needed to load my revolvers that hung empty, one in each hand. The Rebs might be soon pushing our own boys back. I did not want to be again caught unprepared if opportunity again presented itself. Neither did I want to be killed. How I had escaped death or significant injury could be no other than an act of providence.

"Thirsty?" queried Jason.

"Ya, real thirsty," I replied trying hard to forget everything else.

We helped no one, Jason and I ignored everyone put ourselves. Their pleas, their pleading, their pathetic plights were ignored. They fell on deaf ears. Blind were our eyes to their suffering. We two had survived. That for the moment was sufficient for us. We wanted a drink of water and meant to have it.

Jason and I walked upstream in the creek passed the bodies of men and animals. The waters still ran red with their very life blood. Doctor's Creek they had called it. Those we saw in it were no longer in need of his services. At least a half mile we walked before we passed the last floater. Then we moved still further upstream before we found water fit to drink.

Cold was the water, cold and pure. We drank our fill then some more. Other men began to join us, men with both blue and gray uniforms. They came as singles, pairs, and groups. They drank then walked away; some went south, others, Jason and I included, returned to the north.

Neither a shot, nor word of animosity was exchanged by the drinkers. Men just quenched themselves then left. Not an hour prior these factions had killed each other without thought, without guilt. As I thought this over only one common factor stood out. Not one of the former combatants wore brass bars. They were all just soldiers, just men who were lucky enough to have survived.

Most of the rest of the day we spent trying to locate and reorganize what was left of our unit; few now in numbers we were. That night we counted heads. Our miniature saber waving boy lieutenant was not among us. There were seven of us left out of the original twenty-four. I counted them myself; me, Jason, Emerson Blankenship, Louis Blanc, Dirksen Knoll, Quincy Adams, and passing me the mostly full bottle was, Bob Reed.

The bottle was uncapped and unlabelled but its brown wet contents would warm me, body and soul. I let the first mouthful slosh back and forth between my teeth before I swallowed it. On the second pull, I skipped the sloshing. The third and fourth pulls were but hurried gulps as others were waiting their turn on what remained of the diminishing elixir.

Reed never seemed to mind that I almost always took more than my fair share. He had learned a long time ago that there was a relationship between my consumption of his whisky and his assignment of camp duties. The more he gave the less he had to do. Apparently it was easier to buy, steal, or beg a bottle of whiskey than it was to dig a latrine. Reed was no dummy.

Emerson Blankenship, however, was. He was six feet seven if he were an inch. He towered over me. He never talked or smiled; he just stared straight ahead and did what he was told. He had uncommon strength of body. Many a time he was told to do things generally assigned to two or three soldiers. Blankenship would grab, lift, and move whatever it was without comment or effort. How he had survived thus far was a mystery to us all. He was what I called cannon fodder, just someone to send up the hill first, which I often had. Despite his being out front and his immense target presentation not a single mini ball had nicked his person. No one had ever recalled seeing him fire his weapon. What damage he did, if any, to the Rebs was a mystery to me. We always skipped Emerson when we passed the bottle. It seemed a waste, and as he never talked, he never made a complaint.

Louis Blanc, Whiteboy, was young, too young to be a soldier. He wasn't of mentionable size or weight, but he always took a pull when the bottle came his way. Then he would make the most god awful faces, gag, and hack. Then he would giggle a little and wait for the elixir to come back around. After three passes Whiteboy would be fast asleep.

Dirksen and Adams had paired up months ago. They seemed to be the best of friends, mostly keeping to themselves. On occasion both would imbibe. Curiously they would wipe the bottle with a cloth or sleeve when it was passed to either one of them; but they never wiped it when it went from one to the other. They were certainly a pair of odd ducks, good soldiers though; followed orders and kept the pace. "I guess we will be needing replacements," McCormick said as he passed the bottle my way again.

"I suspect so; seven men can not accomplish much."

McCormick was in the talkative mood, "Do you ever wonder why some men fall and others do not."

"Every second," I most truthfully replied, "every second."

"Here, take these, Bud," he said, handing me a small waterproof satchel. "These are your letters from Lydia. I've been carrying them for you. You should have them, you know, just in case."

"Just in case?"

"Ya, just in case."

"You know I can't read a lick, what good are they to me?"

"They are yours."

"Okay," I said only to appease him. I took another pull on the passing bottle before I stuck the satchel up under my shirt. As I did, I saw a face in the smoke from the campfire. It was Helga's. She wasn't smiling.

Chapter 27

▼

Burial detail was always the worst of chores. I hated it almost as much as the battle. At Doctor's Creek we used a long trench. It wasn't very deep as there wasn't much soil; about three feet was all we could dig before we hit solid rock.

Blacks and locals were used to carry the bodies to the wagons and caissons which moved the once living to the trenches. This work was seen as unfit for white men or Yanks. It was only proper that the stinky grotesque task be carried out by Rebel supporters and or the colored. Both appeared to us equal to the task. Occasionally they would find a man still alive. He would be taken to the infirmary, then later to the trenches. The trenches were separated, deeper ones for Yanks, shallower ones for the Rebs. When on occasion a man got dumped into the wrong trench; there he stayed for eternity. No one was going to touch him again. We said nothing, we just kept shoveling. More than a thousand men had died; and for what, I kept asking myself, a drink of water. Our much decimated unit was given replacements. Most were green recruits, but a few were veterans from other units. No discipline problems did I have. Somehow word spread quickly among the rank and file. Sergeant Daggit was no one to mess with. McCormick was made Sergeant for the grand total of one week, and then he was promoted to Lieutenant. It seemed that the ability to read and write was essential in that position. I was good with the promotion, but sad too. My good friend's longevity had been decreased. Officers, especially Lieutenants, were the first to get shot.

McCormick's first order was directed towards me. He made me his first sergeant, what ever that meant. It didn't really matter to me; all I wanted was to find a big blond with a scar, a red headed lieutenant, and another bottle of whiskey. The one I had was now an hour empty. There just wasn't much more in this war for me. I kept a weathered eye for all three.

After the "Creek" we spent several months recuperating; licking our wounds as it were. We trained and drilled daily but for the most part we were not involved in any major battles.

Skirmishes, however, were common as both sides moved and probed; looking for their opponent's weaknesses and strengths. Chattanooga was the key to Dixie. Even a dumb sergeant like me could see it clear on a map. Everything and everyone had to pass through Chattanooga. The Army of the Cumberland was going to go get the key to Dixie. The prospect pleased me little.

McCormick turned out to be a genius in the tactical art of avoiding battles and conflict. I marveled at how his unit continued to find itself in reserve or lesser roles. During the entire rest of the campaign for Chattanooga we found ourselves guarding munitions, horses, food, stores, and contraband. Whiskey was considered just that and of course it was like putting the fox in the hen house. Life was just not so bad.

For months we stayed well sotten. Drunk though I might have been, my blurry eyes searched constantly for my prey. Somehow I knew there would be another chance to redeem my poor marksmanship.

We were in and around Chattanooga for months. We had it, we lost it. Chickamauga had been a horrible defeat for us. I blessed the day McCormick was born as we stood back in reserve and watch the horror from afar. We were there, we were ready; we just never got the nod. McCormick thought it prudent not to volunteer. Not a soul in our squad was lost in battle. Two of the new recruits and one veteran, however, died from disease; one suffered with ague, the other two typhoid fever.

I dug the veteran's grave myself. Carefully, very carefully, I laid a mostly full bottle of spirits on his chest. Then with an issued blanket I gently covered my friend for his long rest. Bob Reed was a good man and I would miss him.

Despite McCormick's best efforts and much to my disappointment in November we found ourselves south of Chattanooga at some place called Missionary Ridge. A general named Grant had taken over and things were changing. Sherman had an army to the east; Hooker had one to the west. We were stuck right in the middle looking up a god awful high mountain full of Rebs.

The Confederates had the high ground and for some reason Grant wanted it. Me, I was for leaving those Rebs up there and just going home; but no, someone was calling us to formation.

God, I hated the sound of drum and bugle. I hated them almost as much as the sound of cannon shot or the crack of rifles. All of it meant men were about to die. It was the screams of those men that I hated the most. I did not know who nor how many, but men would surely die this day because Grant wanted to be on top of that ridge.

As we formed our ranks I could look up and see our goal. It was the top of a big tree covered hill on the south side of Chattanooga. Lookout Mountain was to my right. Yesterday Hooker's outfit had run the Reb's off of it. Grant was just plain greedy, he wanted both mountains.

"Sergeants report," Jason ordered.

"Report," yelled his aide.

I and three other sergeants stood the line.

Jason began his instruction with little enthusiasm of confidence, "We will be spearheading the assault."

There was a silence.

"Us," I gulped, looking up at the hill.

"Yes, us, Bud."

"Why us?"

"I ran out of excuses," he said.

"Damn," I said again looking at the mountain. I could see at least three distinct horizontal lines of rifle pits. They stretched from can see to can't. There were cannon emplacements everywhere. We could see them plain as day. They had the high ground and could rain shot on our cannon before they could get close enough to hit them.

"Damn," was all Jason said as he looked up the same hill. "They call it Missionary Ridge."

We just looked up at the mountain.

"Our orders," Jason began again, "our orders are to advance up the ridge and take that first rifle line. We are to hold it. Sherman's main army and most of Hookers are to assault the flanks. That is all I know."

"When do we march?" asked Sergeant Johnston, a replacement from some Wisconsin regiment.

"Within the hour, ready your squads."

We turned to our tasks.

"Bud," it was Jason pulling me aside. "Here," he said handing me another letter. "It came yesterday. It's from Lydia. She wants to marry you after the war."

"She what?"

He was chuckling, "Yes, sir, she is bonified topsy turvy in love with you. She says that she will be waiting at the Svenson's for you to come home. She says it doesn't matter how long it takes either."

"She's nuts."

"You have said that before. You keep your head down today. You have a woman waiting for you back in Hutchinson."

"Marry her!" I couldn't believe it. I hardly knew the woman.

"Yes, marry her. You'll have to, you know." Jason snickered.

"And why is that?" I retorted.

Because I wrote her back and said that you would."

He was laughing now, that deep infectious laughter that comes from within. He couldn't stop.

Despite my pending doom on the ridge or my matrimonial fate back in Minnesota, I too was caught by his hysteria. It was indeed at my expense, but funny is funny. I was still laughing when I gave the order.

"Forward, forward men, at a walk"

Chapter 28

▼

Our laughter was short lived as both sides began their pre-assault bombing. Cannon from both sides tried to soften the other. As the Rebs had their artillery on the higher ground they had the longer range and the advantage which they were using to good effect.

Men were being blasted from our lines even before we began our actual assault.

To my left an entire squad literally disappeared in a blast of fire and shrapnel, only to be replaced by the squad behind it. They stepped over the dead as they filled in their rank.

I heard a trumpet blare and we were moving again. The cannon blasts were now behind us, but I knew well they were making adjustments. Our only hope was to move quickly and try to out pace their ever rising trajectory. Rarely were we successful. We had nearly a half mile to cover before we even hit the base of the ridge. Many would be our dead and wounded.

At first we marched, then McCormick yelled for a double step. Men still fell to the cannon blasts, blasts that shattered men and spirit. Terror and horror became our world as we raced for the mountain.

And race we did as McCormick yelled, "Charge!"

"Charge!" I yelled though I didn't know if I was heard over the explosions all around us.

The last quarter of a mile was an out and out sprint as we tried to out run the cannon fire that rained death upon us.

As we hit the base of the tree covered ridge we were greeted with mini balls from the first line fire pit that we were assigned to capture. Men screamed and fell as the deadly rifle fire took its toll. The Rebs were in unison with their first rifle volley. Men all around me were mowed down like wheat. Still we advanced; maybe another twenty seconds through an eerie smoke filled silence. Our lungs were pounding with exertion.

"Ready!" It was McCormick taking charge.

"Ready!" I yelled to my squad.

"Aim!" screamed McCormick.

"Aim!" I repeated as loud as I could.

We were still advancing as the Rebs in the trenches were reloading.

"Now!" ordered the Lieutenant.

"Fire!" I yelled as I discharged my rifle at the pit.

The timing had been just perfect. As the newly reloaded Rebs were bringing their rifles to bear we blasted them hard with a volley of our own. Our targets were small but we scored many hits.

"Get yourself behind a tree," I yelled, put your backs to a tree and reload."

My squad did as directed, shielding themselves as they reloaded. Other near by squads were following our lead. Some trees protected 3 or 4 men as they reloaded. As we reloaded the Rebs cut loose with a volley of their own. Few were their targets; harder still was it to hit anyone in the now building dense smoke of the battle field. As soon as the Rebel volley diminished I heard the Lieutenant give the order again to advance.

"Advance!" I yelled.

I heard the order repeated across our lines as we again moved up the hill.

"Ready!"

"Aim!"

"Fire! I yelled, timing the order with the Reb's reloading of their rifles.

Again we shocked their ranks with our mini balls as they were taking aim. Every hit we made was a head shot as that was the only target presented. Every hit was a dead man.

"Behind the trees," I yelled again.

Again we used the cover of the trees to reload our rifles.

The noise and the terror of the battle was horrendous. The cannon, however, had abated. We were well up the hill rendering the artillery useless. To be of service the pieces would have to be fired at a down hill angle. They could not do this without hitting their own positions. We were but twenty five yards now from the trenches. They could not elevate high enough to drop rounds on us. We were past the last point of effect.

"Fix bayonets!" was the order.

"Fix bayonets!" I yelled as did the other sergeants and corporals.

Even with the shots from the thousands of Confederate rifles being fired at us I could hear that metal on metal clinking noise as those long pig stickers were snapped into place.

"Ready!" I yelled to McCormick when the last of my squad was fixed.

"Ready, ready, ready!" came the yells from other squads.

A heavy rifle barrage cut loose from the trench ahead. Few were their targets as we were hidden behind trees or bellied out. They could be seeing little or nothing. As the barrage finished I heard the order plain as day.

"Charge!"

We did the last twenty five yards, our rifles at the ready. As the Rebs brought their guns to bear we fired at will. We did not stop to reload; we just kept the assault moving. So many were we, so thick and menacing were our stickers, the Rebs could do little but fall back to their second line of trench.

Their uphill retreat kept the second rifle trench from being able to fire with any effect as their comrades were shielding us. The retreating first trench soldiers were actually running interference for us.

I don't know who sensed the advantage; we were thousands strong, but we did not stop at the first rifle pit as we had been initially directed.

"Remember Chickamauga!" someone yelled.

"Chickamauga, Chickamauga!" became a battle cry up and down our advancing line. We must have looked like rolling blue wave coming up that hill; a wave that would not stop. There was no order to charge. There was no command to do anything. Captains, lieutenants, sergeants and soldiers advanced; each was a fighter onto himself.

"Chickamauga!" they yelled.

If a man went down and lost his flag; another man grabbed it and continued the advance. I saw it over and over. If a man fell, those behind him stepped around him, on him. There was no stopping the assault. Uphill we moved.

The second trench was cleared by a screaming horde of blue clad savages. I was but one of many. The fighting was hand to hand. I stuck a man with my bayonet, withdrew the blade, and then despite his pleading eyes, I stuck him again where he lived. I advanced on another man. Someone else shot him. My bayonet, still in motion, pierced an already dying man. A mini ball exploded the fore stock of my rifle, the force of which numbed my left hand. A pistol from my belt immediately filled my right hand. It was making noise and I was making hits. As I advanced I put a shot into any Reb that presented a target. When that pistol was empty, I grabbed my spare and continued the insanity. Few were my misses. Our attack was without mercy, it was vicious, up close and personal. Now running up the hill from the second trench were the survivors of the first trench assault and now the second trench assault.

Once again their retreat blocked fire from the remaining top trench. Their own men were again running interference, and we were right on their butts all the way up the hill.

"Chickamauga!" we yelled as we cleared out the top trench without much opposition.

The Rebs were running down the other side of Missionary Ridge when our men reached the top. Little more could we do but fall to our knees and gasp for breath. Our exhaustion was complete. Grant now had both hills. I hoped he was happy.

Chapter 29

▼

I had not been the first man to reach the top of the summit, but from what I saw I wasn't too far behind him. I thought I might never catch my breath again. Labored was my breathing, each breath of air was a conscious effort. Twice I thought I might vomit but the feelings eventually passed.

When finally I quit gasping and could stand, hundreds of men, all in blue, covered the top of the ridge with me. They were shouting in triumph; their weapons, arms, and flags filled the sky.

No live Rebs did I see.

To the north and south of us, Hooker and Sherman were still involved in their assaults. I could hear the sound of their cannon.

Most of the men on the ridge were strangers to me. I looked for men of my unit. I had been in charge of twelve men at the onset; I didn't see any of them, not a single man.

As I looked down the ridge towards the captured rifle trenches I saw that the ground was literally covered with bodies. They were both blue and gray of uniform. Many too were the wounded. Those who could were trying to make their way back down the mountain. As the noise of gun fire abated, the wails of agony took its place.

"Form rank," ordered a captain.

He was among the revelers on top of the hill. He and a few lieutenants were trying to reorganize the units. Perhaps they were trying to prepare for a counter-assault. They were having great difficulty as the survivors of the attack were so loud with their jubilations. So happy were they to be alive they paid the officers no mind.

Neither did I. I started back down the hill. I was looking for our men, my men. I was looking for McCormick, wishful of Reed and his libations. I needed a drink.

I saw not a single face that I recognized among the dead in the top rifle pit. I did find a bottle of sour mash. I put it to my lips and as per my manner; I allowed it to slosh back and forth between my teeth before swallowing it. Little did it do to quench the dry acrid taste in my mouth. Little did it do quench the thirst that comes with exertion. Much, however, was the warming relief to my very soul as the fluid traveled downward to where I lived. I took another pull, then a third. I corked my prize before continuing down the ridge.

I kept looking for my squad. I told myself anything could have happened during the assault. I might have gone left while they went right. In the confusion men always got lost. Not all of them could have been killed. The further down the hill I went the more bodies I encountered. I began to see some men who looked familiar. They could have well been my soldiers; death does much to distort the faces.

In the second trench I found two dead men that I knew for sure, new recruits, Alexander and Smithson. Several men who wore our colors had no face or were so blood covered I could not make any identification. There were scores of Rebels dead and wounded among our own. None of the living wished further confrontation. Their boys cried, moaned, and pleaded as much as our own.

As I rose from the lower side of the second trench a huge man presented himself. He was tall, slim, and most familiar; our cannon fodder still lived. Blankenship stood there; his arm was around a wounded man whose face I could not see.

"Emerson," I yelled out.

The wounded man he was holding lifted his face and made eye contact with me. It was Jason McCormick.

"Damn you Daggit," I think you killed the entire Confederate Army.

I passed him my prize.

As Jason took a pull, I saw a bloody stump where his foot used to be.

"Put me down Emerson," he said.

As the quiet giant sat my friend on the ground I looked desperately for bandaging material. His wound was bleeding but not near as badly as one would think. I'd seen it before countless time. The body seems to know how to shut off blood to missing parts. Apparently there is something in there that tells it the part is gone and needs no further fluid.

I did what I could with material salvaged from soldiers who had no further need of it. While I bandaged and wrapped, McCormick finished off my bottle.

"This is the end of the line for me Bud," he said. "If I don't die of the gangrene, little in life is there for a one legged man."

"You'll do just fine," I lied. "You'll do just fine."

Jason was trying hard not to cry, agony must have been his world. I thought again of our earlier talks. No rhyme or reason was there for whom the owl called.

Chapter 30

▼

"Daggit, Sergeant Daggit!" yelled the new Lieutenant from within his tent. We, Blankenship and me, had been assigned to his unit as we were the only survivors of our squad. Missionary Ridge had taken its toll.

"Daggit!"

Bennett was his name. He was tall, stocky, blond, and an ass. His given name was Phillip Bennett. His men called him Big Beanie, and that was not out of respect.

I just called him Lieutenant and as few times as possible. The Lieutenant was a man to stay clear of. Abrasive and arrogant would be just two of his better character traits. The man was immensely disliked by one and all.

"Daggit!" he yelled again.

"Sir," I responded as I presented myself in front of his tent.

"Break camp and prepare to march," was his order. Then he added, "Have my breakfast brought to me."

"Yes sir," I responded.

"Go to hell and die," was what I thought.

As I turned away he yelled again, "Daggit!"

"Sir," I responded as I turned to face the incredible mind reader.

"You don't like me much, do you?"

"Sir," the man was uncanny.

"You may respond," he said in the most condescending manner.

"Sir, army sergeants are not permitted the luxury of personal opinion."

"Daggit, you have been assigned to my unit a total of three weeks now and quite frankly, I don't care for your attitude."

"I shall endeavor to improve," I lied.

I seethed inside. This man had to go. I had already killed more men than he had fingers and toes. That did not even include Lakota. One more would not matter to me. There was no promised land for me. The only thing I had to lose was the opportunity to dispatch a big blond and a red head. This no mind had just transferred in from quartermaster corp. The army was desperate for officers. As I looked the Lieutenant in the eye; well I realized they had scraped rock bottom.

"I expect you will or I'll have a piece of your hide."

"My hide, sir?"

"Your hide, you heard me."

I was so mad my leg was shaking. Within but a few seconds of contemplation I had shot, stabbed, and strangled to death this dirty, rotten, no good, son of Satan himself. It took all the restraint I had to not act. My quest was more important. I would just put the Lieutenant on the list. He was number three, and I would be coming back for him.

"By your leave, sir," I responded.

I walked away biting my tongue. Men had heard the confrontation. Men also knew it was suicide to strike an officer, no matter the justification.

Within minutes tents were falling. Mad as I was no one wanted a part of me.

"Nelson," I had the attention of an older soldier. He was near my age, big and well muscled. Willard was his first name. We had talked and I had a liking for the man.

"The Lieutenant would like his breakfast served to him at his tent." I continued.

"I heard, replied Nelson. "The whole camp heard."

"You will find him something to eat?"

"Oh yes I will, I have always wanted to give the Lieutenant his just," Willard caught himself, "breakfast, sir, I will get his breakfast."

Over the past several years I had learned that soldiers left to their own devises generally do just fine. I made no suggestion as to what the good Lieutenant might like to eat. Nelson just whistled as he strolled through the camp toward the commissary tents. I saw him take a pouch from his pocket and seemingly weigh it in his hand. I could see him chuckling to himself as he tossed the pouch back and forth, hand to hand.

Well practiced we were, within but an hour's time our camp was dismantled and racked up on the wagons. My men were dressed, packed, with their toes on the line.

As we waited for our assigned position within the south bound cavalcade I had time for contemplation. Always with the military, it is hurry up and wait. We were on the march with General Sherman, Atlanta was our destination.

Our mission was to pierce the heart of Dixie. We were going to burn Atlanta to the ground. Twice in the past few weeks the Rebs had positioned their ranks to block us; twice we easily out flanked them, both times forcing a retreat on their part without confrontation. We had not fired a shot.

One flanking maneuver was just outside of Dalton. The Rebs had set up for a fight. We just slipped around a small range of mountains then right through someone's farm yard. I did not know how the route was discovered, but it was slick. Some said it was the work of Northern spies who had infiltrated the region. I never knew for sure.

What I did know was that we were two weeks south of Chattanooga, stealing, robbing, and burning everything we could. We left nothing. What we found we ate, pocketed, or drank. I was partial to the drink. It was easily consumed, much appreciated, and not hard to carry as the weight kept diminishing. Glad I was those southern boys had their sour mash recipes down pat.

Some said that our path of destruction was over a hundred miles wide. I doubted it as the outriders seemed to return to camp each night. It was these outriders I watched with earnest. Somewhere among them was a red headed lieutenant and a big blond with a scar. At least I hoped so.

We were near 95,000 strong. It was a lot of faces to watch, but I gave it my best. I was watching as we waited our position in the march to open. I noticed too that the Lieutenant was missing.

"Fall in!" was the order from the Column Master.

"Sir," I yelled back, "Our Lieutenant seems to be missing."

"Fall in," he yelled back. "A man not in line is a man left behind."

"Fall in line," I ordered as did the other Sergeants.

Well practiced we were. In but a minute, our unit was marching to Atlanta. We were marching without a Lieutenant to lead.

As I looked back down the line of soldiers I caught Nelson's eye. I truly believe I saw a twinkle there in. Across his face, below that bushy blond mustache was just the hint of a smile.

Willard Nelson was a man hard not to like.

We stopped our march early that afternoon at the base of what they called Big Red Top Mountain. Kennesaw was somewhere ahead. Rumor had it that the Rebs would make a stand at the base of that mountain.

Our camp quickly fell into order. Tents were pitched, fires laid, fortifications made, and guards positioned. It always surprised me just how fast routine such as these took place. One would think that an army as big as this would trip and fall all over itself, but it did not. Everyone had assigned labors which were overseen by the cruelest of task masters.

This date, I had to briefly assume command of our unit's encampment; as we were found to be missing a Lieutenant. Many had heard the morning's conflagrations between the Lieutenant and me. Puzzled they might have been, but to a man they left well enough alone. That evening Willard joined me at the fire. He handed me a bottle as he sat down.

"I understand that a bottle of sour mash might keep a soldier out of latrine duty," he said.

He was pretty straight forward, so was I.

"That it does Nelson, that it does," I replied as I uncorked my prize.

I found the contents both brown and warm as I drank it down.

"You may find yourself excused from tomorrow's roster," I smiled.

"As easy as that?"

"As easy as that," I said taking another pull on the bottle. I took a third pull before I passed it back. "Where are you from?"

"Okabena," he answered.

"Where is that, I've never heard of it."

"Okabena is the last two soddies in Minnesota before you step into the Dakotas."

We talked for quite a while as we watched the flickering of the fire. We passed the bottle until it was empty. Willard had four sisters, all blond, all younger. He said they were pretty. They lived in the biggest of the two sod houses that constituted Okabena. They all shared one bed and a life of cold miserable prairie labor. They were so poor even the Sioux left them alone as they were not worth the bother. Nelson had joined the army to improve his station in life. Willard truly believed he had found the promise land. He ate well, had clothes, shoes, and a coat. He wasn't ever cold. He wasn't over worked. And to top it all off, the army even gave him money from time to time. His family wasn't as well off as he was. They were still back there on the prairie choking rabbits to survive.

As we talked one of the other sergeants came by.

"Letter for you Daggit."

He handed me the letter and walked away. I recognized the style of the writing; it looked like all my other letters in the satchel. I put it in my pocket. Nelson made no comment.

"Are you as bad as they say?" he asked.

"What?" he had caught me off guard.

"They say you are hands down the toughest meanest fighting man in the whole Union Army."

"Who says that?"

"Everyone in the Union Army."

"I have never heard such talk," I said preparatory to changing the subject.

"We heard about Old Bud Daggit long before you showed up in our outfit. I even heard about you at the Mankato Lynching."

"Lynchings?" I asked finding opportunity to change the subject.

"Ya, when we hung half the Sioux nation in one afternoon."

"You were there?"

"Yes I was, saw the whole thing. After that hanging you couldn't find an injun anywhere east of the Black Hills. What everyone in Mankato was saying was you started the whole shebang."

"Me?" I was truly surprised.

"That is what they say. Everyone thinks that you killed a dozen or so Dakota men and boys. Most everyone was glad about it too. They say Old Bud riled up those savages just so the army would come and finish up the job right."

"It," I started, but he interjected again.

"They say you killed over a hundred Rebs, that they run when they hear you are coming. Most Minnesota Yanks know it was you and you alone who ran all those gray shirted worthless bastards off Missionary Ridge.

"It wasn't like that," I replied, desperately trying to change the conversation.

Before I could continue Nelson interjected again, "Say what you will Sarge, I was behind you all the way up that slope. You didn't leave me a single Reb, not one.

"What do you suppose happened to Lieutenant Bennett?" I asked still trying to change the conversation.

"I heard he ate something for breakfast that didn't agree with him."

Again I saw that twinkle in his eye. One good turn deserves another, I passed him the bottle back.

Chapter 31

▼

Life in the army revolved around just a myriad of misery. Either it was freezing cold or hot as hell. We were either deluged with rain or as parched as Arabs, whoever they were. We marched, always up hill, through snow, knee deep mud, neck high rivers, and clouds of mosquitoes. Thus far since leaving Minnesota I thought I had endured just every woe this cruel world had to offer; then along came the chiggers. Chiggers were undetectable, unavoidable, minions from hell. The little whatevers would eat into and under your skin in just the most inaccessible and private of places. Then once settled in; they would move to another place, and then move again. The resulting itch was unbearable. Many a man was driven mad with their body infestation. I was unfortunately not excluded from this misery. Typically covered parts of my body were inflamed and red with both blood and scabs; most of my injury being self inflicted as I tried to scratch and claw the vermin from my skin.

"Sergeant Daggit," it was our replacement Lieutenant calling me.

Adams was his name. He was but two days our leader; this was his first time addressing me.

My scratching my left butt cheek as I saluted probably did not produce a good first impression.

"Sir," I managed.

"Sergeant, do you know Lieutenant Cummings by sight?"

"I do," I responded scratching now between my butt cheeks. "His unit is camped to the east."

"Would you find him and deliver this communication. This is important."

"Yes sir," I said taking the letter in hand.

I saluted then set out. I wondered whether I was given the assignment because he knew I could not read it. It seemed logical to me. If I had a written confidential message I would want the messenger to be an illiterate dunce. I had a letter of my own stashed that I could not make heads or tails of. I told myself that this learning to read was something I could do. Someday, someday I would make time. Right now I was doing my best to just survive this insanity.

It was early yet, breakfast and its clean up was still in progress. My pistols, belt, and gear were still in my tent. To have belted up would have enraged the well entrenched chiggery horde that had taken up residency at my belt line and lower. I put off the agony induced by the belt as long as possible.

They said that soaking in brine would kill the beast. Salt was scarce since some fool let the secret out of the bag. Every drop of salt for a hundred miles was somehow being stuffed, rubbed, and soaked in thousands of trousers.

We were probably going to assault Kennesaw before the day was out.

I wondered if chiggers still ate on you when you were dead. If some Reb mini ball struck me down I would be out of my misery. Strange are your thoughts when you are being eaten alive. I wondered if a few well placed mini balls could kill just the little chiggers and not cause me too much harm. I was not alone in my misery. As I walked through the different camps looking for Lieutenant Cummings I saw hundreds of men similarly distressed. I wondered if they had the same stupid thoughts.

More men still I saw with their butts to a rail. Dysentery and diarrhea still killed more men than the Rebs ever could. I could not think of a more horrible death than the combination of runs and chiggers.

Then, in my wondering minds eye I saw just that; a death more terrible than that which I had previously considered. I saw Helga and Hans. I saw them screaming as the flames of our home engulfed them. I could not make the vision go away. I had seen it a thousand times in my minds eye and I was seeing it again. Only the roar of battle could deafen her screams; then as the men cried and moaned with their agonies I would hear her again.

Sometimes, just sometimes, I found relief near the bottom of a bottle of sour mash. Fleeting though these liquid escapes were, they were preferable to the horrors of the battle. It was the safer option, of that I was sure.

No relief was there this day either. The horrible mental images and the digging chiggers made my walk near unbearable. Cummings had his squads near the pines. I had walked the line twice and had not found him. I knew his unit was next to the horse soldiers.

It was the smell of horse manure on my boots that jogged my mental process. Somewhere inside my head something clicked, "Hey Bud," came the voice, "aren't you supposed to be looking for someone."

The glance from my now green covered boot to the face of two men in front of me took but a second. Recognition took but another second. Between second two and second three my hands, both of them, came up empty. Neither had found a pistol. Before me, not a full step away, was a red headed lieutenant and a big, blond, scar faced sergeant.

Both looked surprised, agape, as they too found recognition.

Second four found the Lieutenant's mouth shut and my fist where his chin had once been. His head was going back and his feet were coming up. The Lieutenant's back was hitting the ground when my left fist hooked the Sergeant to the side of his face.

I had whipped him once before, he well knew what was coming again. I didn't disappoint him. My fists and feet took him time and again. I bowled him back with lefts and rights. He tried to defend himself but there was no escape from my pounding fists. Within less than a minutes time he was wobbling on weak knees. I chopped him down with a solid right to the jaw. Intervention from the other soldiers came slowly, fights were entertainment; pure and simple. The red headed Lieutenant had rolled over and was attempting to get up when that green manure covered boot caught the side of his head. Down he went again.

I didn't know if I had successfully killed either one, but if they lived it wasn't for lack of trying on my part. I gave them all I had and then some. Finally I was powered to the ground by the shear weight of what seemed an entire regiment. It was their combined weight that eventually had me in shackles. My only joy was seeing my victims, both men, carried away on gurneys. Neither was moving, both were covered in blood. I wished both men the worst. Whether or not I made my desires vocal I can't remember; my fury and rage were all consuming.

Hours later, still enraged, still shackled, those little minions from hell resumed their feast. I didn't care.

Chapter 32

▼

For at least ten days my chiggery friends and I were held prisoner in an old barn. With us were half a dozen malingerers. Two were sergeants, one was a corporal, two were privates and one was a moron. The last man was completely insane; not a word of sense did he ever make as he paced the inside of the barn like a caged animal. He reminded me of a babbling Emerson. He was tall and lanky. Crazy though he might be, he made no attempt to escape which I thought odd.

As we sat hot and miserable in the fly filled barn we could hear the sound on an all day battle off in the distance. I had no liking for the barn, my shackles, or the chiggers; but two of the three were preferable to the horrors of battle.

Our guards had told us that Sherman had tried to take Kennesaw and got his butt handed back to him. A good many union boys were either dead or wounded. The guards were as thankful as we to have not been involved in the battle. Longevity on the front was short lived. With that thought in mind, our guards took their task most seriously. We were not going anywhere, escape was impossible. Our guards lived as long as we stayed prisoners. Their eyes were on us constantly.

Of the six of us, I was the one most likely to try to escape. It was the firing squad to any man who struck an officer. That inevitable probability and the stories about the beatings administered to Boland and Matthews rewarded me with shackles to both my hands and feet. No chance was taken.

I had had no contact with anyone other than my five fellow prisoners and the guards since the beatings. I did not even know if I had been successful or not in my attempt to beat the men to death. I would truly hate to leave this world with the task unfulfilled. So much yet to do, so little time to do it, were my only regrets.

I had a letter in my pocket to read, but no one to read it to me. These men jailed with me garnered no trust. The letter would have to wait; perhaps I'd even learn to read it to myself. That was if I wasn't shot or hung.

The light from the opening barn door near blinded me. I had to drop my head and turn away from the light. I could not see who came in, but heavy footfalls plodded my direction. My eyes had not yet grown accustomed to the bright light when I was jerked to my feet. Two men, both huge, had with no visible effort lifted me, along with my shackles and chiggers, right off the barn floor.

My eyes were adjusting.

"Daggit, you are to follow me," instructed a young officer.

As he turned to leave, I was given a quick painful punch to my ribs by the man on my right. As I turned to him, the man on the left did the same. They had dropped me to my knees; no breath did I have. These escorts just jerked me up again and headed me towards the door of the barn. Apparently they wanted to make a good first impression. As we exited the barn into the light of day I was able to see their faces. I made a mental note that they were to be put in the book; four and five.

I tried to follow the Lieutenant as best I could. Those shackles did much to slow a man's progress. I was short stepped to a wagon, tossed into the back, then butt bounced a good many miles down a road of misery and woe. I was better off than most I saw. Wounded men were everywhere. Some were walking, some laid on gurneys, and some were moaning or crying. These were the lucky ones. Stacked like cord wood, were rows and rows of dead men. I had seen it before. Each and every time I had hoped to never see it again.

Eventually we came to an established camp. The wagon was driven deep into the sea of tents and munitions. Men were busy at just every task, but having seen this too, so, many times before, it seemed to me; these men were licking their wounds. These men had lost the battle. The wagon stopped in front of a large tent. Three armed men stood the flap. I was taken past these men, through the flap, into the tent, and plopped in a chair.

As we entered, another prisoner, a man near my age, but shorter and darker was being escorted out. He too was in shackles. I saw resolution in the man's eyes. I had no idea what he saw in mine.

From my chair I had just the best view of an army court; and most important, as I was the party who was the subject of this court martial. At the front table sat three officers. Two tables faced theirs; two other officers were seated at each of those tables. I was between one of the tables and the front bench of three. There was a gallery of at least twenty men that sat on benches at the rear of the tent. I did not recognize a single person at the tables nor at the bench. I did see Boland and Matthews in the gallery. Both showed much too little of the beating I had given them. Boland wore a bandage around his head. Matthews sported only a black eye; but it was a good one. I was very much disappointed that either of them still breathed. The shackles I wore prevented my continuing what I had not finished.

There were other familiar faces in the gallery. Lieutenant Adams, Nelson, and Emerson Blankenship were present. I surely wished Nelson had brought refreshment; I needed a drink.

It wasn't five minutes before it began, "If it pleases the court, the prosecution would like to begin."

As he finished the word, "begin," a volley of shots rang out. They were close, not far from the flap of the tent.

The shots caused a pause in the proceedings, six or seven seconds, no more.

"Proceed," replied the center officer at the main table.

There was some rustling of papers, but no one paid even the slightest heed to the volley of fire outside the front flap.

The prosecutor to my left began speaking, "This matter today concerns the court martial of Brewster Ulysses Daggit, Sergeant, Second Minnesota Volunteer Infantry.

"Captain Lee, What are the charges?" asked the center officer at the head table. He was a big man, blond, with a handlebar mustache and more medals, clusters, and foofraw on his uniform than I had seen in my entire military career.

"Major Pendleton," began Captain Lee, "there are four charges; may I list them?"

"Please do."

The Captain wasted no time, "Insubordination, dereliction of duty, aggravated battery to an officer, and the attempted murder of a union sergeant.

Pendleton, the head officer, looked at me and asked, "And how does the defendant plea?"

I was looking him back, dead in his eye. I was about to say, "guilty," when a man at the table closest to me said, "not guilty."

"I what?"

"He pleads not guilty," the man said again. He had the markings of a Captain. His eye contact with me was at the most brief. I found no reassurance at all.

"You will present a defense?" questioned Pendleton.

The Captain defending me began, "That we will Major; we will show the incidents in question, although factual on the face, were each and every one with adequate justification."

I just stared at this guy in disbelief, how he could be so sure, I'd never even talked to him.

"Are you ready to proceed with your case, Captain Lee?" asked Pendleton.

"I am."

Pendleton then looked at the Captain who was defending me, "Are you ready with your defense Captain Jenkins?'

"I am."

"Gentlemen," began Pendleton, "are the shackles on the defendant necessary. We are in a military tribunal; we have men aplenty who might quell any problems that might arise."

I was thinking, "Amen, brother, lets get these chains off, I've a killing to complete and there they sit."

Captain Lee stood up pointing at me, "Major Pendleton, in the interest of justice, prudence, and the safety of all in this room I strongly suggest the shackles remain affixed. If there are additional irons available I would request this demon animal from hell be double shackled incase the first set has worn from his constant gnawing at them."

"Objection, objection, the prosecution has no right to use emotional diatribes, which depict their personal feelings or fears to slander a good soldier. The prosecution is out of order. This hearing is to be considered null and void."

Pendleton took control, "Good point Captain Jenkins. Captain Lee, you shall refrain from all but the facts of this case. Yes, the man remains shackled. Let us proceed with these informalities; we have a war to fight. Cases such as this detract from our bigger mission."

This judge, if that was what he was, had found my defense proper, and then in the same breath ignored it. I was in big trouble.

"Major," started Jenkins.

"We will proceed Captain Jenkins, interrupted Pendleton, "Captain Lee, your case please."

Captain Lee stood, "Sir, we will in short fashion prove the defendant guilty of each charge previously stated. We will present testimony from witness, victims, and superior officers. Our testimony will be both direct and factual. We full well anticipate a ruling of guilty to each offense. Then after your ruling we will justifiably expect the defendant, Brewster Ulysses Daggit, to be marched out the flap of this tent, to that rail across the road and summarily shot dead like the last man.

Captain Lee had my undivided attention.

Chapter 33

▼

Lee wasted no time, "The prosecution calls Lieutenant Adams; the charge dereliction of duty."

I was puzzled but said nothing.

There was a chair straight across the room from me. Adams walked to the chair, stood, faced the Major, stood at attention, and then saluted the court.

"Lieutenant, you may be seated."

"Lieutenant Adams," Lee began, "the defendant in this case, Brewster Ulysses Daggit is in your command."

"He was."

"On the day in question did you give an assignment to Daggit?"

"I did."

"Can you explain the order?"

"I gave him a very important message that he was to personally deliver."

"And?"

"He failed to follow through with my command."

"The letter was not delivered?"

"It was not," responded Adams.

Captain Lee then asked, "And failure to follow a direct order is dereliction of duty?"

"That it is."

"I have no further questions of this officer." said Lee.

"Captain Jenkins, have you a cross examination?"

Jenkins seemed to be in deep thought and did not immediately answer.

"Jenkins!" Pendleton was impatient, that was for sure.

"Excuse me Major, I was momentarily distracted. The Lieutenant has accused Sergeant Daggit of dereliction of duty in that he failed to deliver a very important letter to someone in another camp. My client was in the process of that very mission when other circumstances presented themselves preventing him from making the delivery."

Jenkins looked over at me. "Sergeant Daggit, we have never met, have we?"

"No, sir, we have not."

"You were assigned to deliver a letter, and failed to do so. Would you happen to know where the letter is?"

"Yes, it is still in my front left shirt pocket."

"Have you read it?"

"No, I have not."

"Please Sergeant, you mean you have this very important letter in your possession for well over a week and you have not even looked at it."

"No, I have not."

"And why, Sergeant is that?"

I hesitated with my response, then almost with shame I confided, "I can't read."

"Did Lieutenant Adams know you were illiterate?"

"Maybe, I think they list that in your file."

"I object," Captain Lee, did not like the direction of the testimony.

"Sustained, you will move on Captain Jenkins."

"Very well, no further questions in regards to the letter in the Sergeant's pocket."

Captain Jenkins asked no questions, but he walked over to me, reached into my front left shirt pocket and removed the letter. He opened it as he walked back to his table.

"That's my letter," objected Adams. "It is personal."

"Personal!" Jenkins was on him like stink on dung. "You will have a man shot for dereliction of duty for not delivering a personal letter. Let me see, it says only."

"Objection, objection," Lee was standing, "The court specifically admonished the Captain to discontinue that line of questioning and he persists."

Jenkins didn't miss a step, "The court will note that I have not asked a single question, it was the prosecution's witness who insists the letter to be of value."

"Captain Jenkins, you will give me the letter," ordered Pendleton.

Jenkins gave him the letter then sat down. We watched as the letter was read. I could see the Major's face redden as his eyes went down the page. It must have been a very short letter or the Major was a fast reader.

"Gentlemen, we shall continue. Captain Lee, call your next witness."

"Major," interjected Jenkins, "as a point of legal procedure, that letter was passed to the bench as possible evidence in these proceedings. The court reviewed it. It is military law that if you read it, the prosecution and the defense are entitled to read it."

Lieutenant Adams wasn't saying a word. I don't know how a man could sit lower in a straight back chair. The three officers at the bench put their heads together in consultation. Ten minutes, maybe more, the officers talked back and forth.

Finally Pendleton addressed the court, "Very well, Captain, your point was well taken, considered, and found with basis. The letter issue was initiated by the prosecution, and quite skillfully manipulated into evidence by the defense. Since the court read it, everyone is entitled."

Pendleton picked it up and read, "Pete, I've been there too. It was the best whore house on the Mississippi. I preferred Luella over Lorraine."

All the eyes in the room were on Lieutenant Adams. Sending a man to his death over a message about whores seemed unconscionable to all. I hoped all included Pendleton. I had a respect building for my defense attorney.

Adams was excused. He left the tent with great haste. I highly suspected he would be leading an assault in the near future.

"Captain Jenkins, has the defendant any further rebuttal on the charge of dereliction of duty?"

"No, sir, Sergeant Daggit was carrying out his most important assignment when he was unavoidably detained. He was not nor did he derelict his duty."

"Captain Lee, have you further evidence?"

Lee again stood up, this time he seemed surprisingly more confident than one would have expected, "On the charges of aggravated battery on a superior officer and insubordination, I call Lieutenant Boland.

Boland took the chair. He did not look my direction. Boland only looked at the front table or at Captain Lee. He was putting on a dog and pony show; he held his bandaged head from time to time and acted like he was in great pain, which I hoped he was. He testified that I, without the slightest provocation, attacked him and Sergeant Matthews. So swift and furious was the assault, neither had time to defend themselves. Then he went on and on about the extensive injuries he had received.

I truly enjoyed this part of his testimony.

Once he completed testifying for the prosecution, Captain Jenkins was allowed to question him.

"Lieutenant Boland, he asked, could there be some reason for the assault?"

"Not that I am aware of," was his answer. "He just screamed that he wanted me to die."

I wanted to jump up and call him a murdering son of my mother's dog; but I bit my tongue.

Sergeant Matthews was called to the chair. He gave similar testimony as to the fight, but he had a list of different injuries.

I truly enjoyed his list of agonies too.

"Sergeant Matthews," asked Jenkins, "have you a logical explanation for the assault."

"No, He just said that he wanted to kill me then; attacked without provocation," Matthews answered. He took just a glance in my direction. Well he could see the shackles were still attached.

Matthews was excused.

"Have you further evidence Captain Lee?" asked Pendleton. "We still have a war to fight gentlemen. I could see Pendleton was not impressed. My time was getting short.

"No Sir, our case is basic and simple. Sergeant Daggit was insubordinate, failed to complete an assignment, then attacked and beat both an officer and a sergeant unmercifully. He was heard over and over screaming he wanted to kill them. With the extent of their injuries what they were we can only surmise that he was trying his best to achieve that end.

"Do you have rebuttal witnesses or evidence Captain Jenkins?"

"I do," he said. "May I approach the table; I have a letter to present."

"Yes, please do," Pendleton replied with his voice, but his mannerisms seemed to suggest it was a waste of time.

Jenkins walked to the table and handed Pendleton a letter, the second letter of the proceedings.

"Major, this letter was received by me just yesterday from Lieutenant Jason McCormick, Seocnd Minnesota, Volunteer Infantry. McCormick, as the letter explains, is in Chattanooga still recovering from an amputated foot. McCormick regrets his inability to make this tribunal, but wishes input. An officer who has sacrificed his leg in the service of this country and wishes input has certainly the right to be heard."

Pendleton reluctantly agreed, "Uh, why, yes, Captain, he does have the right. Are you; certain as to the validity of the letter and the existence of McCormick? After all the contents written here are hearsay."

"We have verified both."

Pendleton began reading. Captain Jenkins gave him plenty of time. When Pendleton finished, he handed the letter to the officer to his left. There was a surprised look on Pendleton's face as he looked over at me.

"Is it true?" he asked me.

"I don't know," I replied.

"What do you mean you don't know?"

"Major," I have never seen the letter nor could I read it if I had."

Pendleton turned to Jenkins, "Captain, the Sergeant had no knowledge of this letter?"

"No sir, I had never even seen Daggit until he walked into this tent."

Pendleton looked back at me, "Sergeant Daggit, I have read a letter from Lieutenant Jason McCormick who affirms that you did indeed have sufficient cause to beset both Boland and Matthews. What reason would that be?"

"They killed my wife and son, burned them to death in our cabin."

"That is ample cause, but have you proof."

"I was told by Sergeant Johnson Maher in a dying declaration."

"That is not proof," objected Lee who was now standing."

"It is to me." I was the one glaring Boland and Matthews, as was most of the others present.

"Major Pendleton," continued Lee, "Lieutenant Boland and Sergeant Matthews are not the ones on trial here today; Sergeant Daggit is. We are in the United States Army, Sir; suspicion of a crime does not justify an assault. We are all innocent until we are proven guilty. We, however, have proved Sergeant Daggit guilty of four charges and expect a prompt verdict. We do have a war to fight."

"Have you another witness Captain Jenkins?" asked Pendleton.

I was looking around the room for someone, anyone. Nelson and Blankenship were my only friendly familiar faces. Nelson looked at me, and then he looked over at Captain Lee. He had that twinkle in his eye and that wisp of smile under his mustache. Nelson turned one of his thumbs down. Somehow I knew Lee might have a problem with his digestion.

Blankenship, the simpleton that he was, could be no help. I'd never even heard him utter a single word. His presence at the hearing was indeed strange.

"I," was all Jenkins said as the flap of the tent flew open. In walked two very stalwart sergeant majors. They were clearing a path through the court for a man behind them. The man behind them caused everyone in the tent to rise, go to attention, and salute. I stood, but the shackles much hindered any saluting.

Standing right there in the aisle was Uncle Billy himself, General William T. Sherman.

Chapter 34

▼

"General Sherman," it was Major Pendleton, standing at attention, saluting, announcing to the court what everyone already knew.

"I know who the hell I am. Who is this Sergeant Daggit?"

Sherman was not in a good mood.

"The defendant is to your right sir, the man in shackles," answered Pendleton.

"Shackles?"

"He is a dangerous man General."

"Indeed he is Major, indeed he is," said Sherman as he gave me the twice over. "Are you Daggit?" he continued.

"Yes sir,"

"Well thanks to you Daggit, we lost at Kennesaw."

"Sir?" was all I could say. Befuddled would have been an understatement.

"I know who leads and who follows. I know who fights and who runs. While you sat in some jail we got our butts kicked. Thanks to you a lot of good men are not with us."

"Sir?" I was really taken back, confused.

The General's response was not directed to me, "Emerson, Emerson, where are you?"

Everyone in the room was looking for Emerson, me included. Over the top of the crowd I cold see a head, taller than the rest, moving towards the front of the tent. He stepped from the throng and walked right up to Sherman.

"Good to see you boy!" Uncle Billy had his arms around my Emerson. Blankenship had his arms around the General.

"Come with me, boy," he said to Blankenship. "Gentlemen, a recess please; I may wish to offer a rebuttal in this matter."

General Sherman and Private Blankenship, Uncle Billy and cannon fodder, respectively, left the tent together.

"This Tribunal is in recess until the General returns," said Pendleton.

No one knew what to say but the tent was astir with murmurs aplenty.

What I experienced next was the longest quarter hour of my life. Neither I, nor could anyone in the tent; imagine what General Sherman and Emerson had in common. The whole tent was speculating; guessing, trying to predict what effect Sherman would have on the outcome of the hearing. I was really worried. I had never hesitated to have Blankenship up front on every assault.

I remembered the many times his tall frame had shielded me from the hail of incoming mini balls. I had been confident that the man had no knowledge of the peril we faced. He had always stood tall and stupid as we marched into battle.

Blankenship had over the past years been the butt of many a joke; none initiated by me, though I could have at any time stopped the chiding. I might have even done that had I the slightest idea Emerson knew what was being said.

Why was he here? Perhaps he wanted revenge; to see me shot or hanged. Who knew?

Just a thousand thoughts raced through my mind, each ending with me prone at the base of the fence across the road.

My time on this earth was getting shorter.

They came in as they had before. The stalwart sergeant majors cleared the aisle. General Sherman followed them in. Emerson was right behind the three. Again the room went to attention with everyone resaluting the General. Blankenship peeled off and resumed his position next to Nelson.

General Sherman walked to the witness chair and seated himself. Only then did the rank and file sit.

"General," began the Major.

"Major, I will be brief," interrupted the General, "we do have a war to win."

"Yes sir," replied the Major.

I was awed at the respect General Sherman commanded. Then I considered his power. I knew it took no more than a word or finger and whoever he chose might lead the next charge into cannon and ball.

The General began in a matter of fact manner as he looked the room over, "Gentlemen, we have a serious problem here. Emerson, my wife's sister's boy sent for me; he said to come quick. He sent the message to his mother who sent it to my wife who sent it to me. I came as quick as I could."

The General winked; which resulted in some very reserved chuckling. Most, however, were afraid to comment. The rest of us, me included, saw little humor in the wink.

"Emerson has reported that as a result of this hearing you men are to have Sergeant Daggit shot for a series of unfortunate incidents of which he is probably most guilty."

I was losing heart as he spoke.

"The man you intend to shoot has been in the forefront of every successful assault we have made since 62. He has personally killed more Johnnie Rebs than this room has combined fingers and toes. Emerson confirms it all. The boy rarely talks but he never lies. Emerson said that Sergeant Daggit single handedly took Missionary Ridge."

The General paused as he let his eyes search the room. He was getting no objections.

"Perhaps he did," he resumed, "perhaps he didn't. What I can tell this court is that we did in fact take the ridge. We took everything that involved Sergeant Daggit."

The General paused again, puffed a few times on his cigar, and then continued, "Officers of this tribunal, Daggit is a legend along our Union lines. The men truly believe; so goes Daggit, so goes the war. I try hard to believe that I am more in charge than yon Sergeant; I might be; but I hold no more respect within our ranks. I know I am less feared. Our entire Minnesota contingency threatens to walk off the field should this court execute the Sergeant. If they do walk; so will Wisconsin and Illinois."

Sherman let his diatribe soak in.

Then he began again, "Gentlemen, I have a compromise which should content my Northern Volunteer Armies, keep our war efforts pointed towards Atlanta, and even serve justice.

First, Daggit is no doubt guilty of attacking an officer. This can not be tolerated. He beat up a sergeant, unfortunate, but these things happen. Insubordinate, perhaps, but with six or seven like him the rest of us could just go home. As to dereliction of duty; not in a million years.

I more than strongly suggest that Daggit be found guilty only of striking an officer. He should be sent to the Old Capital Prison in Washington. He will not, am I clear, be shot."

The General was looking Pendleton dead in the eye.

"Am I clear?" he reiterated, this time looking at Lee.

"You are most clear," replied Pendleton.

Lee just nodded.

Then General Sherman, Uncle Billy himself, got up, walked across the room and shook my shackled hand.

"Thank you," I said.

"No sir," he replied, "I thank you."

General Sherman turned and left the room as he had entered; the two sergeant majors leading the way.

Two days later a northbound train was taking me to Washington, D.C. I still had two guards but I was not shackled. The probability of my surviving this war had risen just a tad. Two full years I had been in the thick of the fight. All I had to show for it were bad memories, a few scars, a few friends, and an unread letter in my pocket.

Chapter 35

▼

Four days we traveled north by rail; then another half a day by wagon. My guard and escort for the entire trip was a good old boy. He called himself, Ollie. Ollie had early on explained the program.

"Brewster," he said, "you are the personal prisoner of General Uncle Billy. If you try to run, I won't even stop you. You will, however, be hunted down and shot; no questions, no trial, no nothing. By your departure from custody you will have personally affronted the one most respected General in this whole damn senseless shoot out."

"How long is my sentence?" I asked for the nineteenth time.

"The paper says three years."

"Three years," I sighed for the twentieth time.

I did not want to sit on my butt for three years; I had two very important things yet to do. Time would not be my friend.

"Yup, the letter says you are to be kept locked up for three years. How many times are you going to ask me anyway? I think you should be counting your blessings. You are one lucky son of a gun."

"Lucky?"

"If you are asking me, yes sir, you are as lucky as hell. For the next three years you will be warm, dry and fed. You will not be marching up and down those Georgia hills in the rain and mud. Better still, no reb mini ball will be smashing through your body."

There was much to look at as we traveled. I saw huge farms and manors, most still had blacks aplenty doing various labors. I was giving thought to their plight which hadn't changed much as a result of this war when Ollie found something else for me to focus on.

"There it is, Brewster," he said as he pointed to a huge three story wood and log building. They call it the Old Capitol Prison. She was once a grand building."

I gave my new home the twice over as Ollie tied off the team to a rail. I was not impressed. In my mind's eye I saw myself at a dead run, down the street I was going, hell bent for someplace. It was at that point I realized I had no place to go anyway; I might as well stay here.

Ollie led the way in, right up the front steps and through the open double door.

We passed two guards who were seated at a table near the door; neither bothered to give us much more than a glance. They were much more interested in the game of cards they were playing. One of the guards was my age but very heavy. The other was an older man, thin and weathered of skin. They had rifles, but neither had one close to hand. I was giving thought as to just how easy it would be to grab a gun and make good my escape, but there it was again, just where would I go to do what.

"Is the warden in?" asked Ollie.

Neither guard verbally responded, both were obviously affixed to their game. One did, however, nod as he pointed with his thumb to a door across the hall. With his other hand he reached under the table and grabbed the neck of a whiskey bottle that had been at his feet.

The sight of it caused my mouth to water. Long had been my trip from Georgia to this prison. Not a drop of whiskey had been offered. My guard was either very dedicated or a teetotaler.

Ollie's rap on the closed door did almost distract me from the old man and his bottle.

"Come in," the voice was high pitched, almost squeaky.

Ollie opened the door and walked in. I just followed along

"Afternoon Captain," Ollie said as he saluted.

I followed suit.

"And who do we have here Sergeant Toland?" asked the Captain who was still seated at his desk. He was obviously the owner of the squeaky voice.

"Sergeant Brewster Daggit, Sir, Second Minnesota Volunteer Infantry," was Ollie's reply as he presented my package to the Warden.

"Who's pet project is this?" asked the Warden as he opened my envelop.

The Warden was a tall man, skinny, with a pitted face. Clean shaven, he was, though I couldn't imagine why. Whiskers would have do much to cover up what must have been some terrible teenage years.

"Sherman's sir," replied Ollie.

"Sherman's you say, he hasn't sent us anyone since that Greenhow woman."

We stood the desk as the Warden read my documents. There were two full pages of writing. Once he was finished he opened yet another, it was a personal letter.

"This letter is from the General," he said as he read. "General Sherman always gives us special instruction as to just how he wants his special projects treated. We have plenty of special cells and special assignments for each prisoner. Here at the Capitol, one size does not fit all."

The Warden continued to read.

"Ah hum," he said several times as I watched his eyes scan the page.

My fate I could see was determined by the words there in. As I watched I wished I could have read the contents on the train and planned an escape well before this. I could see that the ability to read was its benefits. I might even be able to know what Lydia had written in the letter that was secure, neatly folded in my shirt pocket. Perhaps the contents there in would have some bearing on an escape plan or attempt.

I was sure that I would not be shot or harmed while in this prison, but what was to be expected had me much unnerved. I could well be in for three years of hard labor before I was free to finish what I had started. Boland and Matthews would have no place to hide.

"Sergeant Daggit," began the Warden, "Captain Tindall is my name. I am not nor will I ever be your friend. You are a criminal, convicted it says for assaulting a superior officer. Your punishment is three years at the Old Capitol. The accompanying letter sent by General Sherman, himself, strongly suggests clean, humane, hospitable treatment. The General says you are a hero extraordinaire and to be treated accordingly."

I felt relief as my mind told my body to relax.

"So, Sergeant Daggit, you will have your own cell, the one recently vacated by Sherman's last project, that Greenhow woman. You will have a guard who will assist you through your sentence; old Pete McDonald will do nicely. But, warn you I will, to escape will mean your death. You sit, you live. If you run, Sherman's protection is null and void. I will have you hunted down and shot. Do we have an understanding?"

"Yes sir."

"Sergeant Toland, you are excused," said Tindall. "As you pass the table out in the hall, tell McDonald to step in here."

As Ollie turned to leave he gave me a wink, "Hang in there Buddy Boy. Three years isn't spit."

Not a second or two later McDonald was in the room saluting, "Captain."

"This is Sergeant Daggit," said Tindall, "he's yours, another package from Sherman. He is to be treated accordingly."

"Yes sir," answered the old man.

McDonald turned to leave, "Follow me Sergeant Daggit he said."

I followed him as directed. As we walked past the table where he had been playing cards he reached down and grabbed the bottle from the floor. He flipped it to me. As I caught it I could see right off it was sour mash and more than half full.

"I know the look," was all he said.

Right off I knew my stay at the Capitol would be most acceptable.

Chapter 36

▼

I had heard men talk about prison; years and years of hard labor, misery and woe they had said.

I had also heard men talk about jail; two hots and a cot.

My stay at the Capitol was more the latter.

I had my own private cell, it wasn't too big, it wasn't too small. It had a window that opened and shut. The door had no lock.

For the most part I came and went as I pleased. McDonald's warning was simple enough. He had said that if I put one foot over that front threshold I would be shot; simple as that. He had told me that my odds of survival would have been better leading every assault for the rest of the war. I had been up front on more than my share of assaults; McDonald got no problem from me. For most of that first year I just stayed warm, dry, fed, and thanks to McDonald, drunk.

McDonald, bless his soul, did not like to drink alone. He said that his kid had his own still "up yonder." That boy made some fine shine. McDonald was in total agreement, our bottle rarely went dry.

Boredom was my enemy. I was always just plain bored. The Warden, a guard, or someone would find physical labors for me, but I had no sustained purpose. A man needs something to do. Most of those around me feared that Sherman's special project, me, might just have too much to do.

It was far better to give out no task than a task that might cause me or Uncle Billy some concern.

McDonald gave me very little work. He did, however, over compensate with that sour mash on demand. His kid was a master.

McDonald often bragged on the boy and his talent, but he boasted more often about his grandkids. It seemed that the kids went to some local school. They had some kind of superior intellect that he did not. He said the kids could read thick books and count immense numbers with little more than a line of beads.

"Can you read old man," I asked.

"Sure, but not near as good as those kids."

"How did they learn?"

"Why in school I suspect," he answered.

McDonald paused a few moments, wondering I was sure, as to where this conversation was going.

"You can't read?" he asked.

"No, not a word, but I've always wanted to learn. I've just never had the time."

McDonald minced no words, "Well Buddy Boy, you have nothing but time now. I believe I can help you some, at least get you started. At home the kids have a primer, a slate, and some chalk. I'll bring them in."

"You would do that?"

"I'd do about anything to keep your nose out of my bottle."

He laughed, took a pull, and flipped it to me. God, his kid made some good whiskey.

McDonald was good to his word. The very next day he had in hand the primer, a real school house slate, and a half a dozen pieces of chalk.

"I talked to the kids, they said that you have to master the alphabet first. You have to practice and practice on the slate until you know all the letters and their sounds. After that you can move on to putting them together."

I opened the primer to the first page. Right there was one of the letters in my last name. It was the second letter in my name. I could see it in my minds eye on the sign that hung in front of our little farm back on Crow Creek. Behind that sign, I could see the little glen down by the creek that held the single grave.

Instantly the rage within me began to stir again. I still had unfinished business. My eyes were no longer on the primer, they were on the door.

"What's got you boy," it was a concerned McDonald. "It's a different look I see on your face, no, it's a dangerous look. I've seen it before when men go out the door."

"Sorry, I was thinking about the wife and boy. He would be about the right age for this book."

"I suspect he might have been," answered the old man.

Then he was quiet for several minutes. Finally he resumed his talking, "Bud, my boy, we have talked many times about the loss of your family and those who did them wrong. Vengeance should be yours, yours alone. I'm not much for believing the Lord will get around to it; he's been much too busy with this damn war."

McDonald took a swig and passed me the bottle.

"The way I see it," he began again, "you need to track down those worthless bastards and show them what God loves and in order to do that; you need an important skill that you do not possess."

"What is that?" I asked, taking a pull off the bottle. I wasn't sure where he was going with the conversation. I could kill those two men as easily as the last fifty.

"You need to take this reading seriously."

"I am. I seriously want to learn how to read."

"Buddy Boy, you need to learn for more than the sake of something to do with your time."

"Why then?"

"When you get out of here, you'll no doubt be on the hunt. In these modern times men don't follow tracks on the ground. The trail you will be following will be words on paper. Men now leave paper trails. Your path will be the words on pieces of paper. These paper trails will lead you to your destination. It will take these words on paper to eventually free your soul."

McDonald had said a mouthful, more than I had ever heard him speak before. As I took stock, I took another pull.

The first letter in the primer was A.

Chapter 37

▼

The war raged on, month after month. We heard rumors aplenty. We were losing; we were winning. We even heard that Lincoln and Davis were about to call it a draw.

The only thing in stone was that Brewster Daggit was stuck in the Capitol Prison. Things could have been worse; others were being killed and maimed.

Me, I just sat around, drank whiskey with McDonald, and worked a little when opportunity presented itself. Mostly though, I labored with my slate, chalk, and primer.

I found the alphabet manageable. There were only twenty six letters to learn. After several weeks of practice I had them down pat; big ones and little ones. Then I tried to compare these with Lydia's letter and found that few matched.

"You are God's own stupid," was McDonald's comment when I confided my confusion with the squiggly letters. "Those are cursive letters."

"Cursive?" I had never even heard the word. "Then what are these?" I asked holding up the primer.

"Those are regular letters."

"Regular."

"Yes, cursive is what adults use so they can write fast and sloppy. Regular writing takes too much time."

"So, why have I spent so much time learning the regular writing?"

"It's just the way it is; books, newspapers, and important things are in regular writing."

"So, do you know the cursive?"

"Some, but not real well; I get by."

"You will help me?" I asked already knowing the answer.

"Pass me back that bottle." was all he said.

Two more weeks were spent with the cursive. Learning to string the letters together posed the biggest problem, but this too was mastered.

Now before me was the true mystery. Just what order did the letters go to form words? I had one word down pat, my name, Daggit. I could write it regular, I could write it in cursive. I wrote it over and over; saying it as I did. Each and every time I saw in my minds eye the sign at the road. Each time I saw an unattended lonely grave on a now over grown prairie. It took much effort to refocus on the problem at hand.

My learning of the words initially came slow, painfully slow, but three months into my studies there sprang forth an epiphany. I began to read; I recognized the words on the papers. These words flowed into sentences, sentences into paragraphs, and paragraphs into books. I read every book McDonald could beg, borrow, or steal. A whole world opened before me; there was so much I had not known. There were people, places, things, and ideas that were all previously unknown to the illiterate Brewster. I began to see what my friend, Jason, had meant; perhaps the pen was mightier than the sword.

I learned that along with the exchange of ideas; the same could be done with feelings and emotions. Poetry was wonderful, I enjoyed so much of it; but more so, I enjoyed the personal letter, especially my letter. I read it at least a hundred times. "My dearest Bud," it said, "Your letters are so heartfelt, so elegant, they near take my breath away. My life now seems to revolve around each and every note you send. You have won over my heart and soul. It is my intention to wait for you as all maidens wait for their lovers who have gone off to war. I will be here doing what I must until at last we can be together again. Yet even with the joy I feel; I have the burden of extending to you my sympathies and regrets. It is with the deepest sadness I must report the passing of the Svenson's. They died as they lived; together. Both fell ill with what we think was the typhoid fever. Nothing we did brought them relief. They were abed for no more than a week before they expired. We will bury them side by side in Hutchinson Cemetery after the spring thaw. I miss them so very much. The Svenson's were family in every sense of the word. I pray every day for your welfare. News comes to us of the fallen; so many young boys have died. Please continue your beautiful loving letters; I cherish each and every one of them. I want you to live and come home to me. I am waiting for your return. Your loving, Lydia"

The news of Svenson's death brought sorrow upon each rereading. They had been such wonderful people; especially the old man.

The news that Lydia loved me shook me to the bone. Over and over I read her letter. I did not see the words, "I love you," but she was saying it none the less. And, she was waiting for me! A beautiful young girl in Hutchinson, Minnesota, was waiting for me as I sat in prison over a thousand miles away.

Young, she was just so young and impressionable. This infatuation with an old man would surely wan. Yet think about her I did. I saw her in my mind, her eyes, her face and oh boy, her figure. She might have only been sixteen, but she had potential, no doubt about it. A man in prison, alone, deprived, and in my case, mostly drunk, sees what he needs to see to survive; and I was seeing Lydia.

Then somewhere in my sotten brain some little mathematician began his work. She was sixteen. I had been gone over two years now. Maybe she was closer to seventeen when we met.

"Sure she was," said the little mathematician as he did his computations.

That little beauty is a full grown woman now; she must be nineteen, maybe even twenty.

"Ding, ding, ding," bells were ringing in my head.

Lydia was prime, fine, and maybe, just maybe, she was mine. Suddenly I wanted out of prison; I wanted to go home.

Home, there it was again. I saw that same mental image of the Daggit sign and the grave that held my family. As much as I wanted to go home, I knew there would be no inner peace, no freedom, no life until I had avenged my Helga and Hans. I would find them, Boland and Matthews. I'd have my revenge, then seek out my hearts desire.

Yet things do not always fall into place. To leave meant to be hunted down and shot; to wait meant my purpose, if they still lived, could disappear. Once they were out of the army they would be hard to track.

As I sat my cell, I realized that even if they were still in the army they would be hard to find.

Chapter 38

▼

The news came to us first as just a rumor; the war was over, Lee had surrendered. We had no confirmation. Then two days later bells were ringing, cannons boomed, their sounds confirming the end to the hostilities.

It was over!

Even in prison I could feel a sigh of relief. The butchery, the horrors of war would be no more.

Yet little did the end of hostilities help my situation. I had been given a three year sentence; I still had more than a year to go. Here I sat.

I thought a lot about Lydia and how much I wanted to be with her. Almost daily I tried to write her back and tell her how I felt. Sometimes I would write most of a page, some days just a few lines. I could never seem to complete an entire letter. It wasn't initially for lack of effort, but as the weeks changed into months my effort became indifference. What beautiful young woman deserved an old ex-convict with absolutely no future?

Besides I was sure there was a waning interest on the behalf of Lydia, as no other letters came. Perhaps she fell in love with someone else. Perhaps she too caught the typhoid fever and died. Most probably she had come to her senses and just plain dumped me.

I eventually gave up all hope and concerns regarding Lydia. As I sat my life away my every thanks went to McDonald, his libations, and the books he found for me to read.

In celebration of the Union victory there was a grand parade in Washington. From my window I watched many or the troops march by; thousands and thousands of survivors they were. Two days after the parade I did not see a soul. They just disappeared, the streets were empty. The men had apparently gone home.

Then again fell a melancholy for me to deal with. Not one man had left their rank to visit me. Surely, I thought, there must have been Minnesotans present for the celebration. I even had a half hearted hope that General Uncle Billy might stop by and get me the hell out of here.

It never happened. I still had time to serve. I'd been forgotten by all but McDonald.

On occasion new prisoners were confined at the Capitol, most came and with little fanfare or notice. Henry Wirtz, however, had my attention. He was alleged to have been the Warden of Andersonville, the dreaded death camp of the Confederacy.

From my cell window I watched them hang him.

Then the President was shot dead; or so it was said. Usurpers and accomplices to the shooting were brought in. All were kept separate and had their own special guards.

"I can't see it," carped McDonald. "I could guard them just fine. We don't need a special crew to do it."

McDonald was drunk as he loudly made his complaint to me. He as well within ear shot of several of the special guard squad, big mean looking soldiers they were, men to stay clear of. I could see right off why they were picked for the assignment. These were men who could not be easily over powered.

"They don't look so tough to me," McDonald said to me, but so loud was his voice I knew for sure he was talking to them. He was taunting them.

"Easy now," I said, "let it be."

McDonald was maybe, forty five or fifty, he was small, and he was God's own drunk.

"Hey there," it was their Lieutenant who had taken both notice and exception. "What is that prisoner doing outside his cell?"

"He's drinking with me." snarled McDonald.

"Drinking!"

"Yes, Bud always drinks with me." McDonald was indignant.

"Well not any more." answered the Lieutenant. "Return that man to his cell. You are drunk and relieved of duty."

The Lieutenant and two big bruisers were walking at us.

"Yes sir," I responded. I could not wait to get back into the cell. Confrontation was the last thing I wanted.

As I turned to go into my cell, they had faced up toe to toe with McDonald. He said something lippy. I heard a crack, turned, and saw McDonald spinning towards the floor. That Lieutenant had apparently socked him in the face.

McDonald hit his knees but his outstretched arms kept him from going prone. There he was on his hands and knees when that Lieutenant kicked him in the side of the face, the force of which flipped McDonald to his back.

The Lieutenant's foot was coming up again, the side of McDonald's face was his target, when I let go with my right fist.

I caught him square to his jaw. He had but one foot planted when I hit him, there was naught to hold him upright. Little good that foot did him. The Lieutenant hit that ground hard. He was flat on his back and oblivious to just how boots to the face felt. I kicked him plenty before the weight of his special squad of goons drove me to the floor.

My three near finished years in prison were rewarded with five more.

Gone were my perks, my books, my own cell, my personal guard, and my whiskey.

I was sent to a new prison. I was sent to hell; they called it the Pea Patch.

Chapter 39

▼

Fort Delaware sat on a three hundred acre island at the mouth of the Delaware River. It's more common name was the Pea Patch. As there were thousands of prisoners confined here, I guessed the name had something to do with the smell. The State of Delaware was to the west bank, Delaware City was just a mile or so down stream. Upstream a few miles was the city of Philadelphia. Across the river to the east was Finns Point, New Jersey.

Finns Point was where I buried the dead.

Day after day we loaded the long boat with dead Rebs, rowed them to the Point, lugged their corpses to the pits and shoveled them in.

The war was over for the Johnnies; all they had to do was swear allegiance to the stars and stripes and freedom was theirs. It was simple as that.

But no; these stupid stubborn sons of bitches chose to sit at the Pea Patch, eat rancid swill if there was any, waste away, incur some disease, suffer and die rather than tell a lie and go home. These idiots were soldiers of the Confederacy, then, now and forever. They vowed to never pledge allegiance to the Union. It made no sense to me. If I could go home with just the telling of a lie, I'd sure do it in an instant. Their lives were naught but want and woe.

My life wasn't much better.

My prison job consisted of disposing of the dead of which there were many. Everyday I rowed, dug, toted, and buried. So dismal was my existence I often thought death might be the better alternative.

The smell of the Pea Patch was of feces, urine, and death. My only relief was the long row to Finns Point. If we were lucky there was a stiff sea breeze to waif away the stench of the corpses that lay the belly of the boat.

I was housed separate from the Rebs as were the near one hundred other Yankee prisoners, all malingers and scoundrels each and every one of them. So vile were my comrades in their speech, mannerisms, and person; I chose not to engage them in conversation or companionship. I just kept to myself and did as directed.

From time to time some fool would try for my crust or swill. Old Bud would then show him, them, and whoever, what God loves. Then I would be left alone for a while, but short lived were their memories. School never recessed for long.

It was in the spring of 67 that the stupid stubborn sons of the South began to learn the virtues of prevarication. Oaths of allegiance were given and I was rowing the live Rebs to Delaware. By the end of the year only a few die hard Rebs remained at the Pea Patch. The rest had gone home or died. Rumor had it that we buried more than twenty five hundred Johnnies at the Point. These men never would go home.

I had resolved that I wouldn't either. Lydia, Hutchinson, Helga, Crow Creek, were but wisps of memories. Try as I might, I was hard pressed to visualize either woman's face. No home did I have to go to.

In 1868 most of the Yank prisoners were dispersed to different Federal prisons or released. I was kept on at the Pea Patch.

They said it was July when the Warden had us row the last four die hard Rebs to Delaware City. These men had never sworn allegiance and vowed they never would. The Warden had said it was just cost effective to give up on them and let them go. Skin and bones, they were; filthy and vermin infested. We put them ashore a mile below town; then just rowed away.

They were free. Free to beg and steal their way home.

Me, I still had two more years to do.

Chapter 40

▼

"Bud! Hey you Bud, for heavens sake get in here," it was Warden Ridgemont yelling. "Bud!"

"Sir," I responded making my way into his office.

There were five of us left on the Pea Patch; the Warden, three guards, and me. Fort Delaware was being decommissioned. It served no purpose so the government was abandoning it. It was our job to take down what we could, salvage what we could, then burn the rest.

"Bud!"

"Yes, Clarence!" I answered. The Warden and I had actually become friends. "I'm coming."

My situation at the Pea Patch had improved. I once again ate real food, slept in a real bed and wore clean clothes. As the only prisoner left, there was no reason to deny me the most basic of amenities. Besides, I did most of the work. If I got sick or died the Warden and the guards would have to whatever themselves. They took good care of me.

"I want you to start carrying those files down to the dock. For some reason the army wants to know who came here, who died and who was discharged.

"Those files?" I asked looking at the cabinets along the wall.

"Yes and the three files that are in my office. You can use the big two wheeler. Put them all in the shed next to the boat dock."

"Yes sir," I responded.

"Say Bud, how much more time do you have to do."

"I'm not sure," I lied. "I got five years, what day is this?"

"September 12th."

"Twelve more days," I responded without need of calculation.

"Twelve, you say."

"Yes sir, twelve days and I'm out of here. September 24ᵗʰ."

"Well you had better get at it, you have plenty to do and not much time to get it done."

"Who is going to do the work when I'm gone?"

"Who cares, when you are gone, so are we. We will just torch what is left and walk away."

"How come I was never sent to another prison like the others?"

"Because I liked you," Ridgemont responded, "now get to work. I'm going to Delaware City. I'll have the boat. You can load the files onboard when I get back. For now just get them to the shed. Orville and Tully are rowing me across the river. Oscar is around here somewhere."

"I guess that leaves me in charge," I laughed.

"Guess it does," he said as he went out the door.

Simple as that, I was alone except for Oscar who was no doubt sleeping somewhere.

I did not earn my status through procrastination. Not two hours later my assigned task was complete. Me and nine file cabinets were resting in the big shed next to the dock.

Boredom, perhaps curiosity, caused me to browse through the file cabinets. I was familiar with a few of the names. I could actually put faces to them. Most of the faces I saw were more distorted and ghastly as my dealing with the individuals was post living.

In one of the cabinets I found a partially consumed bottle of whiskey. Long had been its absence from my world. I gave it a look over and popped the cork. An over the top sniff offered promise. A quick sip confirmed the contents to be the elixir I sought.

I sloshed a big pull of that brown tepid liquor around in my mouth; I moved the fluid in and out of my teeth. Then when I was ready I swallowed it in a gulp. It burned so good; I had another then another before corking it off. The bottle fit quite nicely in my pocket. There it stayed.

The file cabinet from which the liquor came contained the names of Union prisoners. I gave the interior more than a cursory search; it was another bottle I sought. What I found first was my own package.

"Brewster Ulysses Daggit," it said. Besides my name it listed me by my army number. It said that I was from Crow Creek, Minnesota, and a sergeant in the Second Minnesota Volunteer Infantry. Then it listed my offense, assault on a superior officer, five years at the Pea Patch. The start date was 9/23/1865. The discharge date was listed as 9/24/1870.

I spent a little more time being nosey, checking out the names of fellow prisoners that I had known. Most were charged with serious offenses of which they rarely talked. As I read their package I totally agreed with their respective imprisonments. Most should still be locked up. A more heinous group of malcontents and malingers could not have been assembled. Their crimes ran the gamut from simple theft to bestiality and murder.

As I thumbed through the file a name stopped me dead. Stunned, I pulled the file. The tab said, "Clayton Matthews."

He had been incarcerated at the Pea Patch 12/20/63 and discharged 12/21/65. He had spent two years at the Patch for the offense of rape. There were no specifics about his case only the intake and discharge dates. What amazed me most, we were prisoners together for at least three months and our paths never crossed. This was just hard to believe.

As I gave this matter more thought, I gave my lips anther taste. My newly found treasure did little to cool the fire that had just now been rekindled.

For three months we had occupied the same space and I never saw him. He, however, may have seen me and stood clear. That was a possibility. If he were not assigned the burial detail he could have well hid among the hundreds of other Union prisoners.

At least he had survived the war; he was out there somewhere; he and Boland. Even though it was hard to mentally picture my wife's face, I remembered his. I knew it well. I still had an obligation. I had purpose again, and only twelve long days to serve.

I took another pull on that bottle.

Chapter 41

▼

What a man needs is a plan and a stash; something to fall back on, some kind of money. I had nothing, nothing at all. Clarence was setting me free in the morning. I had no money, no decent clothing, and most important; no where to go.

I had no home, the Svenson's were dead, and Lydia had no doubt removed herself from my life.

What I did have was a burning sense of purpose. I would find them, Boland and Matthews. Vengeance is mine sayth the Lord is what the Christians have said. I saw no point to wait him out; I had nothing else to do. It was my special purpose to hasten their judgment day.

A man with no funds is actually better off in prison. At least there is generally something to eat and a place to sleep. These past few months afforded me both. Being the only prisoner was very beneficial. I ate what the Warden ate and I slept in a clean warm bed. I did not relish the idea of being set free then having to beg for drams.

Dusk was upon the Pea Patch and I needed some cash. There was not a penny to be had anywhere on the island. There was nothing left but a few of the buildings and some tools that we used to maintain them.

Little bells and whistles began to chime and blow well back in my brain. Try as I might, the buildings were not going anywhere; but the tools, now that was another story. There were shovels, axes, saws, and hammers. There were picks, drivers, drills, and sledges. A complete carpentry shop was not fifty paces away. These were not run of the mill everyday tools either; these were Federal tools, the best that Federal money could buy.

For the next several hours I lugged and packed every hand tool I could find down to the longboat. Not a guard did I see, they were all asleep in their barrack. Why bother with posting, their only prisoner, me, was free with the morning sun.

When I could find nothing else to add to the pile I decided to make the row to Delaware. If Clarence took exception with my procurements, which I doubted he would even notice, he might just look for me in Delaware City, the closest landing. My dockage would be in Port Penn, several miles further south. I would have both current and tide. My night's row would not be too arduous.

I found pen and paper. I left Clarence a note on his door.

"Dear Clarence, It is morning, I'm free, and I'm out of here. I will leave the boat in Delaware. Thank you, Bud."

I had it all as I put my back to the oars. I had current, an outgoing tide, a mountain of tools to sell, a most serviceable boat, and the fresh smell of the sea in my face.

It must have been an hour before dawn when I slipped south along the coast past Delaware City. There were a few lights popping on here and there. I put my back to the oars; it was at least ten miles to Port Penn.

The current was beginning to wan and the tide rush was over as I pulled beyond the breakers in to Port Penn. I slipped my boat up on a piece of beach away from the docks and tied off to a big rock. No worry did I have of the boat drifting off, the tide would soon be out. Worst case, I'd be beached the rest of the day.

With my boat secured, I went in search of a buyer of tools.

I walked down what appeared to be the main street of Port Penn. There were shops and houses on both sides of the lane. Many were the people who gave me a second glance. It was obvious they took note of strangers.

The sign said, "Lawrence Gray." Under it listed the business as, "Dry goods, Hardware, and Mercantile."

The door was open.

"May I help you?" asked the old bald shop keeper as he looked up from some task.

"Sir, I am looking for a place to sell quality hand tools. I have a boat full of this and that's. It's only a fair price I seek, cash for a new start."

"Stole the stuff did you?"

"Not exactly."

"I have personally used each and every item. I consider each item to be my own personal property."

"Do you now," he was looking me up and down. "You know, I could call the constable."

"Do you have one?"

"No," he smiled, "no, we don't."

"Good."

"And just what variety of goods might you have to sell."

I liked this Gray fellow; he was a man with an eye for opportunity.

"Tools, I have quality tools to sell; a whole boat load. I am looking for a buyer with a discerning eye; some one who will appreciate quality when he sees it."

"And where might these tools be?" he asked, looking beyond me towards the door of his business.

"They are still aboard the boat which is tied off on the sandbar down by the docks."

"Well, let's have a look see."

We walked back to the docks. It wasn't far but we still had time to chat.

"You are him, aren't you?"

"Who?" I replied.

"The last prisoner from the Pea Patch would be my guess," he said as he again looked me up and down.

"It shows?"

He was laughing now, "That it does, plain as the nose on my face. Those are prison pants. That is a prison shirt. What are left of your shoes were no doubt penal specials."

"You know?"

"Sure, I sold clothing and shoes to the Pea Patch, tools too. I heard they only had one prisoner left; and here you are. What I hope you have in the boat are the tools that I sold to them in the first place. The army only bought the best of the best."

"Its quality merchandise," I said, agreeing with him."

We were at that moment in time looking over the gunnels of the longboat.

"That it is," said Gray as he looked over my recently acquired hardware store. "Is the boat for sale too?"

"It is," I affirmed, hoping Clarence would not take exception to the transaction.

"I will give you ten cents on the dollar for the entire load, and fifty dollars for the boat."

"Twenty cents and seventy five for the boat," I countered.

Gray did not bat an eye, "Fifteen cents on the dollar and seventy dollars for the boat."

"Deal," I said.

"Deal," he repeated.

We shook hands and walked back towards the store.

"It will take me a few hours to have all the hardware packed up to the store; another hour or two to get the boat hauled out, hulled, and painted."

"Painted?"

"Damn right, that long boat just screams property of the United States Government. But, you just give me and my boys a few hours and it will be painted, sold, and out of here."

"Is there a place to let; I have need of a bath, clean clothes, a decent meal, and a bed that doesn't move on its own."

"Bad place wasn't it, that Pea Patch took a lot of them; theirs and ours."

"That it was," I replied.

"See that red sign over there?" he asked, pointing down the street.

"The round one?"

"That's it, Port Penn's own Palace Hotel. We call it the Triple P. Tell Maude I've already credited you seventy dollars. She will take good care of you. Come into the store and pick out some new clothing and some decent boots. We will put them on your account."

Not an hour later I was buck naked in a hot bath tub. I was almost chest deep in sweet smelling soapy suds; my second glass of whiskey rested on a stool to my right. The bottle sat the floor next to my new boots. A half consumed beef sandwich sat on another stool to my left. The sun's reflection through the amber colored liquid did much to warm my spirits. I had it all. I thought my station in life could get no better than this. I was warm, fed, and near drunk; and it wasn't even noon yet. Four of the last five years I had done little more than eat swill and bury dead Rebs, but I had not too much to complain about the last year, most of the Rebs were gone, and the food got some better. I just laid my head back and shut my eyes.

No sir, Brewster," I said to myself, "It just doesn't get much better than this."

"Mister," there was a soft voice somewhere in the room.

I opened my eyes to find a beautiful full grown woman standing in the room. She had some years on her, no doubt about it, but she had some left too.

"Mister," she said again, "I work for Gray. I was sent to do what needs done."

"Done?"

"I'm sure that back of yours needs scrubbed; and for a glass of your whiskey I'd be pleased to do just that."

No one had ever accused me of being stupid; I handed her the whole bottle.

L. L. Layman

Just when I had thought life couldn't get much better, it did. It got a whole lot better.

Chapter 42

▼

Diane was her first name; she never told me her last. I never asked. She called me Bud; I called her Di.

It seemed Di was widowed in the war and took her loss to heart. There was a void in her life that left her but a shell. There was a similar void in mine. We both had a need that the other could fill, whiskey did the rest.

From where I stood, a man widowed and alone more than seven years, Di was a most, most remarkable woman, and she had all the right parts in just the right places. Our arrangement was quite amicable. From the Triple P bathtub we moved to a rented room further down the same street. There we stayed for the next two years.

Our life fell into a routine. I worked what seemed to be eight days a week digging drainage ditches, Di tended bar and waited tables in a local eatery. We met each night after our day's labor. She always had with her enough stolen whiskey from the eatery to meet our nightly needs. I had with me enough food to see that we didn't actually die. As the lamp dimmed; our repast and drink consumed, we fell into bed, arm in arm, forever trying to fill that void in our souls.

Then, again, the sun would rise, as would we; and we would do it all over again.

It might have been love, who is to say; but what we had wasn't bad.

My walk home from the ditch job was near three miles, the last two miles bordered the ditch we dug last year. Once the swamp was drained away, the farmers moved in. They did quite well with their vegetables, some of which I would "borrow" from time to time if opportunity presented itself.

Today, my booty consisted of a few carrots, a turnip, and an onion. These along with some cheese, cold meat and bread would make a most adequate dinner. I had to quicken my pace as the shops which offered the cheese, bread, and meats would soon be closed. We had dug longer than normal today; it was either that or start our morning knee deep in mud and slop. We had need but ten more feet to connect our ditch to what they called a terminal. We made the connection in good fashion and headed home with the water running fast towards the sea.

Ditch diggers, me included, were paid daily. I had an extra hours pay in my pocket. I thought I would do a little something special for Di; she had been less than herself for most of a week.

I stopped in Gray's, but he wasn't around. He had become a decent friend. He never complained when Di left his employ and moved in with me. His loss was certainly my gain. Di had once mentioned that it was Gray's wife who more than anything else prompted her to leave his employ. I never questioned or dwelled on the matter; well enough is well enough.

The sun was near set, but there were still a few vendors at the market. I was able to purchase the rest of our dinner along with an apple pie which I hoped would bring a smile to Di's face; it always did mine. A lady was selling cut flowers for the vase, something I had never before considered; not because they wouldn't made a nice gift, but rather the snide remarks I might incur as I carried them past the rogues and ruffians that lined the lane.

Not one of these ruffians did I fear or step aside for. School had been opened many times during these past two years, I had taught a good many students just what God loved. Yet, I knew of their talk. It would be of me and my flowers. A man wanting to avoid problems doesn't invite trouble or ridicule.

This evening, I threw caution to the wind and bought a small bouquet. As I continued home with my bounty I had what they called an epiphany, an original thought. If a man could have flowers delivered to his special interest, more men could avoid the embarrassing walk home. Yes sir, if a man lived by a big city, had access to flowers and made deliveries; he could make a killing.

I was still thinking about this endeavor as I opened the door to our room.

Three things, all unusual, hit me at once. The room was dim, Di was abed, and there was no whiskey on the table.

The first two were easily understood, she had not been feeling well; but having no whiskey set me a reel. Once focused on the problem at hand I remembered my stash and quietly produced a partial bottle from under the bed.

As I had my dinner and drink I could watch Di as she slept in the bed. Covered like she was, all I could see was the shape of her body and her hair as it flowed out across the pillow. I never could decide if it was more red than brown or more brown than red. Whichever, I liked it just fine. I liked the curves of her body under those blankets even more.

"Bud," it was Di calling me softly from the bed.

"Yes," I answered.

"Are those flowers for me?" She was smiling. Her smile was always amazement to me. It was somewhere between infectious and sensuous.

"Yes," I replied, almost embarrassed.

"That's so nice of you; no one has ever got me flowers before. Put them in some water for me."

Her voice seemed weaker than normal. Perhaps she was just very tired. I did as I was told, remarking to myself how out of place the flowers looked on the table. Dingy was our apartment.

"Would you like to eat tonight?" I asked.

"No, I really don't feel well. I want you to come to bed and keep me warm."

"What is wrong with you? How do you feel?"

"I just hurt," she replied. "It's hard to breathe, my chest feels heavy. I just want to lay here. Hurry up and get in bed will you."

Once again I did as I was told and with much haste. Lying with Di had become the high light of my life. Never did we wear night clothes, not that we had any. To feel her body next to mine, to smell her person, brought joy to my life.

Di was all woman, no doubt about it.

This night she kissed me a few times and then just began to talk. She talked and talked. I held her and listened. Di started at the beginning, somewhere just after, "I was born." She rambled on and on.

It seemed that Di was married twice. Her first husband, Joe, was an adventurous sort. He left one day to make their fortune out in the southwest territories. He said that he was going to a place called Arizona. He was going to send for her when he was settled in. She saw him disappear as he turned west on the lane that led from their home. She never saw him again.

After a wait of many years with no word from Joe, she married some guy named Keith. Poor Keith got conscripted and sent off to fight for the Union. She heard from him several times after that, but then he too became silent. She made inquiries and learned that he had been listed as missing in action.

I knew that missing in action included many possibilities. Sometimes the bodies were so mangled, no identification could be made. Men were just buried; their graves marked "Unknown." Sometimes, too, men just walked away. They changed their names and kept on walking. The army was so busy with the war they had little time to immediately chase down absconders. The easiest way to catch the run offs was to simply wait a few weeks then send a detachment to their home. Men who ran learned that they could not go back home for fear of arrest. They had to start new lives in different places. Many did just that.

Diane talked of her widowed years and how hard life was. Apparently she had a child, a girl, who was born during these, "in between years." The child only lived a short time. Her death added much to Di's grief and confusion. Di knew she would never see the child again, but she never knew if either of her husbands would just someday walk back into her life.

She talked about her parents, her old home, and even her dreams.

She was still talking when I drifted off to sleep.

Then, again as always, the sun rose, as did I. It was, however, only me that got out of bed. Di did not rise this day or any other. Sometime during the night, Di had quit talking forever.

Chapter 43

▼

I had said one time that the relationship that Di and I had wasn't love, but I was so very wrong. The sorrow that burst from my inner being nearly killed me. I cried like a baby. I must have been denying my true feelings all along. The grief I felt that morning could have only come from the loss of someone dearly loved. Apparently what we had was love; and it wasn't bad either.

I regretted not a single day; not a single minute of our life together. If I had any regret at all it was in not telling her just how I felt. I should have told her a hundred times, maybe more, that she was the one, the love of my life.

Long was our morning as Di and I waited for the undertaker. She had talked to me on and on the previous night, I was talking to her now. In the silence of our dingy apartment, I told a cold corpse with mostly brown hair what I should have told the warm vibrant woman that I had shared my life with.

I said, "I love you, Di."

She told me just what I deserved; not a word.

Gray came by and helped me wrap her for the undertaker. It was near noon before the man arrived with his hearse and two porters.

"I will need some information for her obituary, funeral instruction, burial location, and of course a nice dress for her to wear," said the most matter of fact undertaker. "I will also need to know what type of funeral you wish. We have a basic fifteen dollar burial. It includes a short sermon provided by my wife, a few flowers, and a five foot deep hole for a standard wood casket."

I didn't answer, I was weighing my options; one, kill this heartless son of a bitch, or two; kill the heartless son of a bitch and both his porters. The decision did not come quick enough as the undertaker had time to continue on with his sales pitch.

"Then, of course, you could have the twenty five dollar deluxe. That includes flowers aplenty, a flannel lined coffin, a six foot hole in either the Catholic or the Methodist cemetery, with an ordained preacher praying."

I just nodded, still deciding if I wanted to kill just this guy or all three.

"Very well," he replied as he gave his horse the whip. The hearse jerked into motion, now carrying the undertaker, two porters, and my blanket wrapped Di.

Gray sat with me a while on the bench outside our apartment door. We talked of this and that, but mostly we talked of Diane and what a great gal she had been.

Eventually Gray left and I had time to write down a few notes for the obituary. It was at this moment in time that I realized that Di had laid it all out for me the previous night. Prior to her ramblings I had known almost nothing of her past. Today, alone on the bench, I knew so much more. Most of all I realized just how much I loved and missed her.

Someone once said that time heals all wounds, little good it was doing for me. All I had were wounds that never seemed to heal.

Three days later my flannel wrapped Diane was laid in her Methodist, six foot deep grave. Unless the stranger praying for her soul had some success, a cold dark lonely world hers now would be. I tried to not dwell on her circumstance, but I might have rather chose to fly like a bird. Her death left such a void in my life, little else was there for me to think about.

That night, the torture of the funeral behind me, I sat a stool in the tavern where she had worked as the barmaid. Many here had been her friends; many too were the condolences and kind words. No drink did I have to buy. Everyone was ever so kind; they ensured that my glass never emptied.

Eventually my fellow mourners left the saloon. Only my amber colored liquid friend and a newspaper with her obituary included therein remained at the now lamp lighted table. I had read it forty times at least. I read it forty one.

"Diane G. DeParte, born 6/18/1829, in Chatham, Massachusetts, to Jorge and Louise Grove, died Saturday last in Port Penn after a short respiratory illness. Diane leaves to mourn her passing her good friend, Brewster Daggit. Diane DeParte had married Joseph Leifer in Boston, 6/14/1849. Leifer had left for the Arizona Territories in 1855 and never returned. He was presumed scalped. She later married Keith DeParte in 1858. Departe left to fight for the Union in 1862. He disappeared and according to the Department of the Army, is listed as missing in action. There is no truth to the rumor that he was last seen in a Greenville whore house with two twin sisters. Diane was preceded in death by both her parents and infant daughter, born sometime between husband number one and husband number two. Diane Departe now rests for eternity in the Port Penn Methodist Cemetary."

That was it, simple and factual. A person lived, loved, conceived, and died. Diane had no accolades; no accomplishments. She just existed, and then died.

I drank another, pondering the meaning of life, and then gave thought to the lack of both; drink and life. One did not hold much without the other. I wasn't in the best of moods. I even gave thought as to looking up the undertaker and his porters.

For need of a diversion, I let my eyes scan the newspaper past the obituary which had held my attention these many hours. An advertisement caught my eye.

"Wanted, Gold Miners!
No Experience Needed.
Top Pay. Six Day Weeks.
Apply at Boland Mines.
Helena, Montana.
James Boland, Proprietor."

The name James Boland hit me like a hammer. There it was right in the paper. McDonald had told me years ago that in these modern times my search for vengeance would be on paper. Here it was, literally in the paper.

I read it again focusing on James Boland, Helena, Montana.

I asked myself over and over, "How many men were there named James Boland, surely more than the one I sought."

I read and reread the advertisement. After each reading my ire grew. I soon forgot about the undertaker, I had a different place to release my anger. Many were the emotions moving through my sotten brain. I had a need, it wasn't new, and it had always been there. I needed to kill something, I needed to kill somebody, I needed to kill James Boland; and just maybe that Sergeant of his, Clayton Matthews.

Late now was the day. The supper hour had passed. I went to Gray's store and found it still open for business. I walked right in, I had a purpose.

"Bud, good to see you," Gray was behind the counter doing some clerical work.

"I'm moving on," I said, "with Di gone I have no reason to stay."

"We will miss you, but I understand."

"Myself as well, I've made some good friends here, but I have a need to move on."

"I understand," said Gray, "and you will have some need for traveling items."

Gray was most astute; he had an eye for opportunity.

"Yes, I will be in need of a few necessities," I replied as I looked into the glass display case. "I would like that Smith and Wesson 44, a box of those brass rounds, that brown holster, and that sheathed pig sticker."

"Where are you going Bud? With these purchases I suspect you are going to be a bank robber."

"No, I am going gold mining at someplace called Helena. Do you have a map?"

Chapter 44

▼

"That will be $13.50, fare from Washington to East St. Louis," requested the station clerk.

He did it with a straight face, never batted an eye.

"The train leaves at straight up noon," he said, reaching his hand out to take my money."

"How long is the trip?" I asked as I counted out the coin.

Diane and I had for the past two years been most frugal with our moneys. Our living arrangements were stark for lack of better description. We "borrowed" plenty, liquor and consumables, probably more often than we paid. Our rent was but a pittance. Our secret stash of cash was substantial, little good it did Di.

"Three days and four hours," replied the clerk as he counted my coin.

"Three days!" I was shocked with the speed. "You mean we can be in St. Louis, Missouri in three days."

"Yes sir," he answered, "and that includes at least a dozen stops."

"Just how fast does this train go," I inquired, still amazed with the speed.

I mentally tried to do the calculations, remembering the four to six miles per day we made as we marched through Tennessee and Georgia. Times were changing, that was for sure. Things just seemed to move too fast in these modern times.

"We average sometimes more than thirty miles per hour," he said, apparently oblivious to mental calculations still bouncing around in my head.

"Will there be layovers for meals?" I asked, meals were an important consideration.

"One meal stop per day," replied the clerk, "and if you are not on the train when the wheels turn again, you will be walking the rest of the way. Most travelers who go the distance pack a few sandwiches and some drink."

"Thank you," I replied as I took my ticket in hand.

The clock on the station wall said 11:05; I had almost an hour to collect provisions. I knew I would need something to drink, three days was a long time. I found what I needed at a small out of the way tavern down the street from the train platform. The bartender must have been familiar with travelers in my situation. He had a bottle ready and sandwiches made. We spent most of the 55 minutes talking about the war and whether the country had accomplished anything by it. He seemed to think that near 500,000 men died for absolutely nothing. Clyde was his name. He seemed fairly astute for a man who probably drank more than he sold. Clyde said that if the North had just let the South succeed; they would have later begged to get back in. The North, he insisted had all the industry, and with it, all the money. The South could have easily been brought back into the Union, simple as hanging a carrot in front of an ass.

"What about slavery?" I asked.

"Slavery, the war wasn't about Slavery, it was about money. That Lincoln did the Emancipation Proclamation as a ruse to divert attention from the truth. I mean, how else could you get a half million dumb asses to march off to their death for the sake of lining someone else's pocket. There had to be a noble cause. Slavery fit the bill."

Clyde got me to thinking, and with three days travel ahead I had plenty of time for contemplation.

Travel by rail was indeed a modern marvel; that first day we crossed most of the Appalachians. From my window seat I could just gaze out at the majestic mountains. There was an appreciation for their beauty that I failed to see as I earlier had lugged my pack and rifle over each peak. Just watching them pass by was certainly more pleasurable than fighting and shooting our way through each pass and valley. Looking out the window, I did give some thought to what Clyde had proposed, but mostly it was too profound for me to comprehend. It was over, so what; there was nothing that I could do about it. What I could do something about was in a place called Helena.

Even a man with purpose can have his attention diverted. As I sat that rock hard seat, the hip and butt wounds incurred years ago began to ache. The liquid fortification that I had obtained from Clyde did much to ease the discomfort; at least I thought it did.

The second day, late in the afternoon, somewhere in Ohio, a trio of young men seated in the same car, began to become annoying. They were drunk, loud, and vulgar. Apparently they had consumed all of their own liquor. All three were eyeballing my bottle that I kept on the bench between my hip and the window. It was a long ways yet to East St. Louis and I wasn't likely to share.

"Hey Pops, how about passing that bottle over this way," blurted out the biggest of the men.

He was a tall fellow, heavy with muscles in the shoulders and arms.

I ignored him.

"Didn't you hear me," he shouted. "We are out of gin and I see you have some whiskey."

He was standing now, moving across the aisle towards me. Thirty other passengers just watched.

"I'll just have a taste," he said, as he reached across my body with his left hand.

Big and strong he was for sure; no doubt used to having his way, but the lad was totally ignorant in the ways of men. He had left his entire torso exposed as he leaned in.

My left hand grabbed his throat and pulled him in as my right fist crashed him square in the nose. Again and again I pasted his face with my fist, getting myself blood soaked for my efforts. His nose and mouth had both let go with gushing red fluid. He had been hit hard.

The man fell to the floor at my feet, but he received no mercy as my boots were steady stomping the back of his head.

His two friends, both well sotten, came to his rescue. Both men, drunk though they might have been, were not stupid. They stopped dead in their tracks as they looked down the barrel of that new Smith and Wesson that had filled my hand.

"No closer boys," I said, getting their undivided attention. "Now drag scooter here out form under my seat."

This they did as I kept them covered with the revolver.

"Now take him to another car at the farthest end of the train. If I see any of you again I'll actually get my butt up off this bench and throws yours off the train."

They were helping Scooter up from the floor when I lost my patience, kicking one of the men square in the butt, sending him flying over Scooter and into the seat across the aisle.

"Move!"

And, they did.

At least sixty eyes watched the trio leave the car; these onlookers focused first on the trio leaving then on me, then back again. Their heads seemed to move in union. One pair of eyes among the fifty-eight others did not follow the rest. Looking to the rear, several benches back on the other side of the aisle sat a woman; a pretty woman, blond of hair and blue of eyes which she had on me.

I heard murmurs and hushed mutterings among my fellow passengers. Quiet though they were I heard my name; both my names. I heard someone call me Old Bud and someone else called me Brewster Daggit.

"Strange," I thought to myself as I took a pull from my bottle, "I didn't remember introducing myself to anyone."

Introduced or not, the blond on the bench seemed to have an added interest upon hearing the name Daggit. At least she seemed to be looking my way more than most ladies ever did. Every time I stood or turned she was making eye contact. I'd smile but never did I initiate any conversation. I could be no more to her than a drunken old bully who had just trounced and embarrassed several young men. Well enough I should leave her alone.

I heard someone call her, Amanda.

The rest of the trip went without incident, at least as best I could recall. My well guarded supply of refreshment had been most adequate.

The train finally stopped in East St. Louis, the end of the line. There was a depot of some size, lots of people that came and went with seemly no purpose. As I stood the platform taking notice, I saw my three young friends leave the train. Two were tending to the third who still seemed much distressed. Most of the debarking passengers were rushing down the dirty street towards the river. Two paddle wheelers were nosed up to the docks. White smoke drifted up from their stacks. These were apparently the ferries that would transport the throng across the Mississippi over to St. Louis on the other side of the river.

Just to the north of the landing was what had to be one of the marvels of these modern times. There was a huge bridge under construction. Over a hundred men were laboring at different tasks. I just stood agape; never could I have even dreamed such an expanse as the mile wide Mississippi could be traversed with a bridge. It was a railroad bridge to boot. Men, wagons, and trains could cross the structure at the same time.

"She's a beauty isn't she?" said an old timer standing next to me.

He was a veteran for sure; his left arm was missing as were most of his teeth.

"Yes she is," I agreed. "I've never seen anything like her."

"She is one of a kind," he replied. "Just look at those lines."

"She's so long, I can't believe it, and she goes all the way."

There was some hesitation in the conversation, but the old man caught up, "I can't speak to that but she just might."

"She sure looks like she could carry the load."

"Yes she surely does," he said.

I just stared; she was an awesome piece of work.

"I bet," I said, "that from the top of her you could look into the gates of heaven."

"I don't know about that Buddy Boy," he said. "Were I on top of her I'd look for heaven a little lower."

"What?" I asked as I turned to face the man.

He wasn't even looking at the bridge. His eyes were following a most curvaceous blond as she made her was towards the landing. I looked from her to him then back to her. Mistaken I might have been but it did seem to me that Amanda was still watching me watching her.

Chapter 45

▼

They called it Ead's Bridge. It had been designed to carry both east and west bound traffic at the same time. It could accommodate horse drawn wagons, pedestrians, and a train, all at the same time. It was an unbelievable sight.

The laborers were busy with tasks aplenty, but most seemed focused on the railroad tracks. What I was seeing first hand was one of the engineering marvels of all time. What I was thinking about was the well built blond who had taken the ferry. What I was feeling was still rage and purpose. I still needed to go west.

No one seemed to notice me as I walked across the bridge. Foot traffic was possible from bank to bank; I and several others were walking from Illinois to Missouri. I must have been fifty feet above the white capped waves of the mighty Mississippi. I was awed. One of the workers I encountered told me that the entire bridge would be finished in less than six more months. Then trains would be carrying people and goods across the river. East St Louis would then become a lesser city as there would be no need to stop there. The ferry boats would also disappear. I hoped not too soon, as it was a paddle wheeler I sought for the next leg of my journey. It was take a boat, ride a horse, or walk to Helena. Sitting a boat seat was indeed the best option.

I found the St. Louis landing amok with ruffians, brigands, and scallywags. Many were the fights I saw. I heard many languages being spoke, but all used the same five or six swear words alternately between just about every word in their conversation. Communication was no problem with the commonality of their adjectives.

As I searched for an upriver bound paddle wheeler I was forced to occasionally add one or two of these adjectives to my inquires in hopes that I might be understood.

It was late in the year for upstream travel, only a few of these river boats were still tied up at the landing. I was able to book passage on the Missouri Star.

"That will be ninety-six dollars," Captain Johnston said without batting an eye.

"Ninety-six dollars!" I was a bit taken back with the price. It was more money than I had paid for my farm back in Crow Creek.

"Let me explain," responded Johnston, "the trip is over two months if all goes well. It is over a thousand miles to Helena as the river winds. During that time you will be given two meals a day and a place to sleep."

"A place to sleep?" I questioned.

"Yes, you can roll out on the deck, drop and flop as you will, just have to keep out of the way of the crew. Or, for an extra ninety-six dollars you can have a berth to yourself. You can pay me now or walk to Helena, it's up to you."

I peeled out the cash.

Then Johnston, my cash in his hand, looked me dead in the eye.

"Are you him?" he asked.

"Him who?" I asked.

"Bud, are you Old Bud?"

"Some call me that." I answered.

"Are you the Old Bud?"

"I don't know if I am the same Old Bud that you think I am." I said, hoping to change the conversation.

"Daggit, are you Daggit?" he asked.

"Yes, my name is Daggit, how did you know?"

"I knew it. Everyone knows of you. They say you are the Jesse Buxton of the North. Word has it that you and Buxton are the two most dangerous men to come out of the Civil War. Most say that we should have just let you and Buxton shoot it out; the rest of us could have just stayed home."

Captain Johnston counted my cash as he talked.

"We leave at first light. You can sleep aboard tonight so as you won't miss the boat in the morning. I make no refunds. No shows make me the most money."

"I will be aboard tonight. I just have to go get a few necessities for the trip; more than two months you say."

Johnston went back to his captaining; I went to town to find a few provisions and a really big bottle.

After purchasing a heavy coat, one of those new sleeping bags and a pony of rye I found myself totally depleted of funds. I was flat broke. It was the deck of the Missouri Star for me this night, I needed a place to sleep and a meal if one could be had.

It was a considerable walk back to the landing. St. Louis was a big town indeed. I saw pretty women aplenty. They were just everywhere. My eye caught sight of just a gorgeous gal walking into a dress shop. The sign said, "Jeannie Lynn's." I wondered if that was Jeannie. As I watched the pretty woman disappear into the store, my mind's eye saw a different woman exit. She was built to go the distance. She was tall, blond, and stunning. And she wasn't really there. I could not believe myself. I was seeing that blond from the depot and she wasn't even there.

I said to myself, "Brewster, you old fool. Diane isn't even cold; you are off to avenge your wife's murder, and you are looking at one woman and seeing another."

Refocused, as best I could, I made my way through the throng of people, heading for the Missouri Star. As I did, yet another female caught my eye.

This one was a red headed girl, not yet twelve, and most nondescript with the exception of her hair and freckles. I just could not remember ever seeing a girl with red hair and freckles. She was walking with probably her father, a young tall lean fellow, one of those men whose strength generally went unnoticed.

As I watched them, still interested in the color of her hair, they were met on the walk by three men. As I approached I could tell they were obviously acquainted. All five moved off into the alley and out of sight.

As luck would have it, I dropped my new coat but saved the pony. I was forced to stop and reposition my load before proceeding to the boat. The pony of rye was three things; heavy, awkward, and essential. A coat was just a coat.

Not a dozen more steps did I take before the sound of gunfire exploded from behind the buildings. There had been a barrage of shots, the firefight concluded with the blast from a shotgun. That sound, the same as my Irving had once made, was a noise well engrained in my brain.

Seconds later, ahead of me, walking from another alleyway was the red headed girl and the tall man. They walked at a steady pace with no regard to the ado behind them in the alley. I could see that the girl was secreting something under her shirt.

They quickly disappeared into a crowd of people coming down the street to investigate the shooting. I looked up the alleyway from which the red head girl had exited and saw three men sprawled on the ground in pools of blood, the same three men who had walked into the alley with the father and his daughter. It was obvious to me all three men were dead. It was readily apparent who had caused their demise. What was even more obvious was the fact that this was none of my affair, I had business in Helena. As other onlookers rushed into the alley, I just walked on. I had no compulsion to tell anyone what I had seen.

I found the open deck accommodations aboard the Missouri Star less than pleasant. That next morning as I groaned and stretched, trying to find my aching back some relief from my nights repose on that hard planking, I noticed a pair of pretty blue eyes watching me with interest. Her hair wasn't blond, nor was she tall and stunning. This girl was short; maybe twelve, freckled, and had red hair.

Looking at me was the same little girl from the alley. She looked me over then moved aft as the Missouri Star's whistle blew two short toots and a long blast. Heavy was the clunk as the paddle wheels engaged into their reverse gear. Everyone went to the rail to watch and wave as we backed the river boat out into the channel.

Two shorts and a long blew the whistle as the arms reversed the wheels. The water churned and boiled as our downstream progress stopped and we started up the river. We moved very slowly at first. We just crept forward at but a snails pace. But within a few minutes time those paddles were slapping water. We were Helena bound; me, my rye, forty or fifty strangers, and an odd pair of killers; one just a little girl with red hair.

Chapter 46

▼

It didn't take but one trip around the rail of the boat to get the lay of it all. Johnston, the captain, posted up on top at the big wheel. The little girl's dad, Buck, they called him, ran the engine room. Some big galoot stoked the furnace for him. A few other hands had some deck functions; I wasn't really sure what they did. Some skinny guy cooked.

I made eye contact with most of the other passengers, none I knew by name. A few were vaguely familiar. I did not know if I was known to any of them, but there did seem to be some hushed talk as I walked away.

After my first miserable night's sleep on that hard wood planking I truly wished I had purchased a berth. Wish, however, was all I could do; I had not a dollar left to my name. What I did have, was a quarter barrel of whiskey, to which I had all intention of depleting in the course of this long voyage.

My wonderings about the boat did not go without reward. I found a space between two large wooden crates that offered sanctuary. The space was above the level of the main deck and well under the cover of the upper deck. It was well out of the way, and most probably would remain as positioned the entire trip. Both boxes were addressed to the Boland Mining Company, Helena, Montana. There was enough room in this small cubicle for me, my rolled out sleeping bag, and my keg. I had found the perfect place. I moved right in. A few more trips around the deck produced a few pieces of unattended tarp which gave some much needed padding to my new sleeping berth. I was happy. I was shielded from the sun, the rain, and Dakota arrows should any be shot our direction.

After two days travel I had the routine down pat. Buck and his laborer, Blue, fired up the boiler each morning just before dawn. As the sun's first light crested that eastern sky, the whistle would blare, the lines were hauled, and the wheels would turn. Then north by northwest we chugged, those huge paddle wheels steadily churning that brown Missouri water.

The Missouri was a treacherous river to say the least. Travel by night was foolish as the sawyers were numerous. Those dead trees, embedded deep in that Missouri bottom, had torn the hull out of many a paddle wheeler. The prudent Captain always tied up just before dusk.

These tie ups had other less important purposes. Passengers could debark, take a walk along the bank, or visit one of the settlements or forts that abutted the river, though few and far between they were. Some of the braver souls even chose to bath in the shallower waters. I had no intention of joining them, at least not for a month or so.

It was the fifth night on the river, after but a short stroll along the bank, I returned to my makeshift berth and found it occupied.

"Hey," I yelled, "this is my spot and that is my whiskey you are drinking."

"So move me old man," was his reply.

It was near dark. He was but a shadow figure sitting well back in my cubby. I could see he was a big man too, he well filled the space. The fact that he wasn't afraid of me was obvious. If he was armed I could not tell; most men were.

The fact remained that he was in my space, on my sleeping bag, and drinking my whiskey.

To get to him I would have to bend my head down, the opening was no more than four feet in height. Dropping my head left me vulnerable.

I remembered a pipe that ran along the bottom of the upper floor deck joists. It was just inside the opening. Not a word did I say to the man, I just stooped, grabbed the pipe with both hands and hurled my body, feet first at the man. My boots took him hard to the chest and bowled him back. If I took his wind I didn't know, I was on him; feet, fists and teeth. Cramped was the space, but he was on the bottom and had almost no mobility. I had the advantage. I smacked, kicked, and bit every target that presented.

No one intervened, no one even gathered outside the entrance to the cubby. Apparently all were still ashore.

After but a minute, the man ceased to move. I gave him a few more for good measure and then drug him out of my berth. His head hit the deck hard, but I didn't stop. I had the momentum and kept him moving, right to the rail. As I lifted him up to the edge of the rail I saw his face, he was a stranger to me. I did not know who he was, I didn't care. He was heavy, but I got him over the rail, gravity took him to the river below.

His subsequent splash took me square to the face.

I wiped my eyes as quickly as I could, looked back, and did not see the man. I initially hoped he was a better swimmer than he was a fighter, and then reconsidered. I didn't care if he could swim or not. The "old man" made his way back to his berth and his drink.

The next day I noticed Captain Johnston walking along the deck. He was looking here and there, talking to quite a few of the passengers. That little red headed girl was with him.

Johnston gave me a visual once over as he passed by but he said nothing and moved on.

Less than an hour later she was standing at the opening to my cubby.

"I saw what you did," she said, "but I didn't tell on you."

"You did, did you?" I replied.

"Yes, I did. The Captain was looking for that man; he paid his fare but had some change coming."

"He did, did he?"

I was wondering where she was going with the conversation. It was hard to believe that if she saw me toss the man overboard she had neglected to tell the Captain.

"He wasn't a very nice man. I was going to tell Buck what he did but you took care of it."

"What did he do?"

"He was nasty, that's all. I'm glad he's gone."

This little red headed girl had a gift to gab. Once you opened the door, she came on in talking and talking. Her name was Lema Moline. The child could ramble, but I sensed there was much more to her. I took notice of the butt of a pistol, close to hand, under the edge of her shirt. As I listened I knew there was more to her than met the eye. The man that went swimming the previous night was lucky I had taken care of him; I think the little girl would have shot him dead.

Lema must have taken a liking to me as thereafter not a day went by without her stopping up for a chat. She came most often early in the day; Buck, her brother, would not allow her around men who had been drinking. Late in the day I was one of those to be sure.

I don't believe that Lema was the least bit fearful of me, liquored or not. Buck wasn't afraid of me either, nor anyone else. He reminded me of myself when I was much younger. Buck Moline was a man to be reckoned with.

Sioux City, Iowa, wasn't much of a stop, but we took on three Helena bound passengers, all women from the same family.

One was incredibly old, one was someone's mother, and one turned every head on the boat. She was just a fine piece of work, from the top of her Lema red head to the tip of her toes; and back up again.

I had my eye on her as did the other fifty plus men on our steamer. Watch we did, but it was that Buck Moline who caught her eye.

Much can be seen by a man well hidden deep back in his cubby.

Chapter 47

▼

Fort Randall was another tie up. As we were now well into Sioux country prudence was the rule. Any night we could lay over at a fort was a plus. The United States Army in its wisdom had seen fit to build a fort about every hundred miles along the Missouri. I was noticing that each fort we passed as further into the interior of the prairie we traveled was progressively less manned. It was an oddity for sure; the closer to St. Louis, the fewer the Indians, the fewer the problems. The farther up river, the greater the danger, the fewer were the soldiers. I saw a real paradox here, but I kept it to myself.

As was our nightly habit, once we were nosed into the bank and tied off; the front gang plank was lowered. Most of the passengers were ashore within minutes, glad of it to be sure. Although travel aboard the Star beat walking, almost everyone was in need of some sort of exercise or diversion.

Once ashore, especially at a fort of some size, a change of diet was sometimes possible. As I had no money, my fare was always whatever was being ladled on board the Star.

This date I had my swill before I took my evening walk ashore. I found early on that a few shots of whiskey did much to enhance its digestion, but little could it do for the taste. Swill was swill, washed down or not.

The fort had but a few planks nailed together to form a very crude dock. I carefully made my way across it then started up the rise towards what appeared to be a wooden stockade.

"Hi Bud," it was Lema.

She and Buck were walking down the path from the fort towards me. Lema had that perpetual smile of hers. Buck seemed more somber than usual.

"Evening," I said in passing. "I think there might be some frost in the air."

"It is a really neat fort up there Bud," she said, "You have to see it. They even have a cannon."

Buck just walked, he said nothing. For sure I thought, the man was deep in some thought.

"I'll have a look," I said, never missing a stride.

My earlier premise was validated. Fort Randall was just the poorest excuse for a military installation that I had ever seen. It wasn't much more than a small stockade surrounded by a few shacks and shanties. The path to the gate was a well worn dusty lane through a sea of waist high weeds and piles of debris.

There was just one soldier at the gate. He was a young little litter throw back for lack of a better description. His filthy uniform was two sizes too big. He had a rusty old rifle that he probably couldn't carry. It leaned against the stockade as did the soldier.

"Can I help you, mister?" asked the guard.

"Just walking and this seemed the way to go."

"Fort Randall aint much but its all we got," said the kid.

"I know the feeling," I replied as I did a quick peek inside the walls.

I could see it all at a glance. He was so very right, it wasn't much at all.

"Nice little fort," I lied.

"She has with stood two Sioux attacks so far," he boasted.

That brought a smile to my face; two Sioux attacks from two Sioux grandmothers was what I was thinking. Three Lakota grandmothers could have breached the walls and scalped the entire garrison. I just nodded to the kid and started to leave.

As I turned to walk away my eye caught the sight of a man back in the weeds. He was just lying there moaning.

My eyes went from the downed man back to the guard.

"He quickly said, "Oh that's old Clayton. Pay him no never mind. He is dying from the syphilis and there is naught to be done for him. He just drinks himself into a stupor then lays down to die; only he never does. Tomorrow he will beg some more whiskey and do it again."

The name, Clayton, had my attention.

I walked over to the man and looked him over. To my amazement it was the devil himself, Clayton Matthews. He wasn't near as heavy as I remembered, his muscle was gone; but it was him. He still had the scar from where the table had busted his head, that, and several others that I had given him.

Lying on the ground was the man who had killed my wife and son.

He was suffering, no doubt about it. The man was delirious with pain.

"Perhaps," I thought to myself, "just perhaps this horrible death is befitting his crime. Maybe I should just let the dirty son of a bitch wreath in his agony until the gate to hell fell open beneath him."

"Hey kid," I said to the guard. "That river boat down there has on it some kegs of candy that are Helena bound. The Captain is selling some of it cheap."

"What kind?" he asked.

"Just about every kind there is. That Captain is always on the prod for profit. I hope he hasn't closed up the lid yet. He's Appolstolic you know, he won't sell anything after dark or on Sunday."

The kid was actually on his tip toes as he looked over the weeds and debris to the river boat beyond. There was actually some drool coming from his lower lip.

"You had better hurry," I said, "it's almost dark."

"You won't tell?"

"Tell who what?"

"I'll be right back," he replied, his feet were already headed down the path.

The soldier boy was kicking dust as he and his rifle disappeared from view.

Clayton was coughing and moaning again. I knelt down and looked him dead in the face. His eyes were closed. I grabbed him by his greasy long blond hair and jerked him up. His eyes came open and he looked at me. We were eyeball to eyeball. Somewhere deep within that pain wracked brain of his there came some essence of recognition.

His eyes widened. I had no idea if he feared death, I just didn't care. I had weighed his plight, duly noting the agony and suffering yet to be endured. Some would have let him continue in his perpetual pain, but I wasn't one of them.

That pig sticker on my belt came easy to my hand. Razor sharp it was.

Clayton's wide eyes got just a little bigger as I plunged the blade deep into his chest. I gave it a twist, pulled it out and then shoved the soon to be lifeless body flat on its back. I watched as the man tried to hold back the blood with his hands. He did a very poor job of it.

James Boland was somewhere farther up the river. I had no intention of being so merciful with him.

Chapter 48

▼

As we pulled the steamer into Fort Rice, the Star crashed into a sawyer, running the log right through the hull. Being laid back in my cubby like I was I didn't see it coming and was caught totally unawares. The force of the impact knocked me forward causing me to hit my head on the same pipe I had used to swing in on the earlier intruder.

I hit it square and hard. My head literally exploded with white lights and pain. I was pretty much a blood soaked mess when my feet hit the deck. Dazed as I was, there was little I could do except try to mentally ready myself for a long swim.

For several seconds, chaos ruled the day. People were yelling and screaming. Many were hurt, many had been tossed overboard.

It was Captain Johnston who kept his head. He was yelling orders to reverse the wheels. Steam we still had and I could hear grinding and clanking as the wheels changed direction. Johnston was able to pull the Star free of the sawyer. As water rushed in the lower deck he had the Star's wheels going forward again. He was making a run for the bank as water filled the boat. We were hard aground less than a few yards from the shore when we lost our steam.

The wreck had been costly. More than a dozen, me included; sustained substantial injury. Three had died. As I looked over their bodies laid out on the bank, I was glad that the beautiful girl, the red headed Mary, wasn't one of them. Most unfortunate for Mary, her mother was.

Johnston estimated that it would take at least a month for the damage to the hull to be repaired. Another upstream steamer came by the next day. Most of our passengers went north with that vessel. I chose to stay with the Star. I still had purpose in Helena, but I had grown rather fond of my accommodation. Despite the problem pipe, my spot nestled between the crates was most comfortable. I would not have such a berth on the other boat, especially with the extra passengers it now carried. Besides, with fewer passengers I'd be less likely to be hit up for a spot of my dwindling elixir.

Worried I was, that pony was now more than half empty. Mentally I computed the distance and time to Helena. I compared that with my intake and volume still remaining in the keg. It was going to be close. Sharing my liquor was not going to be an option.

Buck, a Fort Rice carpenter, and some buffalo soldiers began work on the hole in the hull. It was a monumental project. I felt obliged to stay out of their way. Despite my best efforts I did have to help bale the boat, a labor of many days.

Our layover did much to diminish the closely calculated rationing of my libations. Each day my keg level was lower.

Two shorts and a long blew the whistle. Finally north bound we were, and now thirty one days behind schedule. Talk was, we would be hard pressed to beat the ice up.

Johnston, much to my joy, had paid the soldiers who helped repair the hull with several barrels of Helena destined whiskey. My joy wasn't so much seeing the barrels being hoisted to the bank, but rather in the knowledge that there were two others still aboard. I had not known of their previous existence as they had been stowed deep within piles of other goods. Secreted though they were, their presence just four feet below my very berth did much to free up my own rationing. I was ever so content knowing that when my keg ran out there was another source nearby. Larceny is such a petty crime, especially for an out and out murderer such as myself.

.   Captain Johnston had the Star pointed north. Buck Moline had a new helper in the boiler room. His last laborer had drowned in the Fort Rice wreck. This new stoker was a big black man, one of the buffalo soldiers who held helped patch the hull. The man still wore his army clothing though he had been furloughed or retired. I suspected they were all he had. I did not have much more.

Lack of personal possession did not prevent me from nestling back into my cubby hole. I relaxed and dozed as I watched the western bank of the Missouri River slip by. Many were my thoughts as I sipped away the days.

I thought much about my wife and son. Their horrific deaths caused me to internally burn as hot as Moline's boiler just a few paces away. Yet try as I might, I could no longer picture their faces. I knew their features, I remembered what they should look like, but I just could not mentally see their faces.

I could still see Diane; I even remembered the smell of her hair.

Here I was on a trip of many months; my intention to kill a man, and I could not even remember the face of the woman I intended to avenge.

Time was indeed an evil task master.

Again and again I closed my eyes and tried to see Helga on the back of my eye lids. She just wasn't there. What were on them, however, were little dots that seemed to float across my closed eye lids with neither rhyme nor reason.

I was giving these little moving dots consideration when the distant crack of a rifle caused me to jump. Then there was a heavy thud on the deck above me. Men were running and yelling. I had my pistol in hand as I peered from the safety of my cubby.

"Indians, Indians!" was the cry.

"To arms, watch the port side," it was Buck taking charge as he went up the stairs towards the pilot house.

Watch I did, but not a soul did I see, the dense river willows and cottonwoods could have concealed an entire army, at least this week. The leaves were just every color of reds and browns. Short lived they were; winter was coming.

Finding no target and hearing no other shooting I assumed the danger had passed. I went above and joined others already gathered on the top deck. Captain Johnston was down, blood flowed from his side. I had seen hits like that before and knew his life was now shorter than the leaves on those trees, a lot shorter.

For the next five minutes of his now waning life, Captain Johnston swore and cursed the mothers, daughters, sons, and fathers of every Sioux that ever walked or crawled. Not one demeaning adjective or swear word did he leave out of his final hate filled coughing, blood spewing barrage of Sioux focused profanity. He even requested a pistol in hand so he could kill all the savages that might have sneaked their way into heaven.

I gave him mine.

With my pistol in hand, blood coming from his side, nose and mouth, Johnston cut loose with his final coughing hacking epitaph. He came up with expletives and swear words that I had never even heard.

When it was over Captain Johnston's eyes just stared at the sun and the cursing stopped. His breathing did too. As I was yet bent over him, I brushed his eye lids shut and took back my pistol. I wondered if he was now seeing those strange little dots on the back of his eye lids as I often did. I saw that Johnston had a revolver of his own under his coat. I borrowed it, sticking it in my own belt. No one said a word.

L. L. Layman

Johnston and I had more in common than he ever knew. As I straightened my bent frame and stood, that nagging butt wound from a kid shot arrow many years prior gave me that all too familiar jolt. I also had no use for the Sioux. As I thought of Johnston's vulgar adjectives I was mentally able to add to them.

Chapter 49

▼

Captain Johnston was buried on a knoll on the east bank. As I was well practiced with a spade I dug the hole. I dug it deeper than most; it was square, plumb, and clean. I wondered why I had volunteered for the task, but I knew. The grave somehow justified to myself the theft of the dead man's liquor that I was sure would take place before we got to Helena.

There were but a few of us at the burial. Most were guarding the boat. We respectfully lowered him into his final resting place. If he could have raised his head he would have seen the muddy Missouri he loved so well rolling by. Buck said some nice things that I was sure the man could not hear. Lema tossed in some wild flowers that still grew on the side of the hill.

Then we all went to kicking dirt in the hole. Although that shot had come from the west side of the river, who was to say the shooter was not a good swimmer. Or worse, perhaps he had friends and they were all good swimmers.

When we got back to the boat Buck took the wheel. He just made himself captain, simple as that. The big black took charge of the boiler. Some thin little guy became the tender. I resumed my former position deep back in my cubby. I was good with all four.

Not an hour later we met and tied up with a south bound riverboat. The boat looked like a pin cushion; arrows were stuck into the wood all along her starboard side. Their captain gave us warning of hostiles ahead. That very morning not but a few miles up river they had been attacked by what looked like the entire Lakota nation. According to their captain, there was a place upstream where the current forced riverboats right up against the west bank. He called it the Devil's Oxbow. The bank above the bend in the river was about ten feet high, flat, and ran parallel to the water. The savages waited there for their prey. There was no way to avoid a fight.

I listened as we were told we were too few in number to defend the boat at the oxbow. Buck and the other captain walked off talking. After an exchange which none were privy to, we parted company. The other boat was St. Louis bound; we remained tied up to a tree on the east bank.

I was looking over at the west bank when Buck came up to me.

"Bud," he said, "We have a fight ahead. I'm not turning this boat around. I know you paid your fare, but if you want to live to reach Helena you will need to pitch in. I need your help."

"I'm in." I responded, little choice did I have.

"Good, I need a fighting man at my side, someone who can carry the day."

"Me?"

"You are Brewster Daggit aren't you?"

"Yes."

"You'll do," said Moline, "Rumor has it even Jesse Buxton was but a piker compared to you."

"I'll fight if it's needed," I answered.

I did not particularly like the comparison, but it wasn't the first time that I had heard it.

"Good," he said. "You are my Segundo. If I fall, you are in charge. But, most important, if something happens to me; please do your best to see that nothing happens to Lema."

"I will, but I think that little girl could fare just fine on her own."

"She probably can," Moline was smiling now as he looked aft where the girl was standing. "Yes sir Bud, she probably can."

Buck started to walk away, then abruptly stopped and looked at some crates on the lower deck. I prayed he hadn't espied the two barrels of whiskey.

"Assemble the crew Bud, I have an idea."

He had an idea alright. We began opening crates of US Army uniforms destined for Helena. We did as directed and made ourselves an army of stuffed uniforms. Our grass and leaf filled soldiers were then tied to the port side rails. Another crate was filled with single shot carbines. Lucky us, there was also another crate filled with ammunition for the rifles. That was a surprise to me. Having rifles with the proper ammunition on the same boat headed to the same destination was not something the army I knew could have ever managed.

The rifles were loaded and one was placed next to each dummy.

Buck next began giving orders, "Now when I give the command go down the line and fire every other carbine. Don't aim, just fire as fast as you can.

When you get to the end of the line, go back the other direction and fire the rest of them."

He was pointing to different crew members giving each their assignment.

"You Bud, take the main deck, port side from the galley door to the bow."

He gave each man a position and specific assignment. As he did, I could only mentally smile. Each and every order was given just as I would have.

"Okay men, if everyone understands what needs done, let's head up river. It is about two hours to the Devil's Oxbow."

There was no response from the men, not a sound. There was no enthusiasm; most were no doubt scared stiff. There was but six or seven of us to defend against what might be hundreds of Lakota.

Buck turned to the big black, "Lester, let her rip. Keep her head hot and whistle blowing."

I grabbed one of the extra carbines and a pocket full of rounds for it. As directed I stood the port side rail; me, a carbine, two revolvers, pig sticker, and just a small mug of libation for courage.

Chapter 50

▼

I had hoped there would be time for reflection, but not a full mug of courage had I consumed before the whistle started blaring; two shorts and a long, two shorts and a long. Every Indian west of Brown's Valley knew we were coming.

Ahead I saw a limestone bank on the western side. The river narrowed and cut tight to it, then bended hard to the north and east again.

Atop that bank stood what appeared to be the entire Sioux nation. Those Civil War years of marching towards death's door had made me a fair judge of odds. They were not in our favor. Those savages on the bank out numbered us at least ten to one, and those were the ones I could see. As with all battles, the enemy doesn't show you everything up front. Sioux were no different. Savages they might be, but when it came to removing your hair, they were very adept.

As we drew closer I could see them jumping up and down. They were waving all manner of weaponry; taunting us with their jesters.

These were full grown warriors, twice the size of those I had encountered a lifetime before on the Minnesota prairie. There seemed no uniformity to their person, dress, or choice of weapon. Some were tall, some heavy, some dressed, some naked.

A few with rifles were now beginning to crack off shots at us. I took refuge behind the heavy front draw bridge and listened to the smack of their rounds as they hit the heavy planking.

We were now a hundred yards downstream and closing. I could not yet hear the screams and war cries of the Lakota over the roar of our own whistle and engine.

I found a large knot hole in the bridge planking and stuck the end of my carbine through it. I had found a very nice rifle rest.

I picked out a big naked man wearing a blue brimmed hat. He had a rifle in hand and was trying to reload. I took careful aim, elevated just a tad, and squeezed off a round.

The carbine bucked and the intended just left his feet and disappeared below the edge of the escarpment. I had hit him square. I reloaded, picked out another and squeezed the trigger again. This time a feather bonneted fat man crumpled to his knees holding his chest.

Neither hit made a dent in their number nor had it diminished their ardor.

I reloaded and shot again, this time we were much closer, 30 yards was all that separated us from the horde. As we closed the gap my targets became smaller. The warriors seemed to shrink, all I had were head shots. I picked one, aimed, and cut loose. I saw the man's head literally explode. Then I saw no more as the boat was now next to the escarpment. All were above me well shielded by the bank. They would be coming aboard next; we were not ten feet from the top of the bank.

I left the carbine stuck in the knot hole and grabbed my revolvers. If we were to be boarded it would be now. I was ready.

"Fire!" someone yelled above.

I could hear the crack of carbines from our dummy army. So fast were the reports there seemed to be one continuous roar.

Low like I was on the main deck, the attack would seemingly come from the sky. I had a pistol in each hand as they came flying. Warriors had come at a run, leaping from the top of the escarpment to the decks of the Star eight foot below.

I caught the first air borne savage in mid flight with my right hand pistol. He never made the boat as the impact of the bullet did much to slow his momentum. I shot another as he caught the top of the draw bridge. He fell back into the river. A wild man clad in but a breech cloth hit the deck like a big bird. He rolled and came up, a hatchet in hand. I shot him dead in the chest with my left hand pistol and head bashed yet another with the barrel of my right as his plunging blade found naught but air. He went to his knees at my feet. I shot him in the back of the head.

Two more came from the sky as the boat made its sweep. One I shot, the second landed and drove me back with his shoulder hard into my belly. His arms were around my butt.

I fell backwards onto the deck with the Sioux on top of me. He wasn't a big man, but there was some strength to him. We were at it knuckle and skull, tooth and nail. I got him rolled, and then over and over I bashed him with my right hand pistol. My left hand gun was gone. I tried to shoot the man but I couldn't get the barrel pointed at him. I somehow worked the pistol up between us, pressed it to his head and fired. The round took him right through one eye and out the other, drenching me in blood.

So heavy was my breathing now I almost couldn't get the bloody chunk of meat off me.

As I worked free another warrior came from the port rail. He had a club of sorts in hand and caught me good before I could rise from the floor. He had glanced the club off my head and near busted the bones in my shoulder with the impact. I did not wait for the warrior to hit me again. I drove my body from the deck into his, forcing the man to the rail. Toe to toe we were, my bleeding skull was painting both of us red. He had dropped his club, I had dropped my revolver. A knife came to his hand but I was able to hold it back with my left hand as my own sticker found a gap between his ribs.

I stuck him again and again as I looked into his strangely familiar face. He had but one eye and a horribly scarred face. I was looking at him and that one eye was looking at me.

He should have been dead two times over, but some how his strength was super human. This standing dead man, grabbed me, gave a heave, and over the rail we went into that cold brown Missouri River.

Chapter 51

▼

Strange is the human mind, it works so fast it is hard to comprehend, impossible to control.

At this very moment in time I was hurt, overboard, submerged in the muddy Missouri, drowning with a strangely familiar soon to be dead one eyed Dakota still clinging tight to my body. His last purposeful task was not to leave this world alone.

To make matters worse, if they could be, the Star was cutting hard to the starboard as it made the river bend. No doubt that wheel would within the next second be smashing me and one eye to pieces.

If perhaps I somehow surfaced, my head would be the target of hundreds of arrows and bullets.

Things were just not looking too good for Old Bud.

Despite it all, my brain wanted to comment on the taste and smell of the river water. I'm dying and yet making comment to myself about the quality of the water.

"Bam"

A force so loud I could hear even in the eerie silence of the river, jerked the clinging savage away from me. Up he went.

"Bam," I heard the sound again.

My hip felt shattered. The wheel had caught me at a glance. Then it was gone.

I didn't know how bad I was hurt, I didn't care. If I did not breathe soon I was going to die. My lungs were bursting. If I surfaced I would certainly be shot.

Yet, despite it all, again my brain was still making comments to itself as to just how soft the water was.

"Soft," it kept saying, "isn't this just the softest water."

I could feel the force from the paddles as the water pushed by me. Downstream I went, still submerged, my lungs beyond bursting. I wanted to come up, I was trying but my right leg was not cooperating; numbed I was sure from the smack to the hip. I wasn't even sure it was still attached. My left arm worked but little good it was doing without cooperation from the right which still held fast my knife.

I felt like a fish with fins on one side.

When I felt my lungs could tolerate no more I gasped for air and found it as my face broke the surface.

The Star was forty yards upstream, its nose to the east, that wheel was churning water. She was more than twenty yards from the west bank, safe now from boarding. I could see a fight on the top deck. Buck was bashing someone with that short shotgun he so much endorsed. That sister of his was at the wheel. I could see them plain as day, but they could not see me.

Nor could the Lakota see me; the only good thing to happen to me thus far was surfacing just under the edge of the limestone escarpment. Half the Sioux nation was ten feet above me shooting arrows and guns at the Missouri Star. I was just below them, just out of sight, at least for a man not looking or otherwise engaged.

Downstream from me, bobbing like a cork was a man's head. It had the same one eyed face of the man who would not die; the man who had intended to drag me to hell with him.

As I looked for a place to hide the thought came to me, maybe, just maybe he was the same kid I had shot in the face many years ago.

Where the river's current met the limestone I found a cut into the bank where I could hide. It wasn't much; perhaps less than a foot had been eroded away. Head room wasn't but a few inches.

I squirreled right in, wedging myself up against the limestone wall. Initially I could find nothing to hang on to, but in my frantic search for a hand or foot hold I found two underwater burrow type holes that worked their way back into the limestone. My right arm went deep into the highest hole; my left foot caught the lower. The force of the current forced my face and body tight to the wall.

Precarious was my perch, but I was hopefully invisible from above. The river's swift current forced water up and over the back of my head. I had a small place to breath under my little waterfall. Here I waited for what I had not a clue. Life had thrown its worst at me. For lack of promise, I wondered what other calamity could possibly befall me.

Here I was, one hundred miles north of anywhere, hiding along the base of an escarpment, almost completely submerged in cold deep water, marooned, surrounded by hundreds of savage Lakota Sioux, my hip and leg still near numb, and possibly armed with naught but my knife.

Try as I might, I could not remember if I had somehow secured it in its sheath. I last remembered it in my hand. It wasn't there now.

Even if I by some miracle was able to out last the Sioux and escape down river to a fort, word of a murder at Fort Randall had probably already spread to the other units. If that candy loving soldier kid had put two and two together I was surely named for murder which I was certainly guilty of. Justified or not there was no way to prove my case. I would be hanged for no more than amusement. These soldiers had little else to do with their time.

As I hugged tight that limestone wall I had time aplenty to contemplate the dismal prospects for Old Bud. The best I could do was slim and none.

Chapter 52

▼

The Missouri's cold current kept me well pressed hard to the limestone wall. Time became but a blur as my body slowly lost its heat. To move was to possibly die, but stay remain was to die for sure.

Positioned as I was I could see nothing. The cascade of water, as it came up the back of my head and over my face, blinded me from the dangers that might at any second be upon me. Savages could be preparing to slash my throat. I was blind; totally defenseless.

The little pocket of air between my chin and brow had become my world. I was strangely lonely, incredibly cold, and scared to death. Many times I had faced the enemy in battle, I was terrified each and every time we started up that hill; but there were comrades to the left and right of me. I was not alone and I could see my adversary. This was different. I was hiding for my life and had no idea if I was hid.

Twice I was startled as some creature from the deep waters tried to work its way into my right hand hole. A big catfish wanted in. He wanted to go home, and so did I.

Unlike the catfish, I had no home, no where to go; yet to stay any longer I would be too cold to go anywhere. I was so numb from the cold pounding current that I doubted I could even swim. I had reached the point of no return. I had to take my chances. If I did not drown I'd probably get scalped; maybe both. I had to move.

Slowly, very slowly, I raised my head and took notice of my bleak surroundings. Not a soul did I see. My immediate vista was only that of the brown muddy Missouri. I was eyeball to wave; my vantage was limited at best. If there were savages still on the limestone escarpment above me, I could not tell. I listened but I only heard the slap of the waves on the limestone.

I eased myself along the face of the escarpment, just barely would my bone cold torso respond to my brain's demand. I half swam, drifted, and clawed myself along the rock face. I moved close to a hundred yards; cold, exposed, and terrified of discovery, before I came to a limb and debris filled eddy.

As I worked my way through the maze of sticks and snags I saw it again, that same long haired one eyed head. It startled me at first but those years of war and its mutilations had numbed me to such horrid sights. As I gave the head a once over, I realized that the discovery of the headless body, for sure somewhere down river, would bring searchers this way. Even though old one eye was going to the happy hunting ground headless, his friends would want him there with all his parts.

I needed to move. I needed to hide. Most of all, I needed to be on the east side of the Missouri and headed away from the Lakota.

At this moment in time I was much too cold, numb, and tired to attempt the swim. With no other option than to hide, I worked my way up and out of the eddy, onto the bank, where I tried to walk. I had never been so cold and numb. My legs would barely move, yet they did.

Sometime, eons before, erosion had carved a nook in the limestone wall. I worked my way back into it; it was a place to hide that I sought, but none did I find. The nook widened out and became a ravine which worked its way back up onto the Dakota prairie.

There was a well worn path to follow, probably made by buffalo coming to the water to drink, but I chose to keep well off the trail. I chose to walk through the willow and buck brush. Careful I was not to make a sound or leave a trail.

The no trail thought worried me plenty. What was no trail to me and to a heathen Sioux were two totally different concepts. I had heard they could follow a bug across a smooth rock and be waiting for it on the other side; that was if they were so inclined. Indians were not the most energetic of people. They did what they had to when they wanted to.

Finding their headless buddy might be all the motivation they needed to start looking for that bug.

As I slowly made my way through the brake, the numbness gradually left my body. I began to dry out. The realization of my plight began to manifest. I was alone, armed with but my knife which had somehow found its way into its sheath, and a hundred miles from anywhere. I was without provisions. I was hungry; no I was starved. I was thirsty too; I needed a drink, and it wasn't water I was craving.

The ravine was steadily upward. I followed it a quarter of a mile before I dared my first peek above the rim.

A huge dead cottonwood had fallen from the ravine up and over the rim. Well hidden between the dead limbs I chanced a look out onto the prairie. Off in the distance, miles to the north, I could see a tendril of smoke, most probably from the stacks of the Star. To my right, much closer, I could see the back side of the escarpment from which we were attacked.

Several Sioux were loading bodies onto a travois. I remembered shooting at least two of them. The rest of my hits were adrift somewhere in route to St. Louis.

I slipped back deep into the shadows of the tree. I needed time to think, time to plan, and mostly I needed to not be seen. Long was my wait, these savaged seemed to take forever. They had their bodies loaded yet they did not move them. Other savages on horseback came and went. It was hard to count their numbers from my distant vantage. They were but specks on the prairie.

As I watched I made my plan. It wasn't much, but it was all I could come up with. I would wait them out. After they left, maybe after dark, I would sneak down to the Missouri, swim to the other side, then run like hell for Minnesota.

The plan seemed simple enough; yet it reminded me of another run a lifetime ago. I had little savages to deal with then; these were much bigger. These were full grown fighting warriors; men who were bear strong and hornet mad.

My first run had been but a few miles and I had old Julius to help. This run would be hundreds of miles with but a pair of worn boots for transportation.

My prospects were not improving.

It was the snap of a twig in the ravine just behind me which caused my breath to stop.

"Brewster," I said to myself, "you have just gone from bad to worse."

Chapter 53

▼

He was on the hunt, a lone Lakota. His head was down as he searched for signs of my passing in the leaf litter of the ravine. He was pointing at different spots as he moved along the exact same path I had taken.

I held fast my blade and waited.

The man carried a rusty long gun, rifle or shotgun I could not tell, but he looked as if he were no stranger to its usage.

From my vantage up on the high ground, I could clearly see him; as his eyes were to the ground, he had not yet seen me. It was, however, just a matter of time before he located me. This old codger was not missing a step.

"Old," my brain was now beginning to function.

"One," I said to myself, "is a manageable number."

I then put both observations together, "One old man."

Below me, on the hunt, was an ancient warrior, thin of arm, flail of chest. His legs were but twigs beneath his leather leggings. His skin was almost black of color; his hair a contrasting white.

As he drew closer I could see I had a clear advantage. I had been in many a battle, never had I been bettered by an old man. My advantage would be short lived had he friends or allies close to hand. Try as I might I could see no others.

Behind the old warrior, somewhere back down the ravine was a horse. No Dakota ever walked.

The old man had just what I needed, both a weapon and a horse. Somewhere on his back trail was a ride home.

I waited in ambush as the codger worked out my exact trail. Closer and closer he came; his eyes steady to my passing, his finger constantly pointing out to himself this and that. He was now up and over the rim of the ravine not ten paces from me. He was closing the gap; eight paces, six, two. I held fast my hiding; my very breath seemed to have stopped.

We were not an arms length apart when I came up with my knife. I held it low, blade up, and was driving it home. Yet, no flesh did I find, only the steel of that old long gun as the geezer blocked my thrust with amazing speed. His barrel came around and caught the side of my head. His bashing caused me to fall forward to the ground.

I hit, rolled and came up, my knife still at the ready. I found no target, none but the barrel of that gun as the old man poked and jabbed with that old chunk of steel. He, however, was making contact. Twice he caught me across the arm then once again on the head. He was quick, surprisingly quick. He was hurting me. We circled each other, each trying for the advantage or ideal moment to strike.

With no reasonable impetus or warning he suddenly lunged forward, a butt stroke to the head his intended target. The old man was but a fierce beast moving in for the kill.

"Yieh, Yieh!" he screamed.

The lust and blood of battle had filled his senses. That chunk of long steel in his hands was again moving air out of its way.

I ducked, he missed; and in doing so presented me with a boney rib cage.

I took it, deep I drove that blade into his chest. His lungs seemed to explode; I could see, hear, feel, smell, and even taste the hot blast of bloody froth that spewed from this mouth and covered my own bloody face. He fell to his face, and then tried to rise. He was mortally wounded. He would soon be dead but he had his arms under his torso and was coming up again. The man was still game. In his right hand he still clutched the long gun. I could see that glare in his eyes as I heard the weapon being cocked. I kicked the man hard to the head. Down he went again, the weapon falling from his hand.

The old man tried to raise again, the blood was deeply pooled under and around him. He made it to his knees, glared at me, made a few more guttural sounds then fell to his face. He moved for but a few more seconds, just some twitching of his arms and legs, then no more.

"Damn!" was all I could say as I gasped, my breath still much labored.

I was thinking of the fight; he was as tough a man as I had ever met and at least twice my age.

I picked up the rusty weapon lying next to the body. I had in my hand what appeared to be my very own old ancient shotgun. I had old Irving back, and it was still loaded.

There seemed to be no logic as to why the old man hadn't pulled the trigger. As I looked the weapon over I could see no reason why it would not fire. Perhaps my attack had been too quick for him to get a shot off, perhaps I had kept such close contact during the fight he had no time to aim and fire, or maybe he was one of those Lakota that still counted coup. Who was to say?

If the weapon worked I had but one shot. The old man carried no pouch or additional ammunition that I could see. The only way to know if the gun worked was to test it. To test it would bring the rest of the Sioux on the run. I had not really improved my situation.

I slowly worked my way back towards the river. Somewhere on our back trail there was, hopefully, a horse. As I retraced my ascent, I could see signs of my previous passing; occasionally I saw signs of his. What I was leaving on this trip was a blood droplet trail even a baby Sioux could follow. The old man had bashed me good. I had several holes that continued to bleed.

I would have to do a better job of covering my trail if I were to make it home.

Home, there it was again. I had no home, no wife, no son, no farm; no Diane. I could not even think of a single relative. I had no where to go, no one to go to. The only face that came to my minds eye was that pretty girl from Hoosick, the girl who had written me the letters during the war. Lydia, Lydia was her name.

Strange, I thought to myself, not five minutes had passed since I had ripped the chest out of an old man and I was already thinking about women. A home was what I wanted, a home with my own woman, that, and just maybe a drink of whiskey.

"Whiskey?"

Here I was, a hundred miles from anywhere, Lakota soon hot on my trail, without provision one, not even a glimmer of hope, and I wanted a drink of whiskey.

It was the smell of the river that quenched my thirst and refocused my purpose. The Missouri was no more than a rock's throw away. Two more steps I took, specific sounds drowned now by the sound of the swirl of the eddy. Wary I was. I stopped next to a big cottonwood. In its shadow I took notice of all.

There was movement.

Beyond the brakes was something big, brown and grazing. There was a horse. No, upon closer inspection there were two horses.

I was mentally thanking the gods for the horses and not deducting the obvious.

An arrow suddenly imbedded itself in the truck of the tree just inches from my head.

"Yieh!" screamed a huge Sioux warrior as he came crashing through the brush right at me.

He was notching another arrow as he ran. He drew back the arrow never missing a step. He held his bow low and across his body. His release was slow, saplings and willows blocked his aim.

I had no time to aim, I just cocked Irving, pointed from the hip, and fired. The old shotgun roared. The blast took the man square in the face, the force of which flipped him backwards to the ground. His arrow left the bow and headed for the sun. The big Lakota hit the ground dead.

I looked around, I saw no other savages.

But they were coming, no doubt about it. That shotgun blast could have been heard for miles. They would find two bodies, a floating one eyed head, and the bloody tracks of but one man, me.

Chapter 54

▼

Stupid me, two horses had meant two men. A moron could have made the deduction. I nearly died because I was just plain stupid.

The animals were picketed on a patch of river grass.

One animal was a sway back paint mare; old and gaunt. In the sway of his back was a hide and bone saddle. Two skin bags connected by a cord were draped over the saddle.

The other was a big brown stallion, a formable animal with muscle and girth. He had a big CSA branded on his rump. On his back was a genuine Confederate saddle complete with bags and a rifle scabbard.

I wondered how a Dixie horse made it to the Dakota prairie. His former owner was dead for sure, a fate which did not appeal to me. I needed distance, a lot of it and quick.

Both horses shied as I approached, neither had a liking for the smell of me. I couldn't much blame them.

I untied the paint and gave it a butt slap which sent it up the ravine. I hoped its trail might be a diversion.

The now empty shotgun fit in the scabbard. With it secured and my butt in the Rebel saddle I pointed that Dixie stud right at the eddy and the dirty Missouri. As I kicked him hard in the flanks I hoped he was a good swimmer.

Cold and all too familiar was the water. Initially I thought my plan was naught but folly as the horse submerged below the surface taking me with him. Our heads both returned to the world of air, coughing and snorting. He was swimming and we were Minnesota bound.

L. L. Layman

It was fifty yards to the other shore. The brown four legged Reb found his footing at less than half the distance. We hit the shore line on the fly with that sway backed paint right behind us. Why she followed was a mystery I didn't dwell up. We needed distance.

Two rifle cracks behind us added a more than strong measure of urgency. I put the boots to that horse. The rounds had missed, but there would be more; it was a long, long ways to Minnesota.

For several miles I kept the Reb at a gallop. He was a powerful animal. He had plenty of bottom and decent speed. What surprised me most was the old sway back paint which kept the pace. She stayed on our right flank and matched the Reb stride for stride. When I pulled the Reb up to a walk, he was lathered and blowing hard. The paint just trotted along as if nothing had happened.

My back trail was a rolling prairie. I could see for miles. There was little but grass and a few shrubs to obstruct my view.

Clearly visible on the western horizon was a cloud of dust that moved steadily to the east. They were back there, and they were coming. Just how many and just how mad were they were the questions of the day. As consideration was given to both I whipped up the Reb. We went from a walk to a trot.

I wasn't quite panicked yet, but I needed a plan, a ruse, something.

Try as I might, nothing came to mind. My only thought was run Brewster run.

Another time, a life time ago, I had experienced problems with the Sioux. I made my stand at a creek and tried to drown the little ankle biters. That plan was quickly dismissed as these behind me were much bigger and ten times meaner. One on one I had trouble whipping an old Lakota.

The best I could do was still, run Brewster run.

For most of an hour I pushed that stallion hard. He was beginning to show the wear. The old sway back paint just followed along seemingly without effort.

I stopped on a knoll to let the Reb blow and catch his breath. Behind me, not two miles back, I could clearly see their dust. They were closer than the last time I had seen them. They were gaining ground. They were too far back for me to count their numbers; too close for any comfort.

I gave the Reb the boots. He responded but much slower this time. He was getting tired. I was tired too; tired, hungry, thirsty, and scared. As our trot became but a walk, the light of day also began to wan.

Perhaps darkness could be my friend.

Chapter 55

▼

Due east had been my flight, the only deviation had been an arroyo or ravine too deep to descend or climb. Many were the buffalo that moved from my path. I was hopeful my tracks might become obscured with the hoof prints of these shaggy beasts.

Yet as the sun set on that western horizon, plain as day, my pursers were still behind me. No longer were they a speck of distant dust. I could see them. Six or seven warriors in one tight group were closing the gap.

There was weather coming in from the southwest. Clouds were filling the sky. With them was the smell of rain. Perhaps darkness, rain, and a change of direction would gain me some ground. I tried to be upbeat, hopeful, but well I knew all three would be to no avail.

I gave that Reb another kick, he was getting tired.

A mile, no more, we traveled before we came to a north to south stream. I let the horses drink their fill. As I sat the saddle on my much blistered butt I weighted my options. I had but four; upstream, downstream, straight ahead, or fight. Straight ahead seemed the most obvious, it was after all the most direct route home.

There it was again, home. I had no home, no family, no one, and no place to go.

South, downstream, was option two. There was a fort on the Missouri maybe a day, day and a half, south by southwest. The Lakota might already have that considered and have the path blocked. They could not possibly know my welcome would be a noose.

North, upstream, was option three. Canada was up there somewhere. Canada was cold. I had no provision, no coat. There was no possible way I could survive the cold weather soon to come.

Option four, to fight, was given but fleeting consideration. I had taken on one old Lakota man and he had near beat the bejesus out of me.

I reined up the Reb and pointed him north; heavy came the rain.

Dark, cold, now wet was the night. I was miserable. My saddle weary butt hurt. Then if that wasn't enough, I was hungry.

I pushed the Reb upstream, staying in the water, hoping somehow to hide my tracks. Somewhere I had heard that was the thing to do. As I rode I gave the matter some thought and saw its folly. Trackers, one on each side of the stream just rode along the shore and watched for the tracks to come out. Pretty simple, but it took four men to do the job; two upstream, two downstream. They would find me alright, only there would be two less of them when they did.

Traveling at night was unnerving at best. Every rock, stump, or bush had the appearance of a Lakota. I thought many times that I had ridden into an ambush, yet I was not put out of my misery. I remained tired, hungry, cold, wet, sore, and scared.

We came upon a very dense wall of river willows. As I looked at it, an idea came to mind. I pointed that Reb right into the thickest of the thick and gave him a kick. He had no liking at all for the obstacles but with continued kicking and some choice camp language, he crashed his way through. That rail back paint followed without comment. I hoped my trip through the brakes might fool any pursers. My tracks might be temporarily overlooked. I needed time, distance, rest, and food. I needed to get dry and it was still raining. Little hope did I have for any of it as we moved off into the night.

If I had ever had a more miserable night I could not recall. Dawn came none too soon. I was probably lost, but with all my other complaints screaming for attention, I really did not care.

I pulled up the hang dog Reb's reins deep within a stand of cottonwood trees along the bank of a creek. There was a break between two of the larger trees; I could see the sun as its first rays literally exploded across the horizon. Gone now was the rain. There was not even a cloud in the sky. There was even a faint warming as one of those rays found its way to my right cheek.

We needed to rest. Where we stood looked as good as anywhere else. Besides I doubted the Reb could take another step. He had been rode hard. The other horse, the sway back paint mare, looked no worse for the wear.

I tied off both animals, and then removed their saddles. There was little more I could do than toss their burdens to the ground. I curled between the two saddles and slept.

Chapter 56

▼

My awakening was to a cloudless sky and a mid-day sun. I was cold; chilled to my very bone. I had fallen asleep wet, and the ground had sucked all the warmth from my body. As I shivered I did my best to scan my surrounding for dangers. I saw only my still hang dog Confederate horse and a rail back paint that seemed well rested and ready to travel.

Both animals must have thought me daft or worse as I waved my arms around in the air trying to promote circulation. I needed to work some heat into my body. After considerable gyration I had once again the rewarding feel of life about me; I was a little warmer, but a whole lot hungrier. My brain even began to work. It told me that I was lost, still hundreds of miles from safety, being trailed by savages, and without provision one. And my butt hurt. The prospect of getting back in the saddle had no appeal.

With all my consternation, hunger seemed most pressing; that and perhaps a dram of whiskey to warm my soul.

I gave an eye to that paint. I had eaten many a horse in the big war. Mostly the cooks had called it French beef but we knew better. As I looked the paint over some deep internal instinct caused me to drool.

I still had my knife and I knew what I needed to do.

Logic often times doesn't prevail when a man is lacking sustenance. His brain doesn't always consider all the options. I had every intention of stabbing this rail back paint, hacking off its loins, roasting them and eating my fill. Then it occurred to me that I could not roast a loin without a fire. I had nothing with which to make a fire, and if I did, the smoke would bring the Lakota.

Only then did I remember the Confederate saddle bags and the two skin pouches.

Upon inspection the bags held enough powder, shot and caps for at least four loadings of the shotgun.

The skin pouches contained a broken knife, flint, a few Sioux knickknacks, and most importantly, a huge handful of jerked meats. I wasn't sure what animal had been jerked; I didn't care, I just ate.

The food and the sun brought some much needed warmth to my body. I was still, however, in deep trouble. I gave my surroundings a wary twice over. They would eventually work out my trail, but for the moment; a man who does not move makes no tracks. I walked back to the edge of the cottonwoods. Try as I might, I saw no evidence of my previous nights passing. The nights rain had done much to obscure my tracks, at least to my untrained eye.

I needed a plan. I sat, munched, and thought.

First and foremost, I was still in deep trouble. I was alone, hundreds of miles west of anywhere. Minnesota was the closest sanctuary. Years ago they had put a bounty on the Sioux. There were none east of Big Stone.

I was going east.

Travel during the day was dangerous. I could be easily seen. But travel at night was slow at best. Directions were a problem. On a cloudy night one could easily find himself back where he started.

I was going to chance it and travel by day.

I would need more protection than just a one shot old shotgun and a sheath knife. As I chewed the jerky and soaked up the sun, different weaponry came to mind. I had a few ideas.

I cut a stout piece of willow to the length of a shovel handle. Using one of the strips of leather from the pouches I firmly affixed the broken knife blade to it. My end product was a six foot lance. I had seen cavalry charges led by men on big horses with lances in hand. They had been most effective. Mine was crude, but hopefully it would be just as lethal.

I had my plan, it wasn't the best, but it was a plan. Tomorrow morning, rested, my belly full of jerked meat, and my sore butt in a saddle; I was going east. I was going armed and ready.

As I sat I began to think it over, maybe I wasn't as ready as I thought.

I could see them beyond the cottonwood. Three Lakota were moving their horses north along the east side of the brake. There were two hundred yards off; their eyes to the ground. I moved not a muscle. Even at this distance, movement of any kind can attract the eye.

I was ever so glad I had decided not to move until morning; no tracks would they find.

My horses, hungry like they were, had their heads to the ground, their lips to the grass. The Sioux mounts were too far off to smell. If I was lucky, my horses would not see theirs. A whinny could be the death of me.

The passing by of the Sioux initiated a change of plan and an immediate response on my part. I was getting out of here now.

The Reb was saddled and readied for flight. I had no intention of saddling the rail back, but I took the buffalo hide cover off the bone saddle frame. I opened it up and was much pleased by its size. It already had a hole in the center of it; no doubt it had doubled as a furry poncho. I slipped it over my head.

There was a smell to it that would take some getting used to, but I was noticeably warmer.

As I looked around to make sure I had all my meager belongs packed, I noticed on the ground a most peculiar rock. It was about the size of my fist and had a hole right through the center of it. I picked it up mentally weighing it as I tossed it from hand to hand.

I took the rein from the rail back and tied it through the hole in the rock. I swung it around my head a few times. It would do just fine. I now had a single shot, a sticker, a stabber, and a basher.

"Brewster," I said to myself, "I'm not waiting for morning. I'm going home. I'm going home, now."

Chapter 57

▼

It was near dark when I sent out onto the prairie. It had been several hours since the Sioux had passed. They had not returned.

As I put the boots to that Reb, the word, "home," registered. I had no home, no real place to go. There was no one waiting for me. I told myself that I would be content with just a warm bed, a bed free from danger; that and a bottle of whiskey would suit me well.

I had been a full day without even the thought of whiskey; more than two days since I had last had a drop. Perhaps it wasn't a commodity as necessary to my survival as I thought.

As I peered ahead into the prairie darkness looking for Sioux or worse, I found that my survival needs were now the eyes of an owl, the ears of a bat, the cunning of a fox, and the speed of lightening. Courage would be of some help too, that and a whole lot of luck.

All night I traveled, slow and easy, keeping the North Star high above, just off my left shoulder.

When the sun crested the eastern horizon, dead ahead, I began looking for my day's hideout. I needed a place that offered vantage, concealment, grass, water, and defensibility. The Sioux looking for me would not give up the search. I had taken their blood, and they were going to take mine. The Lakota were coming.

I could see a tree line off to the south. Trees, especially cottonwood and willow meant water. We needed to drink. We were still a trio; me, the Reb, and that sway back mare that had followed the entire night.

I found concealment within the trees; water in the stream. I looked around and found a place where several deadfalls had formed a natural fort. I picketed the Reb on a patch of grass but left the mare to her own endeavors. Within the natural fort, I wrapped myself in the buffalo hide coat, laid down, and remembered nothing else as exhaustion took its demands.

A horse whinnying opened my eyes. The brightness of the sun gave me some insight as to the time of day. A second whinny from my left indicated just about how short that day might be. Reb was picketed to my right, just over the edge of the ravine.

It might be the rail back nickering to my left, but the first whinny had been further away, of this I was sure. I had company. He was either right next to me on the other side of the deadfall, or he was further off and the rail back was on the other side of the log.

Either way I was in deep trouble.

Slowly I reached out and grabbed the shotgun. My knife was still sheathed; but it was close to hand. As quietly as I could I rolled left, rose, and peeked over the top of the deadfall.

Not twelve feet away sitting atop a brown and white paint was the biggest Sioux warrior that I had ever seen. His feet dangled well below the belly of the horse. In his hands at the ready was a rifle. He was looking for me and at that very second in time he found his hearts desire.

The man was swinging his rifle to bear as I touched off my load. The report was deafening; its impact removed the monstrous savage from his mount. He hit the ground hard. His horse reared revealing yet another warrior some fifty feet behind the first.

The second warrior was just briefly stunned by the noise and fate of his companion. In that instant I was over the log and had the dead man's rifle in my hand.

Years of soldiering had left me much conditioned to the fight. The rifle felt like an old friend as I leveled it on the Lakota who was spinning his horse for home or help. I took aim and squeezed the trigger.

The fleeing Sioux took the hit low left, through his buttock I thought, but he stayed his mount and was gone from sight in less than a second.

In but a few seconds more I had the Reb saddled and ready to ride. No telling how soon others would appear.

Before I hit the trail again I took time to pick the pockets, so to speak, of the dead warrior. He had a trade knife and quiver full of arrows. His horse which had stayed the scene carried two skin sacks. One sack contained dried meats and some nasty smelling gruel. The other sack had six extra cartridges for the rifle.

The white paint was a solid enough mount. I quickly fashioned his rein into a lead line then got my butt into the saddle atop the Reb. With my newly acquire horse in tow, my reloaded shotgun in the scabbard and the rifle across my lap, I was once again Minnesota bound.

How much time I had before the one that got away could summon help; I could not say. I prayed he would bleed out before he found the others. Irrespective they would find either one or two of their dead comrades and a clear trail to the responsible party could easily be followed.

Chapter 58

▼

An hour or more I moved to the east, then on the back side of a line of willow I cut to the south. My pace was slow, steady, and measured. Darkness was my new friend. Each tree, stump, and rock still presented itself as a waiting Lakota, but I had learned to just move on. Ever ready was that rifle across my lap just in case I was wrong.

The Reb was responding well. He was a magnificent stallion. The new paint easily kept the pace. The rail back mare just effortlessly tagged along. That nag was an amazement. She was old, thin, but possessed incredible stamina.

After an hour or more of travel to the south I again changed direction, this time heading due east again. We kept the pace and direction as best we could until there was the dawning of a new day on the prairie horizon ahead.

Again I looked for a place to hide and rest. A tree line to the south offered both. I eased my horses into a ravine that lead down to a good sized creek. We all four watered then I led my animals up a different ravine which seemed to have plenty of grass. There was a place to tie off the Reb and Paint where each could graze the morning away. The rail back mare was again left to her own endeavors. Hopefully her vigilance if need be would pay off again.

I ate some of my new jerked meat and just a little of the gruel that came from the slain warriors satchel. The meat seemed palatable but the gruel, a kind of stinky paste, made me sick. As hungry as I was my stomach would not tolerate the goop. Once my stomach settled I wrapped myself in the buffalo robe and slept.

My awakening was to gray dismal cloudy sky. I moved not a muscle as I listened for dangers. Less than a week in the wilderness was honing skills I never knew I had. What I heard was a few birds and the chomping sound of my horses. Reassured, I rose to meet the new day, another exercise in terror and flight I was sure. I was stiff, sore, my butt still hurt, and I was hungry.

I could think of nothing to relieve the first three maladies, but breakfast might cure the latter.

I sat a deadfall and ate the last of the jerked meats. Try as I might, I could not swallow the nasty ball of whatever it was the big warrior had stuffed into the bag. It might have been something called pemmican but I wasn't sure.

I gave it one more smell. It was just god awful. It smelled so bad I began to chuckle. Perhaps, just perhaps, there was a big dead Lakota Sioux somewhere off in his happy hunting ground just laughing hysterically about the dumb white man who was trying to eat his ball of rotted snake crap or whatever it was.

It was near mid-day as best I could tell. I needed to be on the move. I had traveled the previous night only because of fear of being discovered. Savages had been less than a hundred yards off. I had survived to see another day but I had not gained any real distance. As I did the mathematics I saw again a real need to ride. As I traveled at night I might well elude capture or detection, but the pursuers would gain time the next day. They would actually be gaining ground. They could be close, real close.

Again I searched near and far for Lakota.

In that the Sioux would not likely lose my trail again I decided it most prudent to just ride and keep riding.

That is exactly what I did. I got my sore butt into the saddle of the Reb and headed southeast. This day I began to alternate horses, giving the Reb a break. The paint had no liking for the bit, but he got used to it.

Two meal less miserable days I traveled through rain and drizzle covering a goodly distance. I guessed my travel had been a hundred miles or more. The buffalo hide poncho I wore did much to ward off the cold damp weather; though little did it do for my spirits. I was just too hungry to care.

On the morning of the third day I again began to look at the rail back paint in that different light. I could almost smell those roasted back straps as they roasted over a fire which I was still wary about building. My mind was focused on my potential breakfast when the soup de jour's ears pricked up. She was looking south as she whinnied. I was sure it was a diversion on her part, an attempt to cause me to see some other worth or purpose to her existence.

On a whim I let my starving eyes move from her rump to the south.

There, on the rise, not a quarter mile away, sat five mounted Lakota warriors. Even from that distance I could see they knew where I was and that they had a sense of purpose.

"Bless you rail back," was all I could say as I quickly broke camp, saddled up, and prepared myself for a long run.

Not but a few minutes did I take. The Sioux were advancing at a walk. They had some caution about them; at least four of their number had already perished. Steady was their pace. They seemed to be taunting me. It was as if they wanted me to run.

"Why," was a question I asked myself as I got my butt back up on the Reb.

I was being flushed like a rabbit from a brush pile. Five warriors were enough to make anyone run the opposite direction. I looked behind to the north. I saw no one. To run east or west would give them the angle. They could easily cut off my retreat. They wanted me to run north, right into an ambush.

They were giving me no choice. I was going home, right through them if need be, but I was going home.

I slipped my hand under the heavy buffalo poncho and adjusted my sheath knife. The loaded rifle was secured in the scabbard. It was the shotgun I wanted first. I was drawing first blood. At close range I could not miss. With that shotgun in my right hand, my lance in my left, and that leather tagged stone draped over the horn I had every intention of putting the hurts to those Sioux who were now on the move.

I was ready and they were coming.

Five Lakota warriors were a hundred yards in front of me, advancing in a line, five paces apart. They came at a walk.

The distance closed much too quickly as I too advanced at a walk.

I could see their painted faces plain as day; five seasoned fighting men, all intent on a kill. One had a lance. One carried some type of long gun; two had arrows notched in their bows. I could not see what manner of weapon the fifth brandished, but I was sure whatever it was, it would hurt.

At thirty yards I put the boots to the Reb.

I was yelling something I hoped was terrifying.

They were yelling something that was.

Six men, all with but one intention, charged.

My shotgun's blast removed the face of the closest savage as his body went airborne off the back of the horse. I dropped the shotgun from my right hand and focused my attention to my left hand lance just as I was about to get speared. He was drawing his arm back for his thrust as I rammed my horse into his. My lance still in hand stuck him deep before the shaft snapped in my hand. He fell from his mount; his half of my lance was still imbedded in his hip. Where his spear went I did not know. I whipped Reb to the left dropping that piece of stick from my hand as I ducked an arrow narrowly missing my ear.

I was still screaming, profanities aplenty filled the air. I knew nothing of the guttural language of my foe, but I was sure they were matching me tit for tat, as they too screamed.

I charged the Reb at the man who had missed with his arrow. He was nocking another arrow as my rifle came from the scabbard. I brought it to bear as he took aim. We were on the backs of moving animals, but at two yards distance neither of us missed.

My shot took him dead center; his arrow smacked me hard left.

There was another Lakota on my right rear. I had no idea what he was going to do to me as my attention had been on the man now falling from his saddle. I swung the empty rifle in a big sweep attempting to gain space as I again turned Reb hard to the left.

One shot rang out, then another. The black faced man was firing a pistol at me from not five yards. He cracked another shot which somehow ripped the rifle from my grasp. The fifth warrior had another arrow nocked and was taking aim.

I charged my horse into the black faced pistol shooter as I was hit hard again with another arrow.

Screaming I was, every profanity I ever knew was coming out of my mouth. My thong tied rock was now in hand whistling death in circles as I whipped it around and around over my head. The pistol man fired yet another shot as my swinging rock crashed into the side of his head.

Down he went.

The arrow shooter was drawing yet another from his quiver as I crashed my horse into his. I tackled him off the back of his animal. We hit the ground hard. He still had his arrow in hand and repeatedly tried to stab me with it as we rolled on the ground. I still had my leather tied rock in hand. I was bigger, perhaps stronger, but for sure a whole lot madder. I was able to get the advantage; his back was pinned to the ground. He tried to rise but I head butted him to the face. As he drew back I was able to wrap that leather strap around his neck.

I was not merciful.

Chapter 59

▼

My lungs heaved with great gasps as I raised to my feet above the now most dead warrior with bulging eyes.

I stood amidst the carnage, seemingly immune to it. That war had conditioned me to blood and death. Three Lakota warriors were obviously dead, the one bashed with the rock might have been; all I could say was that he was not moving. The fifth, the now blood soaked man with half a lance still protruding from his lower hip, held fast the broken shaft. He was crying out in pain.

I only took notice to see he had no weapon within grasp with which he might cause me harm. I left him to suffer his well deserved fate.

I assessed my own person. I was bleeding from my scalp, two different places I thought; but I could not tell myself from what. I did not remember receiving either injury. I had been arrow shot, of that I was sure. Two times I remembered being hit with arrows. I removed my buffalo coat and saw three arrows still hanging in the heavy hide. I had two bleeding holes; one low, the other high to the shoulder. Neither appeared to be life threatening, just bloody holes which I hoped did not get infected. There were a few extra holes in my clothing that had not been there upon last inspection. All I could say for sure was that I was just a lucky fellow. I still breathed.

I searched the horizon for other Sioux. Seeing none, I removed from the dead what I thought I might need. I took the rifle with at least ten more rounds, and the pistol which apparently did not shoot straight. The man had a holster flap and a pouch full of bullets for the weapon. One of their horses had tied onto its saddle frame a roasted haunch of meat. I suspected it might have been a buffalo calf. I would not go hungry. I was certainly now much better armed.

As I gathered what I could I watched the lanced warrior fall over. He had stopped crying, forever was my guess.

I quickly left the now five lifeless bodies and headed south; me, the Reb, my still tagged paint, and of course my lookout, Rail Back. As we crested the hill I looked back for possible pursuit.

I was being followed; behind me, keeping pace, were five newly acquired four legged friends.

I could never hope to know why six horses, all mares, just chose to follow along but they did. They were all good mounts each and every one of them. My only thought was that the Reb was or had been their herd stud.

Day after day I rode south and east at a mile eating, butt busting, pace. I would alternate horses as one tired. I kept moving.

At night I would stop, rest, and work on that haunch. The morning's sun would find me again south and east.

My fear of trailing Lakota began to wane. There was just no way they could have kept the pace. After seeing the wake of my passing it was hard to believe that there was a Sioux dumb enough to try.

As I rode my loneliness seemed to manifest itself in my thoughts. I longed for a home, someplace safe and warm. I wanted what all men wanted, someone to share their life with, someone to love, someone to love them.

Helga had been my first love. I thought of her often. I thought too of my vengeful purpose and a quest yet unfinished. I still had business in Helena.

I thought of Diane. She had been my second love. She was also gone forever.

I could not say who I missed the most, she who bore my son or she that boarded with me. Both were so different. Both were so very special. Each had filled my every need. Their deaths had made me cry.

"The past is the past," I said to Reb.

The horse did not respond. He and his kind had a different language. He was oblivious to my chatter, I the same to his knickers and whinnies. We were probably saying the same things in different ways. He was the lucky one, he had seven; I had none.

We kept the pace. I had no desire to die. Armed though I was, I had no wish to meet up again with the Sioux. It took but one well placed arrow or knife slice to end ones time on this earth. I did not look forward to death. This life I had was all that I was allowed. A pleasant wonderful hereafter was reserved for the deserving, the believers. Brewster Daggit was not one of those.

"Bud," I told myself, as the horse was tired of listening, "the devil himself doesn't want a piece of you."

My exact destination was unknown. All I wanted was a measure of safety, somewhere east of the Sioux. I wondered if I would ever find someone to spend my few remaining years with. I was after all thirty or forty something.

How old was I? Study as I might, late thirty something was the best calculation I could do.

I did not know where to go to find someone who might want to be with a penniless old man who knew naught but how to kill without remorse and drink to excess.

Drink, I had not even thought about that brown elixir for several days now. I thought that strange, especially with so much time for thought.

I pondered over and over about what I might do to support myself. I had worked for wages when I was with Diane. It took both of our incomes and some stealing to live any type of life at all. That prospect had little appeal. I had tried farming with Helga. The financial advantages there were even less appealing. We had scratched at the ground for several years and ended up little more than rabbit chokers.

South and east was our travel. I had no other destination than the safety of Minnesota. I had no idea what my girls and I were going to do once we got there.

"My girls!" I said to the four legged ladies as I looked back.

There it was; right beside me, right behind me, right under me. I had a magnificent stallion and seven mares. I mentally did the mathematics as rode.

"Seven times two, then maybe twelve times two, added to the original fourteen."

It just might work, it just might.

Chapter 60

▼

I hit the Minnesota River at Big Stone, more navigational luck than design. We followed the river for several more days, homesteads and small bergs were aplenty. I was near awed by the development. When I last left Minnesota there was nothing west of Fort Ridgely, nothing but prairie and Sioux. Now there were fields of wheat and corn. There were even hog farmers.

New Ulm was the first big town that I came to. I found a livery owner that would take one of my rifles in trade. He provided a corral for my herd, feed for two days, and a few coins to boot.

I weighed my coin then walked into town. I hoped New Ulm would be able to provide me with all the comforts of life; a bath, bed, meal, and a bottle. It was the bottle I wanted most. Long and lonely had been my trail. A bath was probably what I most needed.

There was something familiar with New Ulm but I knew I had never been there. I had traveled close but I had never actually been through the town. Then it dawned on me that I had known a man back in the war that was from the town. He had told me much about the place; so much in fact, it was no doubt his descriptions that were jogging a memory that I never knew I had.

Jason, Jason McCormick, was his name. I remembered my tent mate quite fondly; his antics and quick wit brought a smile to my face. Yes, Jason was a piece of work. I was near laughing out loud as I remembered the love letters he wrote in my behalf to Lydia Mackey. He lost his foot down in Georgia, then probably his life. Gangrene took most of the wounded.

As I walked the streets looking for the center of the town, I could well see New Ulm was a safe place to be. No where did I see a Sioux. Jason had told me that before the war the Lakota had besieged the town, many a German and Swede had been killed. The residents of New Ulm, once friendly to the Lakota, now loathed every Sioux; man woman and child. New Ulm had been instrumental in the Minnesota Indian Bounties.

These were people to my liking. We had much in common.

New Ulm had a four corners. There I found a clapboard building which offered all that I sought.

The sign said, "Hermann Haus."

Under that were the four B's of welcome, "Beds, baths, beer, and brauts."

Even though they did not advertise whiskey I knew well I was standing in front of the gates to heaven.

I entered the door full expecting to see a blinding white light and naked angelic women falling before me. I found naught but an empty table near the door. What the patrons saw was an old bearded smelly stranger wearing a buffalo coat come in the door. I took my seat. I was removed far from the others; I hoped they couldn't smell me from that distance.

The waitress was a pretty lady, strangely familiar.

"Dinner or lunch?" she asked. Her voice was just as familiar as her face and figure.

"The sign said, Beer and Brauts," I replied, stalling for time. I knew her, or at least thought I did.

"Our specialty," she replied, giving me the twice over, "is Schell beer and broiled brauts."

She was such a pretty lady I thought as I tried to reply. It just did not seem possible.

"Well," she said most impatiently, "are you going to order something or just whistle Dixie, Brewster?"

"Lydia?"

"Yes, I see you survivied. We had not heard from you in years."

I stood and was rewarded with just the warmest of hugs; and I was hugging her back. She smelled and felt just wonderful. I was wishing she could have smelled something other than an unwashed, hide clad, survivor of the prairie; yet to my joy and her chagrin, my odoriferous self did not seem to offend her. She was not letting me go and neither was I.

I could have held her forever and was trying to do just that when I heard a clip, clop, clip, clop approach of someone to my rear.

"And who is this buffalo skinner who holds tight my wife?" was the voice.

I turned and could not believe my eyes. Before me was a one legged man on a crutch, Jason McCormick

"Jason!"

"Bud!"

My feeling of elation turned at once to exultation. My only friend from the big war had survived his injury. He seemed to share the same feeling as the double hugging turned to a threesome.

Over brauts, beer, a little whiskey from the rear, some laughter and a lot of tears; we three sat the table totally involved in each others stories.

Most of the laughter came from Jason as he retold the stories of our letter writing to Lydia. He said that once home, he hobbled up to Hutchinson to confess the error of his way. Then one thing led to another.

Lydia interjected, apologizing over and over, saying that she had fallen in love with the man who wrote home the letters to her. When she found him, she married him.

Jason said that after they married he moved her home with him. They were the proud owners of the Hermann Haus.

Lydia said that my farm at Crow Creek was sold for back taxes, but she was happy to report that my friends, John and Carol bought the property, built a nice home on it, and faithfully tend the grave site.

Hour upon hour we spent; beer after beer with an occasional whiskey we consumed. Jason and I were always eye to eye. We talked of everything, even Matthews and Boland. I left much out, but both Lydia and Jason said that God most often takes care of issues regarding revenge. I hoped they were right as only half the problem had thus far been remedied.

Lydia occasionally left the table to attend to hotel business but she always returned to add color or comment to the conversation. Jason was truly a lucky man. Lydia had poise, grace, and beauty.

It was well after dark when Lydia offered just the boldest of suggestions.

"Brewster," she said, "at the top of the stairs, third door on the right is room number 4. We have already signed you in. In Room 4 you will find fresh clothing, soap, and a bath tub full of hot water. You will make use of all three."

"Yes, madam," I replied, not eager to conclude the evening, but part company we did.

My dirty self and what was left of the whiskey went up the stairs to Room 4. What I found was the finest, most plush room I had ever seen. It had a private rest room with a bathtub full of hot water. There was a clean suit on the bed along with a night shirt. What more could a man want was all I could think. I had a warm clean bed to sleep in, a full belly, friends, and a bottle of whiskey. It wasn't but a second before I was out of my grimy rags and my well blistered butt was seated deep in that tub of sweet smelling waters. My revolver was close to hand; old habits are hard to break.

I tried to remember when last I had felt such relaxation. Perhaps Diane and I had shared such moments, I tried to remember them as I leaned back with closed eyes. I had but a minute or two of thoughts of her and those wonderful times before a knock at the door opened my eyes.

"Yes," I answered.

"Room service," was the reply, obviously the voice of a woman.

"I'm in the tub," I answered.

"I know, I have more hot water, may I come in?"

"Ok," I replied, some embarrassed, but not too much.

"Excuse me, Mister Daggit," she said as she came into the room.

The woman was tall, blond, gorgeous and familiar. She looked like the blond from the train.

"Lydia sent me," she said again, "Would you like the hot water dumped over your head our just into the tub?"

"People do that for you?"

"Of course, and I can almost do either without looking."

She was smiling which caused me to laugh. Then she started laughing as she dumped the water over my head.

I tried to keep my composure and not sputter as I listened to her.

"We have met before," she said.

"Not formally, but I remember you."

"You do?" she said, "but I could tell she knew the answer.

"We never talked."

"No, but I remember you. You have a way of making a lasting impression. I have never seen a man so well beaten in such short fashion." she said. "My name is Amanda McCormick. Most call me Mandy. Jason is my older brother. I have been hearing about you for years. First it was Jason with his letters, then after Lydia came along, it was Jason and Lydia with Brewster stories."

Mandy was a looker, no doubt about that. She still had curves aplenty in just the right places.

"Lydia said you enjoyed your baths," Mandy said with a chuckle.

"She did, did she?"

"Yes, and she said that you would be a good catch and that I should have a look."

"You peeked?"

"Well yeah, wouldn't you?" she said as she started to laugh.

She was still laughing as was I when she left the room.

That night, clean, safe, and warm, I slept alone but with just the most pleasant of dreams. It would have been a lie to say a big bosom blond wasn't in each of them.

Maybe, just maybe, life still had a few pleasures in store for a new Minnesota horse rancher they called, Old Bud.

Epilog

Cold and wet had been our Minnesota wintering. Its' snows had piled up high against the cabin. It well might have been the most miserable winter on record if it had not been for my Mandy.

She was not only tall, shapely, and blond; she was also my wife. Warm, so very warm, had been my winter.

Love and comfort had become my world, but I still saw a lonely grave and that Daggit sign. Try as I might; I could not make the vision or the dreams go away. A thousand miles away there was a man with red hair who had yet to pay the fiddler.

I remembered my conversation with Lydia and Jason. They had both had said that the Lord handled all things in his own time. I knew in my own mind that the Lord's time table and mine were not the same. Despite my new home, my beautiful wife, and my growing horse herd; I was mentally planning a trip to Helena. It was just something I had to do; unfinished business.

"Bud," it was Mandy refocusing my thoughts.

She was indeed just plain beautiful.

"Look what I have," she teased, waving a newspaper in the air. "I have a paper! I have a paper!"

Indeed she did.

"Where did you get it?" I asked near as excited as she was.

She had in her hand the first paper of the year, least ways one that we could read. Ours was a desolate existence. We were near fifty miles west of anywhere.

"Margot dropped it off. She and Harvey were on their way home from New Ulm and thought that we might enjoy it."

"Here," she said, handing me the paper. "You can start reading while I make us a new pot of coffee."

What I had in hand was the news. Little if anything did we hear from the outside world. It was my intention to read it from front to back, every single word of it.

I was on my second cup of coffee when my eye caught the names. I knew these people. I read.

[Helena, Montana.....Helena has been a city of gold. Fortunes have been made here; fortunes and lives have been lost. Helena has seen it all. Then along came Buck Moline and his young sister, Lema. They brought with them to Helena naught but an allegation of paternity and left with more gold then a person could ever spend. Mr. Moline proved in court that the local gold magnate, James Boland, had fathered out of wedlock young Lema, entitling the child to a percentage of the most successful Boland Mining Company. As the parties settled the financial aspects of the case in the confines of the Miners' Bank of Helena, three men, guns blazing, stormed through the front doors of the bank. All three robbers and James Boland died of multiple bullet wounds. The two attorneys and Buck Moline sustained serious injury. They are expected to recover. Only the child, Lema, and her half-sister, Mary Boland, escaped injury. By all accounts, both females had substantial involvement in the actual shootings.]

"Damn," I said aloud. "I don't believe it."

"Believe what?" questioned Mandy as she looked up from her section of the paper.

"Damn," I said again, comprehension was coming but had not yet set in.

"Damn what?" asked Mandy.

"I just don't believe it."

"Believe what?"

"You remember that unfinished business I had in Helena?"

"Yes, you said you had business, but never once did you tell me what it was."

"Well I no longer have business there; it seems a friend of mine, Buck Moline, took care of it for me."

"So you don't have to go."

"No, it's over."

"Good," she said, "I wasn't going to let you go anyway."

She was looking me dead in the eye. Then, she smiled and simply asked, "More coffee, Bud?"